THE JUDAS WINDOW

THE JUDAS WINDOW

CARTER DICKSON

with an introduction by
MARTIN EDWARDS

This edition published 2025 by
The British Library
96 Euston Road
London NW1 2DB
bl.uk

The Judas Window was originally published in 1938
by William Heinemann Ltd., London.

Introduction © 2025 Martin Edwards
The Judas Window © 1938 The Estate of Clarice M. Carr
Volume copyright © 2025 The British Library Board

For product safety information, please visit shop.bl.uk/pages/
british-library-publishing, or the Publishing pages on bl.uk.

Cataloguing in Publication Data
A catalogue record for this book is available from the British Library

ISBN 978 0 7123 5533 9
eISBN 978 0 7123 6849 0

Front cover image: 'Cabinet de travail' by P. Sigrist, from
Intérieurs en Couleurs (Paris: Éditions Albert Lévy, c. 1925)
© NPL - DeA Picture Library / Bridgeman Images

Typeset by Tetragon, London
Printed in England by CPI Group (UK) Ltd, Croydon, CR0 4YY

CONTENTS

Introduction   7
A Note from the Publisher   11

THE JUDAS WINDOW

PROLOGUE
What Might Have Happened   13

THE OLD BAILEY
What Seemed to Happen   23

I	"And True Deliverance Make—"	25
II	"Look at Photograph Number 5"	39
III	"In the Little Dark Passage"	53
IV	"Either There is a Window, or There Isn't"	62
V	"Not an Ogre's Den"	72
VI	"A Piece of Blue Feather"	80
VII	"Standing Near the Ceiling—"	93
VIII	"The Old Bear Was Not Blind"	104
IX	"Red Robes Without Hurry"	118
X	"I Call the Prisoner"	129
XI	"In Camera"	141
XII	"From a Find to a Check—"	153
XIII	"The Ink-pad is the Key"	167

xiv	Time-table for Archers	182
xv	"The Shape of the Judas Window"	192
xvi	"I Put On This Dye Myself"	203
xvii	"At the Opening of the Window—"	219
xviii	"The Verdict of You All"	236

EPILOGUE

What Really Happened   251

INTRODUCTION

This introduction includes discussion of some of the early plot points in the following novel, so new readers may prefer to treat it as an afterword.

The Judas Window was first published in 1938 and was quickly recognised as one of the finest of all locked room mysteries. The late Bob Adey, who was the pre-eminent authority on this delightful sub-genre, described it as "perhaps the best locked room mystery every written", and in a poll of experts conducted by Edward D. Hoch, the book occupied fifth place in their list of all-time favourites. The novel's legendary status is reflected in its appearance in an episode of the TV sitcom *One Foot in the Grave*, written by David Renwick, whose other series, *Jonathan Creek*, contributed to the revival of interest in locked room mysteries in the modern era.

The author, John Dickson Carr (here using his transparent alias, Carter Dickson) was the most revered exponent of the locked room mystery. He inspired Renwick and plenty of others, and this book shows him working at the height of his powers. Not only does Carr offer a highly ingenious puzzle, he wraps it up in an entertaining courtroom drama, with much of the story taking place at the Old Bailey.

The set-up is terrific, presented in a prologue with events seen from the perspective of young Jimmy Answell. He is in love with Mary Hume, who received congratulations from her father when she told him of her engagement. This was gratifying to her fiancé, who was aware that Avory

Hume was "made up equally of integrity and suspicion". However, by the time Answell calls on Hume at his home, 12 Grosvenor Street, he is beginning to wonder if the course of true love may be about to confront him with one or two bumps. Hume is a keen archer and the wall of his study is adorned with trophies in the form of arrows. He offers his visitor a whisky and soda and wishes him prosperity. But then Answell's head begins to swim. When he comes round, he finds himself alone in the locked and shuttered study—with only Hume's corpse for company. An arrow has been driven into the older man's heart. And Answell has a gun in his pocket and his fingerprints on the murder weapon...

From here on, events are narrated by Ken Blake; he and his wife Evelyn are friends of Sir Henry Merrivale, that larger-than-life impossible-crime-solver who always makes his presence felt in the Carter Dickson books. H.M. (as he is generally known) explains the central challenge facing anyone who believes that Answell is innocent:

> "The door really was tight and solid and bolted; and the windows really were tight and solid and bolted. Nobody monkeyed with a fastening to lock or unlock either. Also, you heard the architect say there wasn't a chink or crevice or rat-hole in the walls anywhere; also true."

An unexpected and memorable feature of this story is that, when Answell is tried for Hume's murder, H.M. acts as counsel for the defence. Suffice to say that his methods of advocacy are far removed from those of Perry Mason, and—even though he is no mere junior barrister, but a King's Counsel—Evelyn is dismayed by his decision to appear in court: "He took silk before the war... but he hasn't accepted a brief in fifteen years, and they'll *eat* him." The seasoned mystery reader will not, however, be too surprised to discover that they don't.

The book's quality was obvious right away, and a host of contemporary reviews are conveniently gathered on Nick Fuller's blog

"The Grandest Game in the World". The *Saturday Review of Literature* applauded "the most ingenious murder device in years" and Torquemada, the renowned critic and cruciverbalist of the *Observer*, felt this book was the best that the author (of whom he was a good friend and an enthusiastic fan) had written. In the *New Statesman and Nation*, Ralph Partridge said: "I regard it as Mr. Dickson's masterpiece to date." Of those whose praise was more guarded, E. R. Punshon remarked primly in the *Manchester Guardian* that: "The book would merit the highest praise if one did not feel it would be a little spoilt for some readers by... a feeling that... is not much to be congratulated on winning the hand of a young lady so partial to pornography in the nude."

John Dickson Carr (1906–77) had a precocious talent for plotting clever mystery stories and also—crucially—for writing them well. It is one thing to come up with a crafty trick, quite another to develop it into a full-length novel that is thoroughly entertaining and capable of standing the test of time. Carr, in the books he wrote under his own name, and also in the Merrivale series, managed to achieve success by creating atmospheric and sometimes unforgettable situations, interesting human dilemmas, and amusing moments that not only entertain but often serve to misdirect the reader from a vital clue to the solution. This combination of skills enabled him to establish a reputation quickly; he was a major figure in the genre on both sides of the Atlantic and elected as the first American member of the prestigious Detection Club before he reached the age of thirty.

Crime writing is as susceptible to the vagaries of fashion as any other walk of life. Over the decades, the locked room mystery has gone in and out of vogue, but enthusiasts have always recognised the particular strengths of Carr's best work. His work has endured when that of many of his fellow locked room specialists has faded into obscurity, and this has much to do with his storytelling flair. The Carr and Carter Dickson novels that have been republished as British Library Crime Classics have enjoyed considerable popularity, and his present-day admirers include not only David Renwick but the American film-maker Rian Johnson, who has achieved great success with the *Knives Out* movies and the TV series *Poker Face*. It is of course debatable whether *The Judas Window* is the best locked room mystery of all time, or even Carr's finest novel. What I know beyond doubt is that I'm very glad to have the opportunity to welcome this enjoyable mystery back into print.

MARTIN EDWARDS
www.martinedwardsbooks.com

A NOTE FROM THE PUBLISHER

The original novels and short stories reprinted in the British Library Crime Classics series were written and published in a period ranging, for the most part, from the 1890s to the 1960s. There are many elements of these stories which continue to entertain modern readers; however, in some cases there are also uses of language, instances of stereotyping and some attitudes expressed by narrators or characters which may not be endorsed by the publishing standards of today. We acknowledge therefore that some elements in the works selected for reprinting may continue to make uncomfortable reading for some of our audience. With this series British Library Publishing aims to offer a new readership a chance to read some of the rare books of the British Library's collections in an affordable paperback format, to enjoy their merits and to look back into the world of the twentieth century as portrayed by its writers. It is not possible to separate these stories from the history of their writing and therefore the following novel is presented as it was originally published with minor edits only made for consistency of style and sense. We welcome feedback from our readers, which can be sent to the following address:

British Library Publishing
The British Library
96 Euston Road
London, NW1 2DB
United Kingdom

PROLOGUE

WHAT MIGHT HAVE HAPPENED

On the evening of Saturday, January 4th, a young man who intended to get married went to a house in Grosvenor Street to meet his future father-in-law. There was nothing remarkable about this young man, except that he was a little more wealthy than most. Jimmy Answell was large, good-natured, and fair-haired. He was just such an easy-going sort as people liked, and there was no malice in him. His hobby was the reading of murder mysteries, like your hobby and mine. He sometimes took too much to drink, and he sometimes made a fool of himself, even as you and I. Finally, as heir to the estate of his late mother, he might be considered a very eligible bachelor indeed.

It will be well to keep these facts in mind during the murder case of the painted arrow.

Here are the facts behind his visit to Number 12 Grosvenor Street. During a Christmas house-party in Sussex, Answell met Mary Hume. Their love affair was sudden and serious. They were mentioning this subject as early as twelve hours after their first meeting, and by New Year's Day they were engaged. On the strength of it Answell's cousin—Captain Reginald, who had introduced them—attempted to touch him for fifty pounds. He gave Reg a cheque for a hundred, and did similar delirious things. Mary wrote the news of their engagement to her father, who wrote back congratulations.

This was gratifying. Mr. Avory Hume, a director of the Capital Counties Bank, and formerly manager of the St. James's office of that bank, was not a man to take such matters lightly. He might be said to be made up equally of integrity and suspicion, which he had shown since the time he began his career at a mill town in the north. Therefore, when on January 4th Jim Answell was compelled to leave the house-party for one day and go to London on business, he intended to call on his future father-in-law immediately. There was only one thing he could not understand. When Mary saw him off at the station at nine o'clock, he could not understand why her face was so white.

He was thinking about it on the way to Grosvenor Street, at a little past six o'clock in the evening. It had not been necessary for him to get in touch with Avory Hume. The old man had himself rung up Answell's flat that afternoon, and invited him to the house. He had been courteous, but of a freezing formality which Answell vaguely supposed proper to the occasion. "Considering what I have heard, I thought it best that we should settle matters concerning my daughter. Would six o'clock be convenient?"

It was not exactly hail-fellow-well-met, Answell thought. The old boy might at least have invited him to dinner. Besides, he was late for the appointment: a raw white mist impeded the traffic, and his taxi had to creep along. Remembering Mary's scared face, he wondered. Damn it all, Hume couldn't be such a terror as all that! If he were, his obedient son-in-law was prepared to tell him exactly where he could get off; and then he told himself that this was nonsense. Why should he be nervous? For anyone to be ill at ease about meeting the bride's family, especially in this day and age, came to the edge of comedy.

It was not comedy.

Number 12 Grosvenor Street was just such a solid yellow-sandstone house, with inconvenient window balconies, as he had expected. A conventional butler admitted him to a conventionally solid hall, filled with the ticking of a grandfather clock whose hands pointed to ten minutes past six.

"My—er—name is Answell," he said. "Mr. Hume is expecting me."

"Yes, sir. May I have your hat and coat?"

At this point, for no reason at all, Jim dropped his hat. It was a bowler, and it bounced clear across to the other side of the hall. He felt himself growing hot round the neckband, especially at the picture of himself standing like a great gawk among the sedate furnishings, and at the calm way in which the butler retrieved his hat. He said the first thing that came into his mind.

"I'll keep my coat on," blurted Jim Answell. As he made this idiotic remark, his voice sounded almost savage. "Take me to Mr. Hume."

"Yes, sir. Will you come this way, please?"

The room to which he was taken was at the rear of the house. As they passed the great staircase in the hall, he could see someone looking down at him, and he thought he could make out the not unpleasing face of a woman in spectacles. This must be Miss Amelia Jordan, of whom Mary had spoken, who had been with her father for many years. He wondered if the old man's brother, Dr. Spencer Hume, were also there to give him a formal inspection.

"—to see you, sir," said the butler.

His guide opened the door of a high room which was furnished like an office, except for the sideboard. There was a modern desk-lamp burning on a modern flat-topped desk in the middle of the room. Another hint of an office (or even a strong-room) was in the two windows: both were shuttered, and the shutters looked like steel. The place had been fashioned out of a tall and rather chilly back-parlour of the last century, having black paper once patterned in gold, and a few grudging chairs. In the wall opposite the door was a white marble mantelpiece, ostentatiously devoid of ornament. The only ornament in the room had been fastened to the wall above this mantelpiece: three target-arrows arranged in the form of a triangle. They had once been painted in different colours, and seemed to have been inscribed with dates; but the three feathers attached to the end of each arrow looked crooked and dry. In the centre of the triangle was a bronze plaque or medallion.

Mary Hume's father got up from behind the desk with the light on his face. He had evidently just closed a chess-board and put the chess-pieces into their box, which he pushed to one side. Avory Hume was a middle-sized, heavy-boned man, vigorous at sixty-odd, with a heavy expression round the eyes. What remained of his greyish-black hair was brushed carefully across a big skull. He wore a grey tweed suit, with a high old-fashioned collar and crooked tie. At first Answell did not like the expression of his rather protuberant eyes, but this changed.

"That will be all, Dyer," he told the butler. "Go and bring the car round for Miss Jordan." His voice was non-committal. The look he turned on his guest was neither cordial nor hostile, but merely non-committal as well. "Please sit down. We have a great deal to talk about, I think."

Hume waited until the door had closed. Then he sat back in the chair behind his desk and inspected his hands. The fingers were thick and blunt-tipped, but well kept. He added suddenly:

"I see you are looking at my trophies."

Answell, flushing again and feeling that something was very much wrong, drew his glance back from the arrows on the wall behind his host. The bottom arrow of the triangle, he noted, was a dusty yellowish-brown, and inscribed with the date 1934.

"Are you interested in archery, sir?"

"When I was a boy in the north, we drew a forty-pound bow as boys here play cricket and football. Here I have found it fashionable." The heavy voice stopped. Avory Hume seemed to consider every idea as though he were walking round it and inspecting it, like a man inspecting a house. "I am a member of the Royal Toxophilite Society, and of the Woodmen of Kent. Those arrows are trophies of the grand target, or annual wardmote, of the Woodmen of Kent. Whoever first hits the gold—"

"The gold?" repeated his guest, feeling that there had been a sinister emphasis on this.

"The centre of the target. Whoever first hits the gold becomes Master Forester of the society for the ensuing year. In twelve years I have won it three times. They are still good arrows. You could kill a man with them."

Answell restrained a desire to stare at him. "Very useful," he said. "But look here, sir, what's up? I didn't come here to steal the spoons, or to murder anyone unless it becomes absolutely necessary. The point is, I want to marry Miss Hume, and—well, what about it?"

"It is an honourable estate," said Hume, smiling for the first time. "May I offer you a whisky and soda?"

"Thanks, sir," said the other with relief.

Hume got up and went to the sideboard. He drew the stopper of the decanter, splashed in the soda for two weak drinks, and returned with them.

"May I wish you prosperity?" he went on. His expression changed a little. "'Mr. James Caplon Answell'," he said, repeating his guest's name and looking at him steadily. "I will be frank with you. That marriage would be advantageous—to both sides, I might say. As you know, I have already given my consent. I can find absolutely nothing against it"—Answell said something to the rim of his glass—"I had the honour to be acquainted with the late Lady Answell, and I know that your family financial position is sound. Therefore I propose to tell you... Man, man, what's wrong with you? Have you gone mad?"

Answell saw his host stop with his own glass half-way to his lips, and an expression of consternation on his face. But he saw it strangely. Something seemed to be burning his throat, and along his shoulders, and up into his temples. His head began to whirl, so that vision spun with it. The desk tilted forwards, and he knew he must be falling against it when he tried to rise. His last wild thought before he lost consciousness was a realisation that his drink had been doctored; but even this was blotted out by the roaring in his ears.

A line of ideas was unbroken even in pain. "There-was-something-in-that-whisky" kept swimming round in his mind, as though it were swimming back to life with him. He sat up, feeling his back cramped in a hard chair. His head seemed to be rising towards the ceiling in long spiralling motions. First, before he could get back his eyesight, he must conquer this sickness at his stomach. It took some time, and the light hurt his eyes. He blinked at it. It was a desk-lamp in a curved green shade.

A moment of complete panic was succeeded by a vague realisation of where he was. Then he got it all at once. As Hume had been in the act of giving a blessing to the marriage, something had knocked his guest out. Hume must have put something into the whisky. But that was nonsense. Why should Hume put anything into the whisky? And where in God's name was Hume?

Feeling suddenly that he had got to find Hume, Answell pushed himself to his feet. His head ached violently; and his mouth tasted as though he had been eating mint and slobbering a little. If he could only *talk* to someone he would be all right. This business was like missing a train, or watching the end of a procession disappear down the end of a street just before you could move. What had happened, and how long had he been like this? He still wore his overcoat, which was clumsy when he groped inside after his watch. When he came into this house, it had been ten minutes past six. An unreal-looking watch in his hand now said six-thirty.

He put his hands on the desk and looked down at the floor to steady his swimming eyesight. That was how, glancing along the bottom of the desk to the left, he saw an old-fashioned laced boot and a few inches of tightly drawn sock. He stumbled over the foot when he walked round the side of the desk.

"Get up!" he heard himself saying. "Get up, damn you!"

And again his own voice, more plaintive: "Get up off that floor and say something!"

Avory Hume did not get up. He was lying on his left side between the windows and the side of the desk, so close to the desk that his sprawled right hand touched it as though he were trying to embrace it. Answell rolled him over on his back. Something rolled up and over with the body, so that Answell jerked back to avoid being touched by it. He also saw blood. A length of thin, rounded wood rose up to some height from Hume's chest. At the end of the arrow, which had been driven eight inches into Hume's heart, were attached three bedraggled and dusty feathers.

The man was dead, but still quite warm. In death the dour face looked surprised and angry; the high collar and tie were rumpled; there was dust on his hands and a cut on the palm of his right hand.

Trying to get to his feet and jump away at the same time, Answell almost fell over backwards. He felt then—though what it was he did not know until later—some sort of bulge in his hip pocket under the overcoat. It was impossible that Hume should be lying in the middle of his own carpet, skewered like a hen, with blood all over his coat. The desk-lamp shed a business-like light over the blotter, over the light brown carpet, and over the dead man's open mouth.

A very panicky young man looked round the room. In the wall behind him was the door. In the wall to his left were the two shuttered windows. Against the wall to the right stood the sideboard. And on the wall straight ahead of him hung the arrows—but there were only two arrows now. The one which had formed the base of the triangle, inscribed with the date 1934, had been driven through Hume's body. Painted a dingy yellowish-brown, it had three feathers; and half the central feather, coloured blue, had now been torn or broken off.

At the back of his mind he had known there was something wrong with this house from the moment he had walked into it. His interview with Hume had seemed fantastic. The grizzled butler, the great clock ticking in the hall, the women leaning over the banisters, all seemed a part of a trap or an illusion. Someone had come in here while he was unconscious, and had killed Hume. But in that case where was the murderer now? He obviously was not here; the room was completely bare, without even a cupboard.

Moving back still further, he became aware of a loud and insistent noise somewhere in the region of his hand. It was the ticking of his watch. He put back the watch in his pocket, and went to the door; but he wrenched several times at the knob before he realised that the door was bolted on the inside.

But somebody got out of here! He went over more slowly to the windows. The steel shutters on each window were also locked, secured with a flat steel bar which had been shoved into its socket like a bolt.

Then he began to hurry round the room. There was no other entrance. The only thing he had not previously noticed was a two-bar electric heater, set into the grate of the white marble mantelpiece. No way in or out by the chimney, either; the flue was only an inch wide and choked with soot which had not been disturbed. The fire seemed to throw out a blaze of heat, and made him conscious of how warm he was with his overcoat on. Also, he was walking fast. Had Hume killed himself? Had Hume gone mad and staged a weird dance of suicide in order to incriminate someone else: a situation very popular in his favourite form of reading? Nonsense! The only other alternative—

But surely nobody would believe *he* had done it? Why should he? Besides, he could easily explain: he had been given a drugged drink. It was true he had not seen Hume put anything into the glass; but the whisky had been doctored somehow and by someone. He could prove it. With a flash of clearness he recalled that he had not even finished his drink. As the first black wave of nausea came over him, he had automatically put down the glass on the floor beside his chair.

He hurried over to look for it now. But the glass was gone, and he could not find it anywhere in the room. Nor was there any trace of the whisky and soda which Hume had mixed for himself.

By this time in a collected, rather abstract state of fear, he examined the sideboard. On it were a cut-glass decanter of whisky, a syphon of soda-water, and four tumblers. The decanter was full to its stopper: not a drop of soda had been drawn from the syphon; the four glasses were clean, polished, and obviously unused.

He afterwards recalled that at this point he said something aloud, but he had no notion of what it was. He said it to cover his thoughts, as though by speaking rapidly he could prevent himself from thinking. But he had to think. Time was going on: he could still hear the ticking of the watch. If the one door and the two windows were both locked on the inside, he was the only person who could have killed Hume. It was like his own favourite novels turned to a nightmare. Only, with the police of this material world, they did not believe in your innocence, and they hanged you. Also, it is all very well to talk of ingenious devices by which a door is bolted on the inside by someone who is actually outside the room—but he had seen this door, and he knew better.

He went back to look at it again. It was a good heavy door of oak, fitting so tightly into the frame and against the floor that the floor was scraped where it had swung. There was not even a keyhole for any flummery: a Yale lock had been set to the door, but it was out of order and stuck fast in the "open" position of the lock. Instead the door was now secured by a long, heavy bolt so stiff from disuse that, when he gave it a tentative wrench in its socket, he found that even for him a powerful pull would be needed to move it at all.

From the bolt he found himself inspecting his own right hand. He opened the palm and studied it again: after which he went over to the light to get a better look. The fingers, the thumb, and the palm were now smudged with a greyish dust which felt gritty when he closed his hand. Where could he have got that? He knew for a certainty that he had touched nothing dusty since he had come into this room. Again he felt the bulge in his hip-pocket; an unaccustomed bulge; but he did not investigate because he was half afraid to find out what it was. Then, from the hypnotic light of the desk-lamp, his eyes strayed down to the dead man.

The arrow, from hanging so long on the wall, had accumulated a coating of greyish dust: except for a thin line along the shaft where, presumably, it had hung protected against the wall. This dust was now broken and smudged in only one place. About half-way down the shaft, there were signs that someone had gripped it. When he bent down to look, even with the naked eye he could make out clear finger-prints. Answell looked back at his own hand, holding it out in front of him as though he had burnt it.

At that moment, he says, there came into his mind some faint notion of what might really have been meant by that telephone-call: of Mary's white face, and certain conversations in Sussex, and a hasty letter written overnight. But it was only a cloud or a ghost, a name that went by his ears. He lost it in Avory Hume's study, standing over Avory Hume's body, for there were other things to claim his attention.

No, it was not the sound of the blood beating in his own head.

It was the sound of someone knocking at the door.

THE OLD BAILEY

WHAT SEEMED TO HAPPEN

At the Central Criminal Court
March 4, 1936

REX

v.

JAMES CAPLON ANSWELL

The Charge:	Wilful murder of Avory Hume.
The Judge:	Mr. Justice Rankin.
The Counsel:	

For the Crown:	Sir Walter Storm, K.C. (Attorney-General).
	Mr. Huntley Lawton.
	Mr. John Spragg.
For the Defence:	Sir Henry Merrivale, K.C.

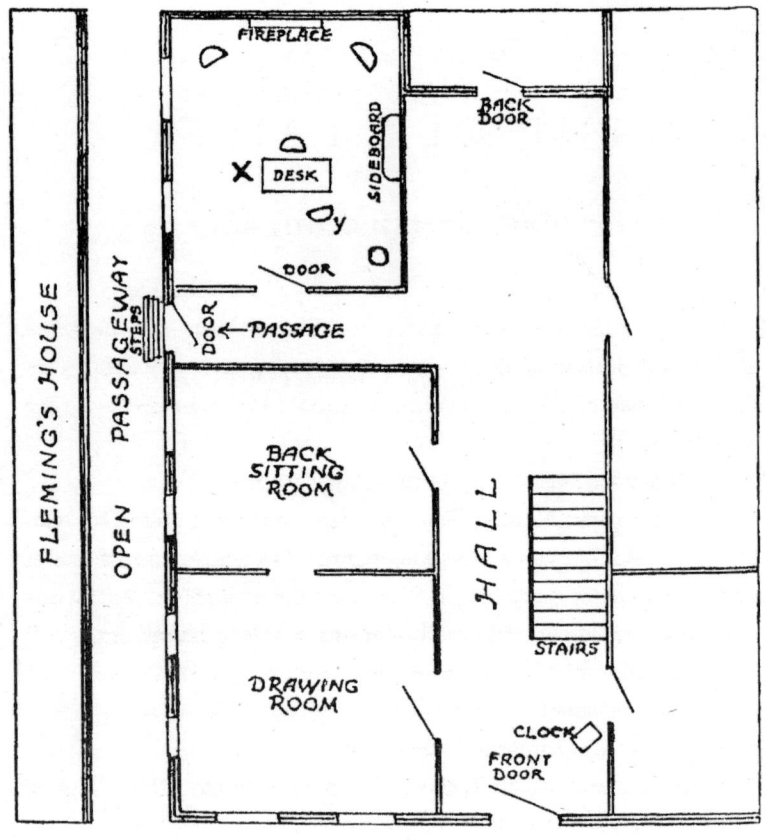

INSPECTOR MOTTRAM'S DRAWING, *with notes:*

1. X, position of body.
2. Answell sat in chair *y*.
3. Two remaining arrows fastened to wall above fireplace; flat against wall.
4. Side door in passage, leading to steps into brick-paved passageway between houses, found closed but not locked. Probably nothing in this; back door unlocked as well.
5. Doors of sideboard in study locked, and keys in deceased's pocket; but sideboard empty. (?)

I

"AND TRUE DELIVERANCE MAKE—"

"*All persons who have anything to do before my Lords the King's Justices of Oyer and Terminer and general gaol delivery for the jurisdiction of the Central Criminal Court, draw near and give your attendance.*

"*God save the King, and my Lords the King's Justices.*"

In Court-room Number One, the "red" judge was taking his seat. Mr. Justice Rankin was a very short plump man whose robe of scarlet slashed with black made him look even shorter and stouter. But he carried it with a swing of briskness. Under a grey tie-wig, fitting him as well as his own hair, his face was round and fresh-complexioned. His little narrow eyes, which should have been sleepy, had an alertness which gave him the air of a headmaster before a form.

To Evelyn and myself, sitting in the reserved seats behind counsel, the place had a look less of a court than of a schoolroom. Even the desks were arranged like forms. Over the court a big white-painted dome ended in a flat roof of glass, blurred with the light of a raw March morning. The walls were panelled to some height in oak. Concealed electric lights under the cornices of the panelling threw a yellow glow up over the white dome; they made the oak look light, and turned the woodwork of the rest of the court to a yellowish colour. This resemblance to a schoolroom may have been caused by the brushed, business-like neatness of the place. Or it may have been the complete lack of haste or flurry, like the pendulum of a grandfather clock.

From where we sat—behind counsel—we could see of the barristers only the backs of their gowns and wigs: a few descending tiers of white wigs, with little ridges of curls like hair buttons. A school, bending towards each other and whispering. Towards our left was the big raised dock, now empty. Immediately across from us—beyond the long solicitors' table in the well of the court—was the jury-box, with the witness-box beside it. Towards our right, the judge's bench showed behind it a line of massive tall chairs: the Sword of State suspended vertically over the chair in the centre.

Mr. Justice Rankin bowed to the Bar, to the officers of the court, and to the jury. His bow was from the waist, like a salaam. The two clerks of the court, at the desk immediately below him, turned round and bowed in unison. Both were very tall men in wig and gown, and their deep bend together was in such sharp timing with the judge's as to give it the effect of a movement in a Punch-and-Judy show. Then the court settled down, and the coughing began. Mr. Justice Rankin arranged himself in the chair immediately to the left of the Sword of State: never in the centre one, which is reserved for the Lord Mayor or one of the aldermen. Fitting on a pair of shell-rimmed glasses, Mr. Justice Rankin took up a pen and smoothed flat the pages of a large notebook. Over the glass roof of the court, March daylight strengthened and then dulled. They brought in the prisoner at the bar.

You cannot look long at the prisoner, standing in that enormous dock with a policeman on either side of him. Or at least I can't. You feel like a ghoul. It was the first time either Evelyn or I had seen Answell. He was a decent-looking young fellow—almost anybody in court might have looked into a mirror and seen his counterpart. Despite the fact that he was well-dressed and freshly shaven, there was a certain air about him which gave the impression that he did not now particularly care a curse what happened. But he stood stiffly at attention. There were a few ghouls from the society columns sitting behind us; he did not glance in our direction.

When the indictment was read over to him, he answered *not guilty* in a voice suddenly edged with defiance. Not an unnecessary word was spoken in the court. The judge seemed to conduct matters mostly by signs.

"I swear by Almighty God"—they were administering the oath to the jury—*"that I will well and truly try, and true deliverance make, between our Sovereign Lord the King and the prisoner at the Bar, whom I have in charge, and a true verdict give according to the evidence."*

It was a schoolroom with a rope at the end of it when you left the headmaster's study. Evelyn, who was troubled, spoke behind her hand. She had been looking down over the blank rows of black-silk backs in front of us.

"Ken, I can't understand it. Why ever does H.M. want to go into court? I mean, I know he's always at loggerheads with people in the government; and he and the Home Secretary practically come to blows every time they meet; but he's hand in glove with the police. That chief inspector—what's his name—?"

"Masters?"

"Masters, yes. He'd take H.M.'s advice before he'd take his own superiors'. Well, if H.M. can prove this chap Answell is innocent, why didn't he just prove it to the police, and then they'd have dropped the case?"

I did not know. It was the one point on which H.M. had preserved a belligerent silence. Though the barristers in front had their backs to us now, it was easy to pick out H.M. He was sitting alone on the left of the front bench: his elbows out-thrust on the desk, so that his ancient gown made him look still broader, and his wig sitting strangely on him. Towards his right on the same bench, counsel for the Crown—Sir Walter Storm, Mr. Huntley Lawton, and Mr. John Spragg—conferred together. Their whispers were inaudible. Though the desk in front of H.M. was comparatively clear, the space before counsel for the prosecution was piled with books, with the neatly printed briefs, with the yellow booklets in which official photographs are bound, and with fresh pink blotting-paper. Every back was grave. Yet under the mask of studied courtesy which marks the Old Bailey, I felt (or thought I could feel) a certain ironical amusement under those wigs whenever an eye happened to stray towards H.M.

Evelyn felt it too, and was furious.

"But he shouldn't have come into *court*," she insisted. "He took silk before the war, but Lollypop told me herself he hasn't accepted a brief in fifteen years, and they'll *eat* him. Look at him down there, sitting like a boiled owl! And if they begin to get under his skin he won't behave himself; you know he won't."

I had to admit he was not the most polished counsel who might have been selected. "It would appear that there was some commotion the last time he did appear in court. Also, I think myself it was indiscreet to begin an address to the jury with: 'Well, my fatheads.' But for some curious reason he won the case."

A creaking and a muttering drone filled the court as the jury continued to be sworn. Evelyn glanced down past counsel at the long solicitors' table in the well of the court. Every seat was filled, and the table was piled with exhibits bound into neat envelopes or packages. Two other and more curious exhibits were propped beyond, near the little cubicle where the court shorthand-reporter sat. Then Evelyn looked up at Mr. Justice Rankin, sitting as detached as a Yogi.

"The judge looks—tough."

"He is tough. He is also one of the most intelligent men in England."

"Then if this fellow is guilty," said Evelyn. She mentioned the unmentionable subject. "Do you think he did it?"

Her tone took on the furtive note with which this is mentioned by spectators. Privately, I thought Answell was either guilty or crazy or both. I was fairly sure that they would hang him. He had certainly done as much as possible to hang himself. But there was no time to reflect on this. The last of the jurors, including two women, had now been sworn without a challenge. The indictment was again read over to the prisoner. There was a throat-clearing. And Sir Walter Storm, the Attorney-General, rose to open the case for the Crown.

"May it please your Lordship, members of the jury."

There was a silence, through which Sir Walter Storm's rich voice rose with a curious effect of seeming to come from a gulf. The woolly top of his wig confronted us as he tilted his chin. I do not think that throughout the entire trial we saw his face more than once, when he twisted round: it was long, long-nosed, and ruddy, with an arresting eye. He was completely impersonal, and completely deadly. Often he had the air of a considerate schoolmaster questioning slightly feeble-minded charges. In his course of remaining impartial, his voice took on a heavy and modulated e-nun-ci-ation like an actor's.

"May it please your Lordship, members of the jury," began the Attorney-General. "The charge against the prisoner, as you have heard, is murder. It is my duty to indicate to you here the course that will be followed by the evidence for the Crown. You may well believe that it is often with reluctance that a prosecutor takes up his duties. The victim of this crime was a man universally respected, for many years an official of the Capital Counties bank; and later, I think, a member of the board of directors of that bank. The man who stands accused of having committed it is one of good family, good upbringing, and of considerable material fortune, having a great many of this world's advantages denied to others. But the facts will be presented to you; and these facts, I shall suggest to you, can lead to no other conclusion but that Mr. Avory Hume was brutally murdered by the prisoner at the bar.

"The victim was a widower, and at the time of his death was living at Number 12, Grosvenor Street with his daughter, Miss Mary Hume; his brother, Dr. Spencer Hume; and his confidential secretary, Miss Amelia Jordan. During the fortnight of December 23rd to January 5th, last, Miss Mary Hume was absent from this house, visiting friends in

Sussex. You will hear that on the morning of December 31st, last, the deceased received a letter from Miss Hume. This letter announced that Miss Hume had become engaged to be married to James Answell, the prisoner at the bar, whom she had met at the home of her friends.

"You will hear that, on receiving this news, the deceased was at first well pleased. He expressed himself in terms of the warmest approval. He wrote a letter of congratulation to Miss Hume; and conducted at least one telephone conversation with her on the subject. You might think that he had reason to be satisfied, considering the prisoner's prospects. But I must draw your attention to the sequel. At some time between December 31st and January 4th, the deceased's attitude towards this marriage (and towards the prisoner) underwent a sudden and complete change.

"Members of the jury—when this change occurred, or why, the Crown do not attempt to say. But the Crown will ask you to consider whether or not such a change had any effect on the prisoner at the bar. You will hear that on the morning of Saturday, January 4th, the deceased received another letter from Miss Hume. This letter stated that the prisoner would be in London on that day. Mr. Hume lost little time in communicating with the prisoner. At 1.30 on Saturday afternoon he telephoned to the prisoner at the latter's flat in Duke Street. The deceased's words were overheard on this occasion by two witnesses. You will hear in what terms, and with what acerbity, he spoke to the prisoner. You will hear that, as the deceased replaced the receiver of the telephone, he said aloud: 'My dear Answell, I'll settle your hash, damn you.'"

Sir Walter Storm paused.

He spoke the words unemotionally, consulting his papers as though to make sure of having them right. A number of people glanced automatically at the prisoner, who was now sitting down in the dock with a warder sitting on either side of him. The prisoner, I thought, seemed to have been prepared for this.

"In the course of this telephone conversation, the deceased asked the prisoner to come to his house in Grosvenor Street at six o'clock that evening. Later, as you will hear, he told the butler that he was expecting at six a visitor who (in his own words) 'might give some trouble, for he is not to be trusted.'

"At about 5.15 the deceased retired to his study, or office, at the rear of the house. I must explain to you that—during his long term of service with the bank—he had constructed for himself a private office at home suited to his needs. You will see that there are only three entrances to this room: a door and two windows. The door was a heavy and tight-fitting one, fastened on the inside with a bolt. There was not even a keyhole: the door being fastened on the outside with a Yale lock. Each of the windows could be covered with folding steel shutters, which, as you will hear, were of a burglar-proof variety. Here the deceased had been accustomed to keep such valuable documents or letters as he had once been obliged to bring home with him. But for several years this study had not been used as a 'strong-room'; and the deceased had not considered it necessary to lock up the room either with door or with shutters.

"Instead, he kept there only his 'trophies.' This, members of the jury, refers to the fact that the deceased had been a keen follower of the pastime of archery. He was a member of the Royal Toxophilite Society and of the Woodmen of Kent, societies which exist for the furtherance of this good old sport. On the wall of his study hung some prizes of the annual matches of the Woodmen of Kent. These consisted of three arrows—inscribed respectively with the dates on which they had been won, 1928, 1932, 1934—and a bronze medal presented by the Woodmen of Kent for a record number of points, or hits, in 1934.

"With this background, then, the deceased went into his study at about 5.15 on the evening of January 4th. Now mark what follows! At this time the deceased called to Dyer, the butler, and instructed him to close and lock the shutters. Dyer said: 'The shutters?'—expressing surprise, since this had not been done since the deceased had left off using the room as an office. The deceased said: 'Do as I tell you; do you think I want Fleming to see that fool making trouble?'

"You will hear that this referred to Mr. Randolph Fleming, a fellow archery-enthusiast and a friend of the deceased, who lived next door: in fact, in the house across the narrow paved passage outside the study windows. Dyer followed the deceased's instruction, and securely barred the shutters. It is worthy of note that the two sash-windows were also locked on the inside. Dyer, making sure that everything was in order in the room, then observed on a sideboard a decanter full to the stopper of whisky, an unused syphon of soda-water, and four clean tumblers. Dyer left the room.

"At 6.10 o'clock the prisoner arrived. You will hear evidence which will enable you to decide whether he was or was not in an extremely agitated frame of mind. He then refused to remove his overcoat, and asked to be taken at once to Mr. Hume. Dyer took him to the study and then left the room, closing the door.

"At about 6.12 Dyer, who had remained in the little passage outside the door, heard the prisoner say: 'I did not come here to kill anyone unless it becomes absolutely necessary.' Some minutes later he heard Mr. Hume cry out, 'Man, what is wrong with you? Have you gone mad?' And he heard certain noises which will be described to you."

This time the Attorney-General's pause was of the slightest. Sir Walter Storm was warming up: though he remained fluently impersonal, and still read out quotations with the same painstaking articulation. His only gesture was to move his forefinger slowly at the jury at each word he read. Sir Walter is a tall man, and the sleeve of his black gown flapped a little.

"At this point, members of the jury, Dyer knocked at the door and asked whether anything was wrong. His employer replied: 'No, I can deal with this; go away'—which he did.

"At 6.30 Miss Amelia Jordan came downstairs, on her way out of the house, and went to the study. She was about to knock at the door when she heard the voice of the prisoner say: 'Get up! Get up, damn you!' Miss Jordan tried the knob of the door, and found that it was bolted on the inside. She then ran down the passage, meeting Dyer who was just coming into it. She said to him: 'They are fighting; they are killing each other; go and stop them.' Dyer said that it might be better to get a policeman. Miss Jordan then said: 'You are a coward; run next door and fetch Mr. Fleming.' Dyer suggested that Miss Jordan had better not be left alone in the house at that moment, and that she herself had better go after Mr. Fleming.

"This she did, finding Mr. Fleming just leaving his house to go out. Mr. Fleming returned with her. They found Dyer returning from the kitchen with a poker, and all three went to the study door. Dyer knocked; after a minute they heard a noise which they correctly believed to be that of the bolt being slowly withdrawn from its socket on the other side of the door. I say 'correctly,' members of the jury. That the bolt was indeed withdrawn at this moment, and that it was a stiffly working bolt which required some effort to draw, has repeatedly been acknowledged by the prisoner himself.

"The prisoner opened the door a few inches. On seeing them, he opened it fully, and said: 'All right; you may as well come in.'

"You may or may not think the remark a callous one under the circumstances. The circumstances were that Mr. Hume was lying on the floor between the windows and the desk, in a position you will hear described. An arrow had been driven into his chest, and remained upright in the body. You will hear that arrow identified as one which, when deceased was last seen alive in the company of the prisoner alone, had been hanging on the wall of the study: this, indeed, has been acknowledged by the prisoner himself.

"With regard to this arrow, we shall demonstrate by medical evidence that it had been driven into the body with such force and direction that it penetrated the heart and caused instantaneous death.

"You will hear, on the testimony of expert witnesses, that this arrow could not possibly have been shot or fired—as, that is to say, one might discharge it from a bow—but that it must have been used as a hand-weapon, as one might use a knife.

"You will hear from police officers that there was on this arrow (which had been hanging for some years against the wall) a coating of dust. This dust had been disturbed at only one place, where there were found clear finger-prints.

"You will hear, finally, that these finger-prints were those of the prisoner at the bar.

"Now, what happens when the prisoner opens the door of the study to Miss Jordan, Mr. Fleming, and the butler? He is alone in the room with the dead man, as they establish. Mr. Fleming says to him: 'Who did it?' The prisoner replies: 'I suppose you will say I did it.' Mr. Fleming says: 'Well, you have finished him, then; we had better send for the police.' Still, they proceed to examine the room: discovering the steel shutters still barred on the inside, and the sash-windows locked on the inside as well. The prisoner, it will be our course to demonstrate to you, has been found alone with a murdered man in a room rendered inaccessible in this fashion; and nowhere, we may say literally, can there be shown a crack or crevice for the entrance or exit of any other person. During the time that Mr. Fleming searched the room, the prisoner sat in a chair with what was apparently complete calm (but you must hear this from the witnesses); and smoked a cigarette."

Someone coughed.

It was an inadvertent cough, since every face in the court wore a strain of gravity; but it caused a stir. How most of the people had taken all this I could not tell. Still, such things have an atmosphere; and this atmosphere was sinister. Behind us in the seats of the City Lands

Corporation were two women. One was good-looking and wore a leopard-skin coat; the other was plain, not to say ugly, and made up her aristocratic face several times. It is only fair to admit that they did not shift round or laugh or make their voices carry; the metallic whispers reached only us.

Leopard-Skin said: "Do you know, I met him at a cocktail party once. I say, isn't it frightfully exciting? Just think, in three weeks he'll be hanged."

Plain-Face said: "Do you find it amusing, darling? I do wish they would give one a comfortable place to sit."

Sir Walter Storm leaned against the back of the bench, spreading out his arms along it, and contemplated the jury.

"Now, members of the jury, just what does the prisoner himself have to say to all this? How does he explain the fact that he, and he alone, could have been with the deceased when Mr. Hume died? How does he explain the presence of his finger-prints on the weapon? How does he explain (a fact which will further be presented to you) that he went to that house armed with a pistol? You will hear in detail the various remarks he made to Mr. Fleming, to Dyer, and to Dr. Spencer Hume, who arrived shortly after the discovery of the body.

"But most of these remarks are contained in the statement he made to Divisional Detective-Inspector Mottram at 12.15 a.m. on January 5th. The prisoner accompanied Inspector Mottram and Sergeant Raye to Dover Street, where he voluntarily made the statement which I now propose to read to you. He said:

"I make this statement voluntarily and of my own free will, having been told that anything I say will be taken down in writing and may be used as evidence.

"I wish to clear myself. I am absolutely innocent. I arrived in London at 10.45 this morning. The deceased knew I was coming, since my *fiancée* had written to him saying that I would take the nine o'clock train from Frawnend, in Sussex. At 1.30 Mr. Hume rang me up on the telephone, and asked me to come to his house at six o'clock. He said he wished to settle matters concerning his daughter. I went to his house at 6.10. He greeted me with complete friendliness. We spent a few minutes talking about archery, and I then noticed the three arrows hanging on the wall. He said that you could kill a man with one of those arrows. I said, meaning it as a joke, that I had not come there to kill anybody unless it became absolutely necessary. At this time I am certain that the door was not bolted, and I did not have any kind of weapon on my person.

"I told him I wished to marry Miss Hume, and asked his consent. He asked me if I would have a drink, and I said I would. He poured out two glasses of whisky and soda, giving me one and taking the other himself. Then he said that he would drink my health, and he gave his full consent to my marriage with Miss Hume."

Sir Walter lifted his eyes from the paper. For what seemed a long time he remained looking steadily at the jury. We could not see his face; but the back of his wig was eloquent.

"The Crown will indeed ask you to believe that the deceased invited him there to 'settle matters concerning his daughter.' You will have to decide whether you think this statement reasonable, or probable, on the face of it. He goes there, they fall to talking of archery as soon as the prisoner enters the room, and Mr. Hume in the friendliest possible manner announces that you could kill a man with one of those arrows. You may think this extraordinary conduct, although it allows the prisoner to make his joke about murder. You may think it still more extraordinary that the deceased, having expressed before other witnesses such sentiments towards the prisoner as you will hear, should drink success to the prisoner and approval to the marriage. But what follows?

"I had drunk about half of the whisky and soda when I felt my head going round, and I knew I must be losing consciousness. I tried to speak, but could not. I knew a drug must have been put into that drink, but I felt myself falling forward, and the last thing I remember is Mr. Hume saying: 'What is wrong with you? Have you gone mad?'

"When I came to myself again I was sitting in the same chair, though I believe I had fallen out of it before. I felt ill. I looked at my watch, and saw it was half-past six. Then I noticed Mr. Hume's foot on the other side of the desk. He was lying there dead, just as you saw him. I called to him to get up. I could not think what had happened. I went round the room, noticing that one of the arrows had been taken off the wall. I tried the door, and found it was bolted on the inside. I also examined the shutters, and they were locked as well. It occurred to me that possibly I might be suspected of having killed him, so I went to look for the glasses of whisky that Mr. Hume had poured out. I could not find them. The decanter of whisky was full again on the sideboard, and the syphon of soda did not seem to have been used. There were four clean glasses: but two of them may have been the glasses we used; I don't know.

"A short time after this I went over and looked at the door again. I then noticed that dust on my hand, as you called my attention to it later. I went back and looked at the arrow. While I was doing so, someone knocked at the door; and I saw there was nothing else to do, so I opened it. The big man you call Fleming came charging in, and the servant behind him carrying a poker, and Miss Jordan hanging about the doorway. That is all I can tell you. I never touched that arrow at any time."

There was a rustle as Sir Walter flipped over the flimsy typewritten sheets, and put them down. That rustle went through the court.

Leopard-Skin whispered: "Why, he's as mad as a hatter."

Plain-Face said: "Do you really think so, darling? How terribly naïve of you. That's what he *wants* them to think, I daresay."

"Ss—t!"

"Members of the jury," continued Sir Walter, spreading out his hands with a gesture of magnanimity and even perplexity, "I shall not offer to comment on that statement, nor on such physical evidence as will be outlined by the witnesses and the police officers. What explanation can be made for these extraordinary statements, what interpretation will be placed on them by the prisoner or by my learned friend, it is not within my province to say. The contention of the Crown is that this man, finding in Avory Hume an angry, unexpected, and determined opposition to a cherished project, quarrelled with him and brutally killed an old man who had done him no harm.

"In conclusion, I need remind you only of this: The matter before you is to determine whether or not the evidence which the Crown will lay before you supports the charge of murder. That is your painful task, and your only task. If you think that the Crown have not proved their case beyond any reasonable doubt, you will have no hesitation in doing your duty. I tell you quite frankly that the Crown can supply no reason for the victim's sudden antagonism towards the prisoner. But that, I shall submit, is not the point at issue: The point at issue is what effect this antagonism had on the prisoner. The antagonism itself is a fact, and you may think a starting-point in the chain of facts we shall lay before you. If, therefore, you think that the case for the Crown has been fairly proved, you will not allow a weakness of character on the part of the prisoner to be turned into a strange link for his defence; and you must have no hesitation in condemning him to the extreme penalty of the law."

II

"LOOK AT PHOTOGRAPH NUMBER 5"

THE ATTORNEY-GENERAL SAT DOWN WITH SOME RUSTLING, AND a glass of water was handed up to him from the solicitors' table below. An officer of the court, who had been tiptoeing past the jury-box with his back bent down so as not to obscure the jury's view of counsel, straightened up. Mr. Huntley Lawton, Sir Walter's junior, rose to his feet to examine the first witnesses.

The first two were official, and were speedily out of the box. Harry Martin Coombe, an official photographer, testified to certain photographs taken in connection with the crime. Lester George Franklin, surveyor to the Borough of Westminster, gave evidence as to his survey of the house, 12, Grosvenor Street, and produced plans of the house. Copies of all these were given to each member of the jury. Mr. Huntley Lawton, whose manner had an innocent pomposity which seemed to go out into a beak of a nose, detained the latter witness.

"I believe that on January 5th, last, at the request of Detective-Inspector Mottram, you made an examination of the room called the study at Number 12, Grosvenor Street?"

"I did."

"Did you find any means of entrance or exit in that room except the door and the windows? That is to say, was there anything in the nature of a hidden entrance?"

"There was not."

"The walls were, in fact, homogeneous?"

Silence.

The little judge looked round slightly.

"Counsel asks you," said Mr. Justice Rankin, "whether there were any holes in the walls."

It was a soft, even voice: and you awoke to several things. You suddenly became aware of a sort of concentrated common sense, whittling down all things to their real values. You also became aware of absolute mastery, which the whole court felt. The judge, sitting perched out on the edge of his tall chair, kept his head round until the witness said: "Holes, my lord? No holes"; then he blinked at Mr. Lawton with some curiosity; and then the pen in his plump hand continued to travel steadily over his notebook.

"There was not," pursued counsel, murmuring a formula, "even a crevice large enough to admit the shaft of an arrow?"

"No, sir. Nothing of the kind."

"Thank you."

There was no cross-examination; H. M. only shook his head and humped the shoulders of his gown. He was sitting down there in the same immobile fashion, and you might hope that he was not glaring in his usual malevolent way at the jury.

"Call Amelia Jordan."

They brought Miss Jordan into the witness-box, that narrow roofed-over cubicle which stands in the right angle between the jury-box and the judge's bench. Ordinarily she must have been a calm and competent woman. But she stumbled in going up the steps to the box, and was on the edge of a bad state of nerves when she took the oath. Whether nerves caused this stumble, or the stumble itself caused the nerves, we could not tell: but she flushed a dull colour. Also, she had manifestly been ill. Amelia Jordan was in her early or middle forties. She had the remains of solid, easy good looks shrivelled a little from their pleasantness by illness, but not detracted from by those streamlined chromium spectacles which contrive to suggest that no spectacles are there at all. She had no-nonsense brown hair and no-nonsense blue eyes. Her clothes caused favourable comment from the two women behind us. She was wearing black, I remember, with a black hat whose brim had a peak like a cap.

"Your name is Flora Amelia Jordan?"

"Yes."

The reply came out in a quick throat-clearing, of her voice trying to find its proper level. Without looking at the judge or the jury on either side of her, she fixed her eyes on the soothing figure of Mr. Huntley Lawton, who was putting forth his fullest personality.

"You were Mr. Hume's confidential secretary?"

"Yes. That is—no, I have not been his secretary for a long time. I mean, he had no use for a secretary after he left— That is, I kept house for him. It was better than having a paid housekeeper."

"My lord and the jury quite understand," said counsel, with a gentle heartiness. Her last words had come out in a rush, and he was even more soothing. "You were a sort of relation, I take it?"

"No, no, we were not related. We—"

"We quite understand, Miss Jordan. How long had you been with him?"

"Fourteen years."

"You knew him intimately?"

"Oh, yes, very."

The first part of Miss Jordan's examination was taken up with producing and proving two letters dealing with Mary Hume's engagement, one from the girl to her father, and one from her father to her. The first of these Miss Jordan had seen; the second, she explained, she had helped to write. Characters emerged. To judge by her letter, Mary Hume was impulsive, flighty, and a little incoherent, just as you would have imagined from the photograph of the blonde with wide-set eyes which had adorned the *Daily Express* that morning; but with a streak of strong practicality in her nature. Avory Hume showed himself as kindly and cautious, with a taste for preaching in pedantic terms. Above all, one idea seemed to delight him. "I trust I do not anticipate the future too many years when I say that I am certain I shall one day have a grandson—"

(At this moment the man in the dock went as white as a ghost.)

"—and I am so certain of this, my dear daughter, that I mean to leave everything I have in trust for the son I know you will have; and I am certain that I can look forward to many years of a happy life in the company of all of you."

There was some uneasy coughing. Answell in the dock sat with his head inclined a little forward, regarding his hands on his knees. Mr. Huntley Lawton continued the examination of Amelia Jordan.

"Do you recall any particular comments Mr. Hume made on the engagement in general?"

"Yes, he kept saying: 'This is a very satisfactory business. I could not wish for anything better.' I always said: 'But do you know anything about Mr. Answell?' He said: 'Yes, he is a fine young man; I knew his mother, and she was very sound.' Or words to that effect."

"In other words, he regarded the prospect of the marriage as definitely settled?"

"Well, we thought so."

"We?"

"The doctor and I. Dr. Spencer Hume. At least I thought so; I can't speak for anyone else."

"Now, Miss Jordan," said counsel, and paused. "Between December 31st and January 4th, did you observe any change in Mr. Hume's attitude?"

"Yes, I did."

"When did you first observe a change?"

"On that Saturday morning, the Saturday he died."

"Will you tell us what you observed?"

She was calm enough now, under Mr. Lawton's hypnotic manner. She spoke in a low but quite audible voice. At first she did not know what to do with her hands: putting them on and off the rail of the dock, and finally clasping them determinedly on the rail. When she spoke of the letter she had helped to write, her eyes had a dry and sanded look; she was keeping back tears with difficulty.

"It was like this," she began. "On the Friday it had been arranged that Dr. Spencer Hume and I should go down and spend the week-end with Mary's friends in Sussex. It was to congratulate Mary in person, really. We were to drive down; but we could not start until late Saturday afternoon, because Dr. Hume is attached to the staff of St. Praed's hospital, and could not get away until late. On Friday evening Mary rang up her father on the telephone from Sussex, and I told her about it. I must tell you all this because—"

Counsel urged her along gently. "Was Mr. Avory Hume to go with you and the doctor on this week-end?"

"No, he could not. He had some business to do on Sunday, I think it was Presbyterian Church accounts or the like; and he could not. But he said to give everyone his regards, and we were going to bring Mary back with us."

"I see. And on Saturday morning, Miss Jordan?"

"On Saturday morning," answered the witness, pouring out what had been on her mind for a long time, "at the breakfast-table, there was a letter from Mary. I knew it was from Mary because of the handwriting. And I wondered why she had written, because she had talked to her father last night."

"What has become of that letter?"

"I don't know. We looked for it afterwards, but we could not find it anywhere."

"Just tell us what Mr. Hume did or said."

"After he had read it, he got up rather quickly, and put the letter in his pocket, and walked over to the window."

"Yes?"

"I said; 'Is anything wrong?' He said: 'Mary's *fiancé* has decided to come to town today, and wants to see us.' I said: 'Oh, then we will not go to Sussex after all'—meaning, of course, that we must meet Mr. Answell, and entertain him to dinner. He turned round from the window and said: 'Be good enough to do as you are told; you will go exactly as you had planned.'"

"What was his manner when he said this?"

"Very cold and curt, which is a dangerous sign with him."

"I see. What happened then?"

"Well, I said: 'But surely you will invite him to dinner?' He looked at me for a second and said: 'We will not invite him to dinner, or anywhere else.' Then he walked out of the room."

Slowly counsel leaned back against the bench. The man in the dock looked up briefly.

"Now, Miss Jordan, I understand that about 1.30 on Saturday afternoon you were passing the door of the drawing-room in the hall?"

"Yes."

"And you heard Mr. Hume speaking to the telephone in the drawing-room?"

"Yes."

"Did you look into the room?"

"Yes. He was sitting over at the table between the windows, where the telephone is. He had his back to me."

"Will you repeat, as nearly as you can, the exact words you heard him speak?"

The witness inclined her head calmly. "He said: 'Considering what I have heard, Mr. Answell—'"

"You will swear to the words, 'Considering what I have heard—?'"

"I will."

"Go on, please."

"'Considering what I have heard, I think it best that we should settle matters concerning my daughter.'"

The judge turned his small eyes towards counsel and spoke in the same unhurried voice:

"Mr. Lawton, do you propose to establish that it was the prisoner speaking at the other end of the telephone?"

"My lord, with your permission, we shall produce a witness who overheard both sides of the conversation on an extension of the telephone at the end of the hall; and will, I think, be willing to testify as to whether or not it was the prisoner's voice speaking."

From the left side of the front bench issued a vast throat-clearing. It had an evil and war-hunting quality. Up rose H.M. leaning his knuckles on the desk. For some reason the tail of his wig seemed to stick up straight behind like a pigtail. His voice was the first human sound we had heard here.

"Me lord," rumbled H.M., "if it's goin' to save the court's time any, we're ready to admit that it was the prisoner speakin'. In fact, we're goin' to insist on it."

After bows, and a curious feeling of wonder in the court, he thumped down. Under iron politeness the amusement among counsel communicated itself to Mr. Lawton's grave bow.

"You may proceed, Mr. Lawton," said the judge.

Counsel turned to the witness. "You have told us that the deceased said: 'Considering what I have heard, Mr. Answell, I think it best that we should settle matters concerning my daughter.' What else did he say?"

"He said: 'Yes, I quite appreciate that'—waiting, you see, as though the other person had said something in the meantime—'but this is not the place to discuss it. Can you arrange to call at my home?' Then: 'Would six o'clock this evening be convenient?'"

"What was his tone when he said this?"

"Very curt and formal."

"And what happened then?"

"He put up the receiver quite quietly, and looked at the 'phone for a moment, and then he said: 'My dear Answell, I'll settle your hash, damn you.'"

Pause.

"And how did he speak these words?"

"The same way he had spoken before, only more satisfied."

"You gathered that he was talking to himself: that is to say, speaking his thoughts aloud?"

"Yes."

Like most witnesses, when coming to tell a story or quoting actual words, she was on the defensive. She seemed to feel that each word she said might be picked up and used against her. Under the shadow of the black hat, with its brim like the peak of a cap, her faded good looks and fashionable glasses seemed to withdraw. If there is such a thing as a severely practical clinging-vine, it was Amelia Jordan. She had a singularly sweet voice, which gave even the mild expletive "damn" a sound of incongruity.

"What did you do after you had heard this?"

"I went away quickly." Hesitation. "I was so—well, so shocked at all this sudden change, and the way he spoke about Mr. Answell, that I did not know what to think; and I did not want him to see me."

"Thank you." Counsel reflected. "'*Considering what I have heard,*'" repeated Lawton, in a ruminating way, but with very distinct pronunciation. "Was it your impression that Mr. Hume had heard something against the prisoner which had caused him to change his mind so forcibly?"

The judge spoke without a muscle seeming to move in his face.

"Mr. Lawton, I cannot allow that. Counsel has already stated that the Crown attempt to show no definite cause in this matter. You will therefore refrain from implying one."

"Beg-lordship's-pardon," said the other with hearty humility, and an immediate turn. "I assure your lordship that it was far from my intention. Let me try again. Miss Jordan: should you describe Mr. Hume as a man whose conduct was governed by whims?"

"No, of all people."

"He was a reasonable man, influenced by reasons?"

"Yes."

"If (let us say) he thought John Smith an intelligent man on Monday, he would not think him a complete imbecile on Tuesday unless he had discovered some good reason for thinking so?"

The judge's soft voice silenced every creak in the court.

"Mr. Lawton, I must insist that you stop leading the witness."

Counsel, in gentlemanly humility, muttered: "If-yr-ludship-pleases," and went on: "Now, Miss Jordan, let us come to the evening of January 4th. At six o'clock on that evening, how many people (to your knowledge) were in the house?"

"There was Mr. Hume, and Dyer, and myself."

"Are there no other occupants?"

"Yes, Dr. Hume and a cook and a maid. But the cook and the maid had the evening off. And I was to pick up Dr. Hume in the car at St. Praed's Hospital as near six-fifteen as I could, because we were driving straight down to Sussex from there—"

"Quite, Miss Jordan," interposed counsel, smoothing away the volubility of nervousness. "Where were you at about six-ten?"

"I was upstairs, packing up. Dr. Hume had asked me whether I would put a few things into a suitcase for him, because he did not have time to come home from the hospital to get them; and I was packing my own valise—"

"Exactly; we quite understand. I believe that at about six-ten you heard the front-door bell ring?"

"Yes."

"What did you do?"

"I ran out to the stairs and looked over the banisters."

"Did you see the prisoner come in?"

"Yes. I—I peeped through the lower part of the banisters," said the witness, and flushed. She added: "I wanted to see what he looked like."

"Quite natural. Will you describe what happened?"

"Dyer opened the door. The—that man over there," with a quick look, "came in. He said his name was Answell, and that Mr. Hume was expecting him. He dropped his hat on the floor. Dyer asked him for his hat and coat, and he said he preferred to keep his coat on."

"He preferred to keep his overcoat on," said counsel slowly. "What was his demeanour then?"

"He spoke very angrily."

"And after that?"

"Dyer took him down the hall, and round the bend of the little passage that goes to the study. He looked up at me as he went past. They went into the study, and that is all I saw. I went upstairs to finish packing. I did not know what to think."

"Just tell us what you did, Miss Jordan; that will be sufficient. Let us go on to a few minutes before half-past six. Where were you then?"

"I put on my hat and coat and picked up the bags and came downstairs. Dyer had been told to bring the car round from the garage in Mount Street and put it at the door. I had been expecting him to call me, but when I came downstairs I could not find anyone. I went down to the study door to find out whether Mr. Hume had any last messages or instructions before I left."

"He had no 'last messages,' Miss Jordan," commented Mr. Lawton, with unscrupulous grimness. "What did you do?"

"I was going to knock at the door when I heard someone behind it say: 'Get up, damn you.'" Again the word fell with some incongruity from her lips. She pronounced it self-consciously, as people do in public.

"Anything else?"

"Yes, I think it also said: 'Get up off that floor and say something.'"

"Was it a loud voice?"

"Rather loud."

"Was it the prisoner's voice?"

"I know now it was. I hardly recognised it then. I associated it somehow with what I had heard Mr. Hume say that morning—"

"Did you try the door?"

"Yes, for a second."

"Was it bolted on the inside?"

"Well, I did not think about its being bolted then. It was locked somehow."

"And then?"

"Just then Dyer came round the corner of the passage with his hat and overcoat. I ran to him and said: 'They are fighting; they are killing each other; go and stop them.' He said: 'I will go for a constable.' I said: 'You are a coward; run next door and fetch Mr. Fleming.'"

"What were you doing then?"

"I was dancing up and down, I think. He would not go; he said that I had better go in case anything happened, and with me alone in the house. So I did."

"You found Mr. Fleming quickly?"

"Yes, he was just coming down the steps of his house."

"He returned to the house with you?"

"Yes, and we found Dyer coming from the back of the hall with a poker in his hand. Mr. Fleming said: 'What is happening?' Dyer said: 'It is very quiet in there.'"

"The three of you went to the study door, I understand?"

"Yes, and Dyer knocked. Then Mr. Fleming knocked and hit harder."

"And then?"

"Well, we heard steps, like, inside; and then someone started to draw the bolt."

"You are positive that the door was then bolted, and that the bolt had to be withdrawn?"

"Yes, to judge by the sound of it. It worked about a bit, you know; and slid, and the door thumped a little."

"How long a time should you say elapsed between the time of the knocking and the time the bolt was drawn?"

"I don't know. Perhaps it was not very long, but it seemed like ages."

"A full minute, should you say?"

"Maybe."

"Please tell the jury what happened then."

She did not tell the jury. She looked at her hands on the edge of the rail. "The door opened a few inches, and someone looked out. I saw it was that man. Then he opened the door up and said: 'All right; you had better come in.' Mr. Fleming ran in, and Dyer walked after him."

"Did you go into the room?"

"No, I stayed by the door."

"Just say exactly what you saw."

"I saw Avory lying beside the desk, on his back, with his feet towards me."

"Have you seen these photographs?" He indicated. "I think you nodded, Miss Jordan? Yes. Thank you. Just take that in your hand, if you will."

The yellow booklet was handed up to her.

"Look at photograph number 5, please. Is that how he was lying?"

"Yes. I think so."

"Believe me, I deeply... yes, you may hand it down. How near the body did you go?"

"No nearer than the door. They said he was dead."

"Who said he was dead?"

"Mr. Fleming, I think."

"Do you recall anything the accused said?"

"I remember the first part of it. Mr. Fleming asked him who did it, and the accused said: 'I suppose you will say I did it.' Mr. Fleming said: 'Well, you have finished him; we had better send for the police.' I remember what I saw very well, but I cannot remember much of what I heard. I was not feeling quite right."

"What was the accused's demeanour?"

"Very calm and collected, I thought, except that his neck-tie was hanging out over his overcoat."

"What did the accused do when Mr. Fleming spoke of sending for the police?"

"He sat down in a chair by the desk, and got a cigarette-case out of his inside pocket, and took out a cigarette and lighted it."

Mr. Huntley Lawton put the tips of his fingers on his desk, remained quiet for a moment, and then bent down to confer with his leader; but I thought that this was a conference for emphasis. The end of that recital was like coming up from under water: you could feel the air drawn into your lungs. At one time or another everyone in court, I think—except the judge—had glanced at the prisoner; but it was a quick and unpleasantly furtive look, which made you glance back from the dock again. Mr. Justice Rankin finished making his neat notes, the pen travelling steadily; he looked up, and waited. The witness now had an air of feeling that she must remain in the box for ever, and of trying to prepare herself for that.

Mr. Huntley Lawton had only one more thrust. A quick rustle, as of settling back, went through the court when he addressed the witness again.

"I believe, Miss Jordan, that soon after the discovery of the body you were sent in the car to bring back Dr. Spencer Hume from St. Praed's Hospital in Praed Street?"

"Yes, Mr. Fleming took me by the shoulder and said to drive over there and get him quickly, because if he had an operation or anything they would not give him a message."

"You are unable to tell us anything more of the subsequent events of that night?"

"No."

"Is this because, on the way back from the hospital, you were taken ill with brain fever and were not able to leave your room for a month?"

"Yes."

Counsel moved his hand over the white sheets of the brief. "I ask you to consider carefully, Miss Jordan. Is there anything further you can tell us, anything at all, that you heard the accused say? Did he say anything when he sat down in the chair, and lighted his cigarette?"

"Yes, he answered something: a question or a statement, I think."

"What was the question?"

"Someone said: 'Are you made of stone?'"

"'Are you made of stone.' And he answered?"

"He said: 'Serve him right for doctoring my whisky.'"

For a brief space of time counsel remained looking at her. Then he sat down.

Sir Henry Merrivale rose to cross-examine for the defence.

III

"IN THE LITTLE DARK PASSAGE"

JUST WHAT LINE THE DEFENCE WOULD TAKE NOBODY COULD TELL: there was a frail ghost in insanity or even manslaughter: but, knowing H.M., I could not believe he would try anything so half-hearted as that. It was possible that his first cross-examination might give some indication.

He rose majestically—an effect which was somewhat marred by the fact that his gown caught on something, probably himself. It tore with a ripping noise so exactly like a raspberry that for one terrible second I thought he had given one. He squared himself. However rusty his legal talents had become, it was in cross-examination, where leading questions are permitted and almost anything within reason may be brought up, that his usual rough-and-tumble tactics would be most deadly. But that was the trouble. This woman had won the sympathy of everyone, including the jury: to pitch into her would have been unwise. We need not have been uneasy. After one malevolent glance over his shoulder at the torn gown, showing the glasses pulled down on his broad nose, he addressed her as gently as Huntley Lawton—if a trifle more abruptly. His big voice put the witness and the court at ease. It was in a tone of sit-down-and-have-a-drink-and-let's-talk-this-thing-over.

"Ma'am," said H.M. off-handedly, "do you believe Mr. Hume heard something bad against the accused that made him change his mind all of a sudden?"

Silence.

"I don't know."

"Still, though," argued H.M., "since my learned friend has sort of eased the question in, let's deal with it. As he said, *if* Mr. Hume changed his mind, it must 'a' been because he learned something from someone, mustn't it?"

"I should certainly have thought so."

"Yes. And, conversely, if he hadn't heard anything, he wouldn't have changed his mind?"

"I suppose not. No, certainly not."

"Now, ma'am," pursued H.M. in the same argumentative way, "he seemed to be in the best of spirits on Friday evening, when he arranged for you and Dr. Hume to go to Sussex next day? Hey?"

"Oh, yes."

"Did he go out of the house that night?"

"No."

"Receive any visitors?"

"No."

"Did he get any letters, 'phone calls, messages of any kind?"

"No. Oh, except Mary's telephone-call in the evening. I answered the 'phone and talked to her for a minute or two; and then he came to the 'phone; but I don't know what he said."

"And at breakfast next mornin', how many letters did he get?"

"Just that one, with Mary's writing."

"Uh-huh. Consequently, if he heard anything against the accused, he must have heard it from his own daughter?"

There was a slight stir. Sir Walter Storm made as if to rise; but instead fell to conferring with Huntley Lawton.

"Well, I—I don't know. How can I?"

"Still, it definitely was after readin' that letter that he seemed to show his first tearin' antagonism towards the accused, wasn't it?"

"Yes."

"The whole thing seemed to start then and there?"

"From what I saw of it, I thought so."

"Yes. Now, ma'am, suppose I told you that in that letter there wasn't one word about the accused except the fact that he was comin' to town?"

The witness touched her glasses. "I don't know what I am supposed to answer."

"Because I do tell you that, ma'am. We've got that letter right here, and at the proper time we're goin' to produce it. So if I tell you there's nothin' in it about the accused except the bare fact that he meant to come to town, does it alter your view of Mr. Hume's conduct?"

Without waiting for a reply H.M. sat down.

He left a much-puzzled court. He had not upset, or tried to upset, one thing in the witness's story; but he left a feeling that there was something in the wind. I expected Mr. Lawton to re-examine; but it was Sir Walter Storm who rose.

"Call Herbert William Dyer."

Miss Jordan left the box, and Dyer stepped gravely into it. It was evident from the first that he would make a good and convincing witness, as he did. Dyer was a quiet man in the late fifties, his head covered with close-cut greyish hair, his manner attentive. As though making concessions both to private life and to his employment, he wore a short black coat and striped trousers: instead of a wing collar, he had an ordinary stiff one with a dark tie. The man oozed respectability, without doing so offensively. As he passed between the jury-box and the solicitors' table, I noticed that he made a grave sign of recognition which was neither a bow nor a nod to a light-haired young man who was sitting at the table. Dyer took the oath in a quite audible voice. He stood with his chin a little tilted up, his hands hanging down easily at his sides.

Sir Walter Storm's heavy voice contrasted with the sharp and pushing tones of Huntley Lawton.

"Your name is Herbert William Dyer, and you were for five and half years in the service of Mr. Hume?"

"Yes, sir."

"Before that I understand that you were for eleven years in the employ of the late Lord Senlac, and at his death you were left a legacy for faithful service?"

"That is so, sir."

"During the war you served with the 14th Middlesex Rifles, and were awarded the D.C.M. in 1917?"

"Yes, sir."

First of all he corroborated Miss Jordan's story about the telephone-call to the accused. There was, he explained, a telephone-extension under the stairs at the rear of the hallway. He had been instructed to ring up the Pyrenees Garage to enquire about some repairs that were being done to Mr. Hume's car, and to make sure the car would be ready for use that evening. At about one-thirty he went to the telephone, and heard the deceased speaking on the other wire. The deceased had asked for Regent 0055, had asked to speak to the prisoner, and a voice which Dyer could identify as the prisoner's replied: "This is he speaking." Making sure that the connection was established, Dyer had then replaced the receiver and gone down in the direction of the drawing-room. Passing the door, he had heard the rest of the conversation described by the first witness. He had also overheard the unfortunate soliloquy.

"When did Mr. Hume next refer to this subject?"

"Almost as soon as he had finished telephoning. I went into the drawing-room, and he said: 'I am expecting a visitor at six o'clock this evening. He may give some trouble, for he is not to be trusted.'"

"What did you say to this?"

"I said: 'Yes, sir.'"

"And when was the next occasion on which you heard of it?"

"At about five-fifteen, or it may have been a few minutes later. Mr. Hume called me into the study."

"Describe what happened."

"He was sitting at his desk, with a chess-board and pieces in front of him, working out a chess-problem. Without looking up from the board he told me to close and lock the shutters. I must have expressed surprise, without meaning to do so. He moved a piece on the board and replied: 'Do as I tell you; do you think I want Fleming to see that young fool making trouble?'"

"Was it his custom to *explain* to you the reasons for his orders?"

"Never, sir," answered the witness emphatically.

"I understand that the windows of Mr. Randolph Fleming's dining-room face those of the study across a paved passage between the two houses?"

"That is so."

The Attorney-General made a sign. From under the witness-box there was produced the first of the two curious exhibits: the steel shutters themselves, fastened to the inside of a dummy window-frame with a sash window. Some excited whispering greeted them. They were constructed after the French style, like two small folding doors, except that there were no slits or openings in them; and across the centre ran a flat steel bar with a handle. They were hoisted up for the inspection of the witness and the jury.

"We have here," continued Sir Walter Storm imperturbably, "the pair of shutters from the window marked A in the plan. They were set up by Inspector Mottram under the direction of Mr. Dent of Messrs. Dent & Sons, Cheapside, who fitted them to the windows originally. Will you tell me if that is one of the pair of shutters you locked on Saturday evening?"

Dyer inspected the exhibit carefully, and took his time.

"Yes, sir, it is."

"Will you now lock the shutters as you did on Saturday evening?"

The bar, which was a little stiff, snapped into its socket with a bump and clang which had a grisly effect in that legal schoolroom. Dyer dusted his hands. More than a window was locked away with the movement of that bar. Behind us the girl in the leopard-skin coat whispered conversationally:

"I say; they draw a bolt, don't they, when the trap goes down on the gallows?"

Dyer pulled back the bar, satisfied. He dusted his hands again.

"Outside these shutters, I believe," the Attorney-General went on, "there were two sash-windows?"

"There were."

"Were these also locked on the inside?"

"Yes, sir."

"Very well. Now tell my lord and the jury what occurred after you had locked the shutters."

"I went round to see that the room was in order."

"At this time did you observe on the wall over the mantelpiece the three arrows which were accustomed to hang there?"

"I did."

"Did the deceased say anything to you at this time?"

"Yes, sir. He asked me, still without looking up from the chess-board, whether we had enough to drink on hand. I saw that there was a full decanter of whisky on the sideboard, a syphon of soda-water, and four glasses."

"Look at this decanter here, and tell me whether it is the same one you saw on the sideboard at about five-fifteen on Saturday evening?"

"It is the same one," answered the witness. "I bought it myself, at Mr. Hume's order, from Hartley's in Regent Street. I believe it is a very expensive cut-glass decanter."

"Did he say anything else to you at this time?"

"He remarked that he was expecting Mr. Fleming there that night to play chess, and that we must always have a suitable amount to drink ready when Mr. Fleming came. I understood him to be speaking in the way of a joke."

"At ten minutes past six, then, you let the prisoner in at the front door?"

Dyer's account of this substantiated the first witness's. Then it grew dangerous.

"I took the prisoner to Mr. Hume's study. They did not shake hands. Mr. Hume said to me: 'That is all; you may go; go and see whether the car is ready.' I went out and closed the door. At that time Mr. Hume was sitting behind his desk, and the prisoner in a chair in front of it. I do not remember hearing anyone bolt the door after I had gone out. I was not exactly alarmed, but I was uneasy. Finally I went back and listened."

It is these shorn words of the court-room which seem to me most powerful. We seemed to see Dyer standing in the little dark passage outside the door. There was not much light in the passage even by day, he explained. At one end of it there was a door giving on the paved brick way between this house and Mr. Fleming's, and there had formerly been a glass panel in this door; but Mr. Hume's love of privacy had made him change that door for a solid one six months before. By night there was only the light from the main hall. Reduced to the form of a statement, Dyer's testimony would have run like this:

"I heard the prisoner say: 'I did not come here to kill anyone unless it becomes absolutely necessary.' I heard little of what Mr. Hume said, because he usually spoke in a low tone. Presently Mr. Hume began talking rather sharply, but I could not make out his words. At the end of it he suddenly said: 'Man, what is wrong with you? Have you gone mad?' Then there was a sound which I took to be the sound of a scuffle. I tapped on the door, and called out to ask if anything was wrong. Mr. Hume called out and told me to go away: he said he could deal with this. He spoke in a voice as though he were out of breath.

"But he had told me to go and get the car, and I did. I had to, or I should have lost my position. I put on my hat and overcoat, and went round to the Pyrenees Garage. It is about a three or four minutes' walk.

They had not quite finished repairing the car, and said they had told us they intended to be even longer. I tried to hurry back, but there was a mist and this impeded me in driving. When I got back it was about six-thirty-two by the grandfather clock.

"Beyond the turning of the little passage that goes to the study, I met Miss Jordan. She said they were fighting, and asked me to stop them. There is not much light in the hall. Miss Jordan fell over a big suitcase belonging to Dr. Spencer Hume; and when I said that it would be more sensible to fetch a policeman, she kicked at me. I think she was crying.

"Then she went to get Mr. Fleming, at my suggestion, while I procured a poker. All three of us went to the door. About a minute after we had knocked, the prisoner opened the door. There is absolutely no doubt that up to this time the door had been bolted on the inside.

"When the prisoner said: 'All right; you had better come in,' Mr. Fleming and I did so. I went at once to Mr. Hume, who was lying as he is in that photograph. The arrow you show me was protruding from his chest. I did not feel his heart, because I did not wish to get blood all over my hand; but I felt his pulse, and he was dead.

"There was no person hiding in the room. I went immediately and looked at the shutters, calling Mr. Fleming's attention to them as I did so. The reason was that even then I could not associate a thing like this with a gentleman such as I had heard the prisoner to be. Both the shutters were still barred, and the windows locked behind them."

Other eyes, other opera-glasses. The Attorney-General took him over confirmation of Miss Jordan's account.

"Now, Dyer, when mention was made of bringing in the police, did the prisoner say anything?"

"He said: 'Yes, I suppose we had better get it over with.'"

"Did you make any comment on this?"

"Yes, sir. I know I should not have spoken, but I could not help myself. He was sitting in that chair with one leg thrown over the arm of the chair as though he owned it, and lighting a cigarette. I said: 'Are you made of stone?'"

"What reply did he make to this?"

"He replied: 'Serve him right for drugging my whisky.'"

"What did you make of that?"

"I did not know what to make of it, sir. I looked over at the sideboard and said: 'What whisky?' He pointed his cigarette at me and said: 'Now listen. When I came in here he gave me a whisky-and-soda. There was something in it, a drug. It knocked me out and someone came in and killed him. This is a frame-up, and you know it.'"

"Did you go over and look at the sideboard?"

For the first time the witness put his hands on the rail of the box.

"I did. The decanter of whisky was just as full as when I had left it, and the syphon of soda was also full: there was the little paper fastener still over the nozzle. The glasses gave no sign of being used."

"Did the accused exhibit any sign or symptom which led you to think he had been under the influence of a drug?"

Dyer frowned.

"Well, sir, I cannot say as to that." He raised eyes of candour; he violated the rules, he was instantly corrected for it, and he drove a long nail into the scaffold of James Answell. "But," said Dyer, "I overheard your police-doctor say the accused had not taken any drug at all."

IV

"EITHER THERE IS A WINDOW, OR THERE ISN'T"

AT SHORTLY PAST ONE O'CLOCK, WHEN THE COURT ADJOURNED for lunch, Evelyn and I went downstairs gloomily. The Old Bailey, full of those shuffling echoes which are thrown back from marble or tile, was crowded. We got into the centre of a crush converging at the head of the stairs to the Central Hall.

I voiced a mutual view. "Though why the blazes we should feel so much prejudiced in his favour I don't know, unless it's because H.M. is defending him. Or unless it's because he looks so absolutely right: that is, he looks as though he'd lend you a tenner if you needed it, and stand by you if you got into trouble. The trouble is, they all look guilty in the dock. If they're calm, it's a bad sign. If they're wild, it's a still worse sign. This may be due to our rooted and damnable national belief that if they weren't guilty they probably wouldn't be in the dock at all."

"H'm," said my wife, her face wearing that concentrated expression which betokens wild ideas. "I've been thinking…"

"It's inadvisable."

"Yes, I know. But do you know, Ken, while they were stringing out all that evidence, I kept thinking that nobody could *possibly* be as loony as that chap seems to be unless he were innocent. But then along came that business of his having taken no sleeping-drug at all. If they can prove that by medical evidence… well… unless H.M. will try to prove insanity after all."

What H.M. wished to prove was not apparent. He had subjected Dyer to a singularly long and singularly uninspired cross-examination, directed chiefly to proving that on the day of the murder Hume had been attempting to get in touch with Answell by telephone as early as nine o'clock in the morning. H.M.'s one good point concerned the arrow with which the crime had been committed, and even this was left enigmatic. H.M. called attention to the fact that half of the blue feather attached to it had been broken off. Was that feather intact when Dyer had seen the arrow on the wall before the crime? Oh, yes. Sure? Positive. But the piece of feather was missing when they discovered the body? Yes. Did they find the other half anywhere in the room? No; they had searched as a matter of form, but they could not find it.

H.M.'s last attack was still more obscure. Were the three arrows hung flat against the wall? Not all of them, Dyer replied. The two arrows making the sides of the triangle lay flat on the wall; but the base of it, crossing the other two, had been set out on steel staples about a quarter of an inch.

"And all that," Evelyn commented, "H.M. asked as quietly as a lamb. I tell you, Ken, it's unnatural. He buttered up that little butler as though he were his own witness. I say, do you think we could see H.M.?"

"I doubt it. He'll probably be having lunch at the Bar Mess."

At this point our attention was forcibly called. Who the man was (whether he was someone attached to the courts or an outsider with a thirst for imparting information) we never learned. With an effect like a Maskelyne illusion, a little man thrust himself out of the crowd and tapped me on the shoulder.

"Want to see two of the Ones in the Big Case?" he asked in a whisper. "Just ahead of you! That there on the right is Dr. Spencer Hume, and that there on the left is Reginald Answell, 'is cousin. They're right amongst us, and they'll 'ave to go downstairs together. Ss-t!"

Back went the head. By the convergence of the crowd on the big marble stairs, the two men he indicated were swept to a stiff march side by side. The bleak March light showed them not too favourably. Dr. Hume was a middle-sized, rather tubby man with greying black hair parted and combed to such nicety on his round head that it gave the effect of a wheel. He turned his head sideways for a brief look; we saw a nose radiating self-confidence, and a gravely pursed-up mouth. He carried, incongruously, a top-hat, which he was trying to prevent being squashed.

His companion I recognised as the young man whom I had seen sitting at the solicitors' table, and to whom Dyer had given a sign of recognition. He was a good type; lean, with a fine carriage of the shoulders and sharply defined jaws. The tailor had done well by him, and he was absently hitting the edge of his hand on a bowler hat.

The two took a quick look at each other, and descended with that shuffle-fall which is the march of the Old Bailey. They decided to notice each other's presence. I wondered whether the atmosphere would be hostile; but, as they spoke, they appeared to decide. The atmosphere between them, palpable and sticky as glue, was hypocrisy.

Reginald Answell spoke in that tone exclusively reserved for funerals.

"How is Mary taking it?" he inquired in a hoarse whisper.

"Pretty badly, I'm afraid," said the doctor, shaking his head.

"Too bad!"

"Yes, unfortunately."

They descended another step.

"I didn't see her in court," observed Reginald out of the side of his mouth. "Are they calling her as a witness?"

"The prosecution aren't," said Dr. Hume in a curious tone. He looked sideways. "And I notice they're not calling you?"

"Oh, no. I'm not concerned in it. The defence aren't calling me either. I couldn't do him any good. I only got to the house after he—you know, fainted. Poor old Jim. I thought he was made of stronger stuff than that, big as he is. Mad as a coot, of course."

"Believe me, I quite appreciate that," murmured Dr. Hume, looking quickly over his shoulder; "and I myself should have been only too willing to testify—but there seems to be some doubt on the part of the Crown, and he himself, you know, says—" He stopped. "No hard feelings?"

"No. Oh, no. There *is* insanity in the family, you know."

They descended nearly the whole flight.

"Nothing much, of course. Only like a touch of the tar-brush a few generations back. I wonder what he's eating?"

The doctor was sententious. "Ah, that's difficult to say. I expect *'"He's drinking bitter beer alone," the colour-sergeant said.'*"

"Why the hell," asked the other quietly, "do you bring up the army?"

They stopped.

"My dear fellow, it was only in a manner of speaking! Besides, I didn't know you were any longer connected with the army," Dr. Hume told him, with an air of concern. They stopped under the great rotunda and dim mural paintings of the Central Hall; Dr. Hume became gravely kind. "Now let's face it. It's a sad business. I've lost a brother myself, you know. But there it is: the world must keep on, and men must work, and women must weep, as they say. So the most sensible thing to do is to get this unpleasant matter off our minds and forget it as soon as possible, eh? Good-bye, captain. I'd better not be seen shaking hands with you; it wouldn't look seemly, under the circumstances."

He bustled off.

For they've done with Danny Deever; you can hear the Dead March play;
The regiment's in column, and they're marching them away—

There is something about the atmosphere of this place which impels people to moralise in just the way those lines were going through my head. It was dispelled in a moment by the surprising and welcome spectacle of Lollypop, H.M.'s blonde secretary, pushing her way through the crowd towards us. Evelyn was beginning to say: "For God's sake, let's get out of here—" with her very attractive face flushed, when she stopped.

"Hooray!" said Evelyn, expelling her breath.

"It's H.M.," said Lollypop, rather unnecessarily. "He wants to see you."

"Where is he? What's he doing?"

"At the moment," said Lollypop doubtfully, "I should think he was breaking furniture. That's what he said he was going to do when I saw him last. But by the time you arrive I expect he'll be eating his lunch. You're to go to the Milton's Head Tavern, Wood Street, Cheapside—just round the corner, it is. Oh, dear."

H.M.'s extensive knowledge of obscure eating-houses is due to his extensive knowledge of obscure people. Everyone seems to know him, and the more disreputable the better. The Milton's Head, tucked up into a crazy little alley off Wood Street, looked as though it had not had its little-paned windows cleaned since the Great Fire. There was now a great fire burning in the tap-room against the raw March cold, and artificial geraniums in the windows emphasised that cold. We were directed upstairs to a private room, where H.M. sat behind an immense pewter tankard and a plate of lamb-chops. With a napkin tucked into his collar, he was chewing at the side of one lamb-chop in that fashion which popular film-tradition attributes to King Henry the Eighth.

"Ar," said H.M., opening one eye.

I waited, to see which way the mood would go.

"Well," growled H.M., only half-malevolently, "I suppose you're not goin' to keep that door open all day? You want me to die of pneumonia?"

"In the past," I said, "you've got out of some almighty tight places in the face of evidence. Is it possible that you can get out of this one?"

H.M. put down the lamb-chop and opened his eyes wide. Over his wooden face crept an expression of amusement.

"Ho ho," he said. "So you think they've got the old man licked already, hey?"

"Not necessarily. H.M., is this fellow guilty?"

"No," said H.M.

"Can you prove it?"

"I dunno, son. I'm goin' to have a very good try. It depends on how much of my evidence they'll admit."

There was no raising of defences. The old man was worried, and almost showed it.

"Who's instructing you in the case?"

He rubbed his hand across his big bald head, and looked sour. "Solicitor? There's no solicitor.* Y'see, I'm the only feller who'd believe him. I got a fancy for lame dogs," he added apologetically.

There was a silence.

"What's more, if you're lookin' for any dramatic last-minute eruption of the hidden witness bustin' into court and causin' a row, get it out of your heads. You'd no more cause a row in Balmy Rankin's court than you'd find one on a chess-board. It's all goin' to be on the table all the

---

* As a rule, counsel for the defence may appear at the Old Bailey only on instructions from a solicitor. But there are two exceptions to this: "legal aid" cases, and "dock briefs." In legal aid cases, counsel is appointed by the judge for a prisoner having no money to employ it. When no legal aid is granted, it becomes a "dock brief," or "docker"; the accused has the right to be defended by any counsel, sitting in robes in court, whom he may select. In Answell's case there was, of course, no question of a lack of money. But since Answell—as will appear—refused to have anything to do with anyone except H.M., it became technically a dock brief. I am told that this procedure, though unconventional, is strictly legal. The ordinary dock brief is one of the best features of the impartial Central Criminal Court. Any counsel, however eminent, must serve if selected; it is a point of honour that he must put his best efforts into the defence; and his fee must be—neither more nor less—£1 3s. 6d.

time—and that's how I want it. One quiet move to another. Like chess. Or maybe like hunting. You remember the way the lines swing in *John Peel*? 'From a find to a check: from a check to a view: from a view to a kill in the morning'."

"Well, good luck to you."

"You could help," roared H.M. suddenly, wishing to get this off his chest.

"Help?"

"Now, shut up, dammit!" insisted H.M., before I could say anything. "I'm not playing any games now, or gettin' you thrown into gaol. All I want you to do is take a message, which won't compromise you any, to one of my witnesses. I can't do it myself; and I've got a suspicion of telephones since I've heard what they've done in this business."

"Which witness?"

"Mary Hume... Here comes your soup, so eat and keep quiet."

The food was excellent. At the end of it H.M.'s tension had relaxed, and he was in such a (comparative) good humour that he had fallen to grousing again. There was a good fire in the dingy grate: H.M., with his feet on the fender and a large cigar drawing well, broached the subject with a scowl.

"I'm not goin' to discuss this business with anybody," he said. "But if there's anything about it you'd like to know that won't concern what the defence knows or has had the gumption to find out—meanin' me—

"Yes," said Evelyn. "Why on earth did you have to bring this business to court? That is, of course, if you could show the police—?"

"No," said H.M. "That's one of the questions you can't ask."

He sniffed, staring at the fire.

"Well, then," I suggested, "if you say Answell isn't the murderer, have you got any explanation of how the real murderer got in and out of the room?"

"Burn me, I should hope so, son! Or what kind of a defence do you think I'd have?" asked H.M. plaintively. "Do you think I'd be such an eternal blazin' fathead as to go chargin' in without an alternative explanation? I say, it's a funny thing about that, too. It was the girl herself—this Mary Hume—who put the idea into my head when I was dead stumped. She's a nice gal. Well, I was sittin' and thinkin', and *that* didn't seem to do any good; and then she mentioned that the one thing in prison Jim Answell hated most was the Judas Window. And that tore it, you see."

"Did it? What's the Judas Window? Look here, you're not going to say there was any hocus-pocus about those steel shutters and locked windows, are you?"

"No."

"What about the door, then? Are they right in saying that the door really was bolted on the inside: and that it was a good solid door, so that the bolt couldn't be and wasn't tampered with in any way from the outside?"

"Sure. They're quite right in sayin' all that."

We all took a drink of beer. "I won't say it's impossible, because you have been known to pull it off before. But if this isn't some kind of technical evasion—?"

Some inner irony seemed to appeal to H.M.

"No, son. I mean exactly what I say. The door really was tight and solid and bolted; and the windows really were tight and solid and bolted. Nobody monkeyed with a fastening to lock or unlock either. Also, you heard the architect say there wasn't a chink or crevice or rat-hole in the walls anywhere; also true. No, I'm tellin' you: the murderer got in and out through the Judas Window."

Evelyn and I looked at each other. We both knew that H.M. was not merely making mysteries: he had discovered something new, and he turned it over and over in his mind with fascination. "The Judas Window" had a sinister sound. It suggested all sorts of images without a definite one emerging. You seemed to see a shadowy figure peering in; and that was all.

"But damn it," I said, "if all those circumstances are true, there can't be any such thing! Either there is a window or there isn't. Unless, again, you mean there was some peculiar feature in the construction of the room, which the architect didn't spot—?"

"No, son, that's the rummy part of it. The room is just like any other room. You've got a Judas Window in your own room at home; there's one in this room, and there's one in every court-room in the Old Bailey. The trouble is that so few people ever notice it."

With some difficulty he hoisted himself to his feet. He went to the window, his cigar fuming, and scowled out at the clutter of roofs.

"Now, now—" continued H.M. soothingly. "We got work to do. Ken, I want you to take a letter to Mary Hume in Grosvenor Street. Just get an answer yes or no, and come back straightaway. I want you to hear the afternoon sittin', because they're first going to put Randolph Fleming in the box, and I've got some very searchin' questions to put to him—about feathers. Fact is, if you follow very closely the testimony that has been given and will be given in court, you'll see just where I went to get my witnesses, and why."

"Any instructions?"

H.M. took the cigar out of his mouth and contemplated it. "Well... now. Considerin' that I don't want you to get into any trouble, no. Just say you're an associate of mine, and give the note I'll write for you to Mary Hume. If the little gal wants to talk about the case, go right ahead and talk, because your knowledge is pretty limited. If anyone else tackles you about it, let your tongue rattle freely, and it wouldn't do any harm to spread an atmosphere of mysterious disquiet. But don't mention the Judas window."

It was all I could get out of him. He called for paper and an envelope; he scribbled a note at the table—and sealed it. The problem seemed to be one of words as well as facts, in those three words of the Judas window. When I went downstairs I had a confused idea of thousands of houses and millions of rooms, piled into the rabbit-warren of London: each respectable and lamp-lit in its long lines of streets: and yet each containing a Judas window which only a murderer could see.

V

"NOT AN OGRE'S DEN"

THE TAXI-DRIVER WHO SET ME DOWN BEFORE NUMBER 12 Grosvenor Street eyed the house with interest. It was one of those narrow dun-coloured places in whose windows there are nowadays many *To Let* signs, set up from the street inside a little paved patch of yard with an iron railing round it. A narrow paved passage separated it from the house on the left. I went up the steps to the vestibule, out of a raw wind that was raking Grosvenor Street at the turn of the afternoon. The trim little maid who answered the doorbell began to close the door before the words were out of my mouth.

"Sorry-sir-can't-see-Miss-Hume-ill—"

"Will you tell her I have a message from Sir Henry Merrivale?"

The maid darted away, and the door wavered. She had neither invited me in nor closed it on me, so I went inside. In the hall a great grandfather clock looked at you with a no-nonsense air, and seemed to rustle rather than tick. By an agitation of draperies on an arch to the left you could follow the maid's flight. There was a slight throat-clearing inside, and Reginald Answell came out into the hall.

Seeing him now face to face, an earlier impression was confirmed. His long-jawed and saturnine good looks seemed to give him a darkish tinge which did not go well with his light hair. Under a long slope of forehead his eyes were a little sunken, but completely straightforward. Though subdued, he was not now bowed down by that thick humility-before-death he had shown on the stairs of the Old Bailey, and I judged that ordinarily he would be engaging enough.

"You're from Sir Henry Merrivale?" he asked.

"Yes."

He lowered his voice and spoke with some intensity. "Look here, old chap: Miss Hume is—not very well. I've just come round to see about it. I'm a—well, I'm a friend of the family, and certainly of hers. If you have any message, I could easily take it."

"Sorry, but the message is for Miss Hume."

He looked at me curiously, and then laughed. "By gad, you lawyers are a suspicious lot! Look here, I really *will* give her the message, you know. This isn't an ogre's den or a—" He stopped.

"Still, I think it would be best to see her."

At the rear of the hallway there was a sound of footsteps descending the stairs quickly. Mary Hume did not look ill. On the contrary, she looked strung up under a sort of hard docility which you could swear was assumed. The newspaper photograph had been surprisingly accurate. She had wide-spaced blue eyes, a short nose, and a plump chin: which features should not make for beauty, but in her they did. Her blonde hair was parted in the middle and drawn to a knot at the nape of the neck, but without an effect of curtness. She wore half-mourning, and displayed an engagement-ring.

"Did I hear you say you had a message from H.M.?" she asked without inflection.

"Miss Hume. Yes."

Reginald Answell had begun to rummage in a hat-rack. His face appeared round the ring of hats with a smile of broad charm.

"Well, I'll be pushing off, Mary."

"Thanks for everything," she said.

"Oh, that's all right. Fair exchange," he told her with jocularity. "It's all agreed, though?"

"You know me, Reg."

During this cryptic little exchange she had spoken in the same tone of affectionate docility. When he had nodded and gone out, closing the front door with considerable care, she took me to the room at the left. It was a quiet drawing-room, with a telephone on a table between the two windows, and a bright fire burning under the marble mantelpiece. She took the envelope, and went close to the fire to break the seal. When she had read the brief message inside, she dropped it carefully into the fire, turning her head from side to side to watch until each corner had burned. Then she looked back at me, and her eyes were shining.

"Just tell him yes," she said. "Yes, yes, yes!—No, please; just a moment; don't go. Were you in court this morning?"

"Yes."

"Please sit down for a moment. Have a cigarette. In the box there." She sat down on the broad low seat round the fender, and tucked one leg up under her. The firelight made her hair look more fluffy. "Tell me, was it—pretty awful? How was he?"

And this time she did not refer to H.M. I said he was behaving very well.

"I knew he would. Are you on his side? Do have a cigarette, please do. There," she urged. I offered her the box, and lit one for her. She had very delicate hands; they were trembling a little on the cigarette, which she held with both hands, and she looked up briefly over the matchflame. "Did they prove very much? How would you have felt if you had been on the jury?"

"Not very much. Besides the opening speech, there were only two witnesses, because the examinations were fairly long. Miss Jordan and Dyer—"

"Oh, that's all right. Amelia," said Mary Hume with practicality, "doesn't really dislike Jimmy, because she's too obsessed with love's young dream; and she'd like him even better if she hadn't liked my father so much."

She hesitated.

"I—I've never been at the Old Bailey. Tell me, how do they act to the people who go as witnesses? I mean, do they go and yell in their ears, and storm and rave the way they do in the films?"

"They certainly do not, Miss Hume. Get that idea out of your head!"

"Not that it matters, really." She looked sideways at the fire, and grew more calm. But a long puff of cigarette-smoke blew out against the flames, billowing back again, and she turned round once more. "Look here, tell me the truth before God: he'll be *all right*, won't he?"

"Miss Hume, you can trust H.M. to take care of him."

"I know. I do. You see, I was the one who went to H.M. in the first place. That was a month ago, when Jimmy's solicitor refused to have anything more to do with the case because he believed Jimmy was lying. I—I hadn't been keeping anything back deliberately," she explained incomprehensibly, but evidently thinking I knew. "It was only that I didn't know or guess. At first H.M. said he couldn't help me, and raved and thundered; and I'm afraid I wept a bit; and then he roared some more and said he'd do it. The trouble is, my evidence may help Jimmy a little; but it won't get him out of that awful business. And even now I haven't the remotest idea how H.M. intends to do it." She paused. "Have you?"

"Nobody ever does know," I admitted. "Honestly, the very fact that he's so quiet about it means that he's got something up his sleeve."

She gestured. "Oh, I suppose so. But I can't feel easy about something I don't know. What good is it just to say everything will be all right?"

She spoke with great intensity. Getting up from the fireside seat, she walked round the room with her shoulders hunched and her hands clasped together as though she were cold.

"When I told him as much as I knew," she went on, "the only two things that seemed to interest him at all were things that simply made no sense. One was something about a 'Judas Window',"—she sat down again—"and the other was about Uncle Spencer's best golf-suit."

"Your uncle's golf-suit? What about it?"

"It's gone," said Mary Hume.

I blinked. She made the statement as though it ought to convey something. My instructions were to discuss the case if she offered to do so, but here there was nothing to do but apply the spur of silence.

"It ought to have been hanging up in the cupboard, and it wasn't: though," said the girl, "I can *not* see what the ink-pad can have had to do with it, can you?"

I could quite agree with that. If H.M.'s defence in some fashion depended on a Judas Window, a golf-suit, and an ink-pad, it must be a very curious defence indeed.

"That is, the ink-pad in the pocket of the suit, that Mr. Fleming was so keen to get. I—I hoped you'd know something. But the fact is that both the suit and the ink-pad have gone. Oh, my God, I didn't know there was anyone in the house!"

The last words were spoken so low that I barely heard them. She got up, throwing her cigarette into the fire; and an instant later she was a composed, docile hostess turning on her guest a face as blank as a dumpling. I glanced over my shoulder, and saw Dr. Spencer Hume had come in.

His tread was brisk but subdued, as though it became the situation. Dr. Hume's round face, with its well-brushed hair having a parting that must have been a quarter of an inch wide, showed domestic worry as well as sympathy. His rather protuberant eyes—like those in the pictures of his dead brother—passed incuriously over me, and seemed to study the room.

"Hello, my dear," he said lightly. "Have you seen my eyeglasses anywhere?"

"No, uncle. I'm sure they're not here."

Dr. Hume pinched his chin. He went over and looked at the table, and then on the mantelpiece; finally he stood at a loss, and his glance towards me was more interrogative.

"This is a friend of mine, Uncle Spencer. Mr.—"

"Blake," I said.

"How do you do?" said Dr. Hume without inflection. "I seem to recognise your face, Mr. Blake. Haven't we met somewhere before?"

"Yes, your face is familiar too, doctor."

"Perhaps at the trial this morning," he suggested. He shook his head, and glanced meaningly at the girl; you would never have recognised in her the vital personality of a few minutes ago. "A bad business, Mr. Blake. Don't keep Mary too long, will you?"

She spoke quickly. "How is the trial going, Uncle Spencer?"

"As well as can be expected, my dear. Unfortunately"—I was to learn that he had a trick of beginning speeches with a hopeful assertion, and then saying "Unfortunately" with knitted brows—"unfortunately, I'm afraid there can be only one verdict. Of course, if Merrivale knows his job properly, he'll have medical evidence there to prove insanity beyond any doubt. Unfortunately—by Jove, yes! I remember where I've seen you now, Mr. Blake! I think I noticed you talking to Sir Henry's secretary in the hall of the Old Bailey?"

"Sir Henry and I have been associates for a good many years, Dr. Hume," I said truthfully.

He looked interested. "You are not appearing in the case, though?"

"No."

"H'm, yes. May I ask (strictly between ourselves) what you think of this unfortunate business?"

"Oh, he'll be acquitted, undoubtedly."

There was a silence. Only the firelight illumined this room; the day had turned black and windy. What effect I was having in pursuing my instructions to "spread a little mysterious disquiet" I could not tell. But Dr. Hume thoughtlessly took a pair of black-ribboned eyeglasses out of his waistcoat pocket, fitted them on his nose with some care, and looked at me.

"Guilty but insane, you mean?"

"Sane and not guilty."

"But that's preposterous! Utterly preposterous! The boy is mad. Why, his evidence about the whisky alone—I beg your pardon; I suppose I really shouldn't be discussing this. I believe they expect to call me as a witness this afternoon. By the way, I always had an impression that witnesses were herded together and kept under surveillance like jurymen; but I learn that this is so only in some cases. The prosecution does not think this is one of them, considering that the—er—issue is so clear."

"If you're a witness for the prosecution, Uncle Spencer," said the girl, "will they let you say Jimmy is crazy?"

"Probably not, my dear; but I shall manage to suggest it. I owe you that much, at least." Again he looked at me meaningly. "Now see here, Mr. Blake. I quite appreciate your position. I know you want to give Mary all the comfort you can, and keep her spirits up at a time of great trial. But to encourage false hopes is—confound it, sir, it's heartless! That's what I said: heartless, and there's no other word for it. Just remember, Mary, that your poor old father is lying out there, dead and murdered and under ground; and that will be all the support you need." He allowed a pause, after which he consulted his watch. "I must be getting on," he added briskly. "'Time and tide wait for no man,' as they say. Er—by the way, Mary, did I understand you to be talking some nonsense about my brown tweed suit, that old suit?"

She was sitting on the fender-seat, her hands clasped round her knees. Now she looked up briefly.

"It was a very good suit, Uncle Spencer. It cost twelve guineas. And you want to get it back, don't you?"

He regarded her with concern. "Now there, Mary, is a fine example of the way people will catch at trifles at a time of—of bereavement! Good Lord, my dear, why are you so concerned over that suit? I've told you I sent it to the cleaner's. Naturally, afterwards, I was not concerned with an old golf-suit when there were so many other things to think of! I simply neglected to call for it, and it's still *at* the cleaner's, so far as I know."

"Oh!"

"You understand that, do you, my dear?"

"Yes," she said. "Did you send it to the cleaner's with the ink-pad and the rubber-stamps still in the pocket? And what about the Turkish slippers?"

There would seem nothing in this calculated to disturb anyone, though it was not very intelligible. But Dr. Hume removed his eyeglasses and put them back into his pocket. At the same time I noticed that the draperies at the doorway had stirred, and a man was looking through. The light was not strong enough to see him well: he appeared to be a thin man with white hair and a nondescript face: but one hand was holding to a fold of the curtain, and seemed to be twisting it.

"I suppose I must have done so, my dear," said Dr. Hume, in such an altered voice that it was like the sudden grip of that hand on the curtain. Yet he was trying to speak lightly. "I shouldn't trouble about it, if I were you. They are honest people, these cleaners. Well, well, I must be getting along. Er—? Oh, I beg your pardon. This is Dr. Tregannon, a friend of mine."

The man in the doorway dropped his hand and bowed slightly.

"Dr. Tregannon is a mental specialist," explained the other, smiling. "Well, I still must be getting along. Good day, Mr. Blake. Don't stuff up Mary's head with nonsense, and don't let her do the same thing to you. Try to get some sleep this afternoon, my dear. I'll give you some medicine tonight, and it will make you forget all your troubles. 'Sleep that knits up the ravell'd sleeve of care,' doesn't Shakespeare say? Yes. Quite so. Good day."

VI

"A PIECE OF BLUE FEATHER"

THE MAN IN THE WITNESS-BOX OF COURT-ROOM NUMBER ONE, Central Criminal Court, had a large and confident voice. He was in the middle of a sentence when I came creeping in.

"—and so, of course, I thought of the ink-pad. Like 'precautions to take before the doctor comes,' you know. Only this was a policeman."

Mr. Randolph Fleming was a large, burly man with a stiff red moustache which forty years ago would have been remarkable even in the Guards. He had a bearing of the same sort, and was not abashed. With the darkening of the day, the concealed lights under the cornices of the oak panelling threw a theatrical glow up over its white dome. But, crawling in some minutes after proceedings had begun, I thought not so much of a theatre as a church.

Evelyn glowered at me, and then whispered excitedly: "Sh-h! He's just confirmed all Dyer said about finding the body, up to the time Answell swore he had taken a drugged drink; and they found none of the whisky or the soda had been tapped. Sh-h! What was the blonde like?"

I shushed her in reply, for heads were turning towards us, and that mention of an ink-pad had caught me. Mr. Randolph Fleming took a deep breath, expanding his chest, and looked round the court with interest. His enormous vitality seemed to enliven counsel. Fleming's large face was somewhat withered, with a pendulous jowl dominated by the stiff red moustache; his eyelids were wrinkled, and the eyes very sharp. You felt that there should be a monocle in one of them, or some sort of helmet on his stiff brown hair. At intervals in the questioning—when there was a cessation of movement like the clogging of a motion-picture film—he would study the judge, study the barristers, and look up to study the people in the gallery. When he spoke, Fleming's jowl moved in and out like a bull-frog's.

Huntley Lawton was examining.

"Explain what you mean about the ink-pad, Mr. Fleming."

"Well, it was like this," answered the witness, drawing in his jowl as though he were trying to smell the flower in the button-hole of his pepper-and-salt suit. "When we had looked at the sideboard and seen that the decanter and the syphon were both full, I said to the prisoner, I said"—pause, as though for consideration—"'Why don't you be a man and admit you did it? Look at that arrow over there,' I said. 'You can see there are finger-prints there; and they'll be yours, won't they?'"

"What did he say to that?"

"Nothing. Ab-so-lutely nothing! Consequently, I thought of taking his finger-prints. I'm a practical man; always have been; that's how I came to think of it. I said to Dyer that if we had an ink-pad—you know the sort of thing: one of those little pads that you press rubber stamps on—we could get a good clear set. He said that Dr. Hume had just recently bought some rubber stamps and an ink-pad, and that they were upstairs in one of the doctor's suits. He remembered because he had intended to take the stamps out in case they soiled the pocket, so he offered to go upstairs and fetch—"

"We quite understand, Mr. Fleming. Did you get the ink-pad and take the prisoner's finger-prints?"

The witness, who had been thrusting out his neck with earnestness, seemed ruffled at the interruption.

"No, sir, we did not. That is, not that particular ink-pad. Dyer couldn't find the suit, it seems, or it wasn't there. But he did manage to fish up an old one from the desk, in violet ink, and we got a set of the prisoner's finger-prints on a piece of paper."

"This piece of paper? Show it to the witness, please."

"Yes, that's the one."

"Did the prisoner make any objections to this?"

"Yes, a bit."

"What did he do?"

"Nothing much."

"I repeat, Mr. Fleming, what did he do?"

"Nothing much," said the witness in a heavy growl. "He caught me off balance. He gave me a sort of shove with his open hand. My feet were off balance, and I went over against the wall and fell down a bit."

"A sort of shove. I see. What was his manner when he did this: angry?"

"Yes, he was in a devil of rage all of a sudden. We were trying to hold his arms down so we could get his prints."

"He gave you a 'sort of shove' and you 'fell down a bit.' In other words, he struck hard and quickly?"

"He caught me off balance."

"Just answer the question, please. All of a sudden he struck hard and quickly. Is that so?"

"Yes, or he wouldn't have caught me off balance."

"Very well. Now, Mr. Fleming, did you examine the place on the wall of the room, shown in photograph 8, from which the arrow had been taken down?"

"Yes, I went all over it."

"Did the small staples—the staples that held the arrow to the wall—show signs of having been wrenched out violently, as though the arrow had been suddenly jerked down?"

"Yes, they were all over the floor."

Counsel consulted his brief. After this little brush, Fleming squared his shoulders, lifted his elbow, and put one fist on the rail of the witness-box. He took a good survey of the court, as though challenging anyone to question his answers; but his forehead was ruffled with small wrinkles. Once, I remember, he happened to look straight into my eyes from across the room. And I wondered, as you always do on these occasions, "What's that fellow really thinking?"

Or, for that matter, you might wonder what the prisoner was really thinking. He was much more restless this afternoon than he had been this morning. Whenever a man in the dock moves in his chair, you are conscious of it; like a movement on an empty dance-floor such as the dock resembled. A shifting, an unquiet stealing of the hands, seems to come close to you. Often he would glance towards the solicitors' table—in the direction, it seemed, of the grave and cynically preoccupied Reginald Answell. The prisoner's eyes looked rather wild and worried; his big shoulders were stooped. Lollypop, H.M.'s secretary, was now at the solicitors' table, wearing her paper cuffs and poring over a typewritten sheet.

Counsel cleared his throat to resume.

"You have told us, Mr. Fleming, that you are a member of several archery societies, and have been an archer for many years?"

"That's so."

"So that you could describe yourself as something of an authority on the subject?"

"Yes, I think I could safely say that," returned the witness, with a grave nod and a bull-frog swell of the throat.

"I want you to look at this arrow and describe it."

Fleming seemed puzzled. "I don't know what you want me to say, exactly. It's the standard type of men's arrow: red pinewood, twenty-eight inches long, quarter of an inch thick, iron pile or point footed with bullet-tree wood, nock made of horn—" He turned it over in his hands.

"The nock, yes. Will you explain what the nock is?"

"The nock is this little wedge-shaped piece of horn at the end of the arrow. There's a notch in it—here. That's how you fit the arrow to the bowstring. Like this."

He illustrated with a backward gesture, and banged his hand against the post supporting the roof of the witness-box: to his evident surprise and annoyance.

"Could that arrow have been fired?"

"It could not. Out of the question."

"You would call it definitely impossible?"

"Of course it's impossible. Besides, the fellow's finger-prints were the only marks on—"

"I must ask you not to anticipate the evidence, Mr. Fleming. Why is it impossible that the arrow could have been fired?"

"Look at the nock! It's been bent over and twisted so much that you couldn't possibly fit it to a string."

"Was the nock in this condition when you first saw it in the deceased's body?"

"Yes, it was."

"Will you just pass that along for the inspection of the jury? Thank you. Having established that the arrow could not have been fired: in the coating of dust you tell us you observed on the arrow, did you observe anywhere—*anywhere*—any marks except those which you knew to be finger-prints?"

"I did not."

"That is all."

He sat down. While the arrow travelled among the jury, a long and rumbling throat-clearing preceded the rise of H.M. There are sounds *and* sounds; and this one indicated war. It struck several people, for Lollypop made a quietly fiendish sign of warning, and for some reason held up the typewritten sheet over which she had been poring. Trouble blew into that room as palpably as a wind, but H.M.'s opening was mild enough.

"You've told us that on that Saturday night you were goin' next door to play chess with the deceased."

"That's right." (Fleming's truculent tone added, "And what of it?")

"When did the deceased make an appointment with you?"

"About three o'clock in the afternoon."

"Uh-huh. For what time that night?"

"He said to drop in about a quarter to seven, and we'd have a bit of cold dinner together, since everybody else in the house was out."

"When Miss Jordan ran over and brought you, you've told us you were already on your way to keep that appointment?"

"Yes. I was a bit early. Better early than late."

"Uh-huh. Now take a dekko—HURRUM—just glance at that arrow again. Look at those three feathers. I think I'm right in statin' that they're fixed edgeways to the arrow about an inch from the nock-end, and they're about two and a half inches long?"

"Yes. The size of the feathers varies, but Hume preferred the biggest ones."

"You notice that the middle feather is torn off pretty clearly about half-way down. Was it like that when you found the body?"

Fleming looked at him suspiciously, on guard behind his red moustache.

"Yes, that's how it was."

"You've heard the witness Dyer testify that all the feathers were intact and whole at the time the accused went into that study at 6.10?"

"I've heard it."

"Sure. We all did. Consequently, the feather must 'a' been broken off between then and the discovery of the body?"

"Yes."

"If the accused grabbed that arrow down off the wall and struck Hume, holdin' the arrow half-way down the shaft, how do you think the feather got torn off?"

"I don't know. In the struggle, probably. Hume made a grab at the arrow when he saw it coming—"

"He made a grab at the end of the arrow opposite the end that was threatenin' him?"

"He might have. Or it might have been torn off when the arrow was pulled off the wall, from those little staples."

"That's another theory. The piece of feather was broken off either (1) in a struggle; or (2) when the arrow was pulled down. Uh-huh. In either case, where is it? Did you find it when you searched the room?"

"No, I did not; but a little piece of feather—"

"I'm suggestin' to you that this 'little piece of feather' was an inch and a quarter long by an inch broad. A whole lot bigger than half a crown. You'd have noticed half a crown on the floor, wouldn't you?"

"Yes, but this didn't happen to be half a crown."

"I've said it was a lot bigger. And it was painted bright blue, wasn't it?"

"I suppose so."

"What was the colour of the carpet?"

"I can't say I can swear to that."

"Then I'll tell you: it was light brown. You accept that? Yes. And you agree that there was very little furniture? Uh-huh. But you made an intensive search of that room, and you still didn't find the missin' piece?"

Hitherto the witness had seemed rather pleased at his own wit, set to shine, and at intervals tickling up the corners of his moustache. Now he was impatient.

"How should I know? Maybe it got lodged somewhere; maybe it's still there. Why don't you ask the police-inspector?"

"I'm goin' to. Now let's draw on your fund of information about archery. Take those three feathers at the end of the arrow. Have they got any kind o' useful purpose, or are they only decorative?"

Fleming seemed surprised. "Certainly they have a purpose. They're set at equal intervals, parallel to the line of flight; you can see that. The natural curve of the feathers gives the arrow a rotary motion in the air—zzz!—like that. Like a rifle-bullet."

"Is one feather always a different colour from the rest, like this?"

"Yes, the guide feather; it shows you where to fit the arrow on the string."

"When you buy these arrows," pursued H.M., in a rumbling and dreamy tone, while the other stared at him, "are the feathers already attached, or do you fasten on your own?"

"As a rule they're already attached. Naturally. But some people prefer to put on their own type of feathers."

"Am I right in thinkin' that the deceased did?"

"Yes. I don't know how you know it; but he used a different type. Most arrows have turkey-feathers. Hume preferred goose-feathers, and put them on himself: I suppose he liked the old grey-goose-feather tradition. These are goose-feathers. Old Shanks, the odd-jobs man, usually fastened them on."

"And this little joker here: the guide-feather, you call it. Am I rightly instructed when I say he used a special type of dye, of his own invention, to colour the guide-feather?"

"Yes, he did. In his workshop—"

"His workshop!" said H.M., coming to life. "His workshop! Just where was this workshop? Get the plan of the house and show us."

There was a general ruffling and unrolling of plans among the jury. Several of us stirred in our seats, wondering what the old man might have up the sleeve of that disreputable gown. Randolph Fleming, with a hairy red finger on the plan, looked up and frowned.

"It's here. It's a little detached building in the back garden, about twenty yards from the house. I think it was intended to be a greenhouse once; but Hume didn't care for that sort of thing. It's partly glass."

H.M. nodded. "What did the deceased keep there?"

"His archery equipment. Bows, strings, arrows, drawing-gloves; things like that. The odd-jobs man dyed the feathers there, too."

"What else?"

"If you want the whole catalogue," retorted the witness, "I'll give it to you. Arm-guards, waist-belts for the arrows, worsted tassels to clean the points with, a grease-pot or two for the drawing-fingers of the glove—and few tools, of course. Hume was a good man with his hands."

"Nothing else?"

"Nothing that I remember."

"You're sure of that, now?"

The witness snorted.

"So. Now, you've testified that that arrow couldn't 'a' been fired. I suggest to you that that statement wasn't what you meant at all. You'll agree that the arrow could have been projected?"

"I don't see what you mean. What's the difference?"

"What's the difference? Looky here! You see this ink-well? Well, if I threw it at you right now, it wouldn't be fired from a bow; but you'll thoroughly agree that it would be projected. Wouldn't it?"

"Yes."

"Yes. And you could take that arrow and project it at me?"

"I could!" said the witness.

His tone implied: "And, by God, I'd like to." Both of them had powerful voices, which were growing steadily more audible. At this point Sir Walter Storm, the Attorney-General, rose with a clearing of the throat.

"My lord," said Sir Walter, in tones whose richness and calm would have rebuked a bishop, "I do not like to interrupt my learned friend. But I should only like to enquire whether my learned friend is suggesting that this arrow, which weighs perhaps three ounces, could have been thrown so as to penetrate eight inches into a human body?—I can only suggest that my learned friend appears to be confusing an arrow with an assegai, not to say a harpoon."

The back of H.M.'s wig began to bristle.

Lollypop made a fierce wig-wagging gesture.

"Me lord," replied H.M., with a curious choking noise, "what I meant will sort of emerge in my next question to the witness."

"Proceed, Sir Henry."

H.M. got his breath. "What I mean is this," he said to Fleming. "Could this arrow have been fired from a cross-bow?"

There was a silence. The judge put down his pen carefully. He turned his round face with the effect of a curious moon.

"I still do not understand, Sir Henry," interposed Mr. Justice Rankin. "What exactly is a cross-bow?"

"I got one right here," said H.M.

From under his desk he dragged out a great cardboard box such as those which are used to pack suits. From this he took a heavy, deadly-looking mechanism whose wood and steel shone with some degree of polish. It was not long in the stock, which was shaped like that of a dwarf rifle: sixteen inches at most. But at the head was a broad semi-circle of flexible steel, to each end of which was attached a cord running back to a notched windlass, with an ivory handle, on the stock. A trigger connected with this windlass. Down the centre of the flat barrel ran a groove. The cross-bow, whose stock was inlaid with mother-of-pearl, should have seemed incongruous in H.M.'s hands under all those peering eyes. It was not. It suddenly looked more like a weapon of the future than a weapon of the past.

"This one," pursued H.M., completely unself-conscious like a child with a toy, "is the short 'stump' cross-bow. Sixteenth-century French cavalry. Principle's this, y'see. It's wound up—like this." He began to turn the handle. To the accompaniment of an ugly clicking noise, the cords began to move and pull back the corners of the steel horns. "Down that groove goes a steel bolt called a quarrel. The trigger's pressed, and releases it like a catapult. Out goes the bolt with all the weight of

Toledo steel released behind it... The bolt's shorter than an arrow. But it could fire an arrow."

He snapped the trigger, with some effect. Sir Walter Storm rose. The Attorney-General's voice quieted an incipient buzz.

"My lord," he said gravely, "all this is very interesting—whether or not it is evidence. Does my learned friend put forward as an alternative theory that this crime was committed with the singular apparatus he has there?"

He was a trifle amused. The judge was not.

"Yes; I was about to ask you that, Sir Henry."

H.M. put down the cross-bow on his desk. "No, my lord. This bow comes from the Tower of London. I was illustratin'." He turned towards the witness again. "Did Avory Hume ever own any cross-bows?"

"As a matter of fact, he did," replied Fleming.

From the press box just under the jury, two men who had to make early afternoon editions got up and tiptoed out on egg-shells. The witness looked irritated but interested.

"Long time ago," he added with a growl. "The Woodmen of Kent experimented with cross-bows one year. They weren't any good. They were cumbersome, and they hadn't got any range compared to arrows."

"Uh-huh. How many cross-bows did the deceased own?"

"Two or three, I think."

"Was any of 'em like this?"

"I believe so. That was three years ago, and—"

"Where did he keep the bows?"

"In that shed in the back garden."

"But you forgot that minute ago, didn't you?"

"It slipped my mind, yes. Naturally."

They were both bristling again. Fleming's heavy nose and jaw seemed to come together like Punch's.

"Now let's have your opinion as an expert: could that arrow have been fired from a bow like this?"

"Not with any accuracy. It's too long, and it would fit too loosely. You'd send the shot wild at twenty yards."

"*Could* it have been fired, I'm asking you?"

"I suppose it could."

"You SUPPOSE it could? You know smackin' well it could, don't you? Here, gimme that arrow and I'll show you."

Sir Walter Storm was on his feet, suavely. "A demonstration will not be necessary, my lord. We accept my learned friend's statement. We also appreciate that the witness is merely attempting to express an honest opinion under somewhat trying circumstances."

("This is what I meant," Evelyn whispered to me. "You see? They'll bait the old bear until he can't see the ring for blood.")

It was certainly the general impression that H.M. had badly mismanaged things, in addition to proving nothing. His last two questions were asked in an almost plaintive tone.

"Never mind its accuracy at twenty yards. Would it be accurate at a very short distance—a few feet?"

"Probably."

"In fact, you couldn't miss?"

"Not at two or three feet, no."

"That's all."

The Attorney-General's brief re-examination disposed of this suggestion and cut it off at the root.

"In order to kill the deceased in the way my learned friend has suggested, the person using the cross-bow must have been within two or three feet of the victim?"

"Yes," returned Fleming, thawing a little.

"In other words, actually *in* the room?"

"Yes."

"Exactly. Mr. Fleming, when you entered this locked and sealed room—"

"Now, we'll object to that," said H.M., suddenly rearing up again with a wheeze and a flutter of papers.

For the first time Sir Walter was a trifle at a loss. He turned towards H.M., and we got a look at his face. It was long and strong, dark-browed despite its slight ruddiness: a powerful face. But both he and H.M. addressed the judge as though speaking to each other through an interpreter.

"My lord, what is it to which my learned friend takes exception?"

"'*Sealed.*'"

The judge was looking at H.M. with bright and steady eyes of interest; but he spoke dryly. "The term was perhaps a little fanciful, Sir Walter."

"I readily withdraw it, my lord. Mr. Fleming: when you entered this unsealed room to which every possible entrance or exit was barred on the inside—"

"Object again," said H.M.

"Ahem. When you entered," said the other, his voice beginning to sound with far-off thunder in spite of himself, "this room whose door was firmly bolted on the inside, and its windows closed with locked shutters, did you find any such singular apparatus as that?"

He pointed to the cross-bow.

"No, I did not."

"It is not a thing that could be readily overlooked, is it?"

"It certainly is not," replied the witness, with jocularity.

"Thank you."

"Call Dr. Spencer Hume."

VII

"STANDING NEAR THE CEILING—"

FIVE MINUTES LATER THEY WERE STILL LOOKING FOR DR. SPENCER Hume, and we knew that something was wrong. I saw H.M.'s big hands close, though he gave no other sign. Huntley Lawton rose.

"My lord, the witness appears to be—er—missing. We—ah—"

"So I observe, Mr. Lawton. What is the position? Do I understand that you move an adjournment until the witness shall be found?"

A conference ensued, in which several glances were directed towards H.M. Then Sir Walter Storm got up.

"My lord, the nature of the Crown's case is such that we believe we can save the time of the court by dispensing with his testimony and continuing with our evidence in the ordinary course."

"The decision must rest with you, Sir Walter. At the same time, if the witness is under subpoena, he should be here. I think the matter should be investigated, and I will have steps taken in that direction."

"Of course, my lord..."

"Call Frederick John Hardcastle."

Frederick John Hardcastle, a police-constable, testified as to the discovery of the body. While he was on duty in Grosvenor Square at six-forty-five, a man whom he now knew to be Dyer approached him and said: "Officer, come in; something terrible has happened." As he went into the house, a car drove up; the car contained Dr. Hume and a woman (Miss Jordan) who seemed to have fainted. In the study he found the prisoner and a man who introduced himself as Mr. Fleming.

P.C. Hardcastle said to the prisoner: "How did this happen?" The prisoner replied: "I know nothing at all about it," and would say nothing more. The witness then telephoned to his divisional police-station, and remained on guard until the arrival of the inspector.

There was no cross-examination. The prosecution then called Dr. Philip McLane Stocking.

Dr. Stocking was a lean and bushy-haired man with a hard, narrow mouth but a curiously sentimental look about him. He got hold of the dock-rail and never let go of it. He had an untidy string-tie done into a bow, and a black suit which did not fit too well; but his hands were so clean that they looked polished.

"Your name is Philip McLane Stocking, and you are Professor of Forensic Medicine at the University of Highgate, and advising surgeon to C Division of the Metropolitan Police?"

"I am."

"On January 4th last, were you called into 12, Grosvenor Street, and did you arrive there at about seven-forty-five?"

"I did."

"When you arrived, what did you find in the study?"

"I found the dead body of a man lying between the window and the desk, face upwards, and very close to the desk." The witness had a rather thick voice, which he had difficulty in keeping clear. "Dr. Hume was present, and Mr. Fleming, and the prisoner. I said: 'Has he been moved?' The prisoner answered: 'I turned him over on his back. He was lying on his left side with his face almost against the desk.' The hands were growing cold; the upper arms and the body were quite warm. Rigor mortis was setting in in the lower part of the left arm and in the neck. I judged he had been dead well over an hour."

"It is impossible to be more definite than that?"

"I should say death occurred between six and six-thirty. I cannot say closer than that."

"You performed a post-mortem examination of this body?"

"Yes. Death was caused by the iron point of an arrow penetrating eight inches through the wall of the chest and piercing the heart."

"Was death instantaneous?"

"Yes, it must have been absolutely instantaneous. Like that," added the witness, suddenly snapping his fingers with the effect of a conjuring trick.

"Could he have moved or taken a step afterwards? What I wish to put to you," insisted Sir Walter, extending his arm, "is whether he would have had strength enough to bolt a door or a window after being struck?"

"It is definitely impossible. He fell almost literally in his tracks."

"What conclusion did you form from the nature of the wound?"

"I formed the conclusion that the arrow had been used as a dagger, and that a powerful blow had been struck by a powerful man."

"Such as the prisoner?"

"Yes," agreed Dr. Stocking, giving a brief and sharp look at Answell.

"What were your reasons for this conclusion?"

"The direction of the wound. It entered high—*here*," he illustrated, "and sloped down in an oblique direction to penetrate the heart."

"At a sharp angle, you mean? A downward stroke?"

"Yes."

"What do you think of any suggestion that the arrow might have been fired at him?"

"If you ask me for an expression of a personal opinion, I should call it so unlikely as to be almost impossible."

"Why?"

"If the arrow had been fired at him, I should have expected it to have penetrated in more or less a straight line; but certainly not at any such angle as the arrow stood."

Sir Walter lifted two fingers. "In other words, doctor, if the arrow had been fired at him, the person who fired it must have been standing somewhere up near the ceiling—aiming downwards."

It seemed to me that he just refrained from adding, "like Cupid?" There were overtones in Sir Walter's voice that piled thick ridicule without a word being said. I could have sworn that for a second a brief and fishy smile appeared on the face of one of the jury, who usually sat as though they were stuffed. The atmosphere was getting colder.

"Yes, something like that. Or else the victim must have been bent forward almost double, as though he were giving a low bow to the murderer."

"Did you find any signs of a struggle?"

"Yes. The deceased man's collar and tie were rumpled; his jacket was humped up a little about his neck; his hands were dirty and there was a small scratch on the palm of the right hand."

"What might have caused this scratch?"

"I cannot say. The point of the arrow might have caused it."

"As though he had put out a hand to defend himself, you mean?"

"Yes."

"Was there any blood from this scratch on the dead man's hand?"

"It bled a little, yes."

"Did you, in the course of your examination, find a stain of blood on any other object in the room?"

"No."

"Therefore it is likely that the scratch was, in fact, caused by the arrow?"

"I should deduce so."

"Will you tell us, doctor, what took place immediately after your first examination of the body in the study?"

Again the bushy-haired witness glanced at the prisoner; his mouth had an expression of distaste. "Dr. Spencer Hume, with whom I have some acquaintance, asked me whether I would look at the prisoner."

"Look at him?"

"Examine him. Dr. Hume said: 'He tells us some absurd story about having swallowed a drug; I have just examined him and I can find nothing to support it.'"

"What was the prisoner's demeanour during this time?"

"It was collected, much too calm and collected; except that he would occasionally run his hand through his hair, like this. He was not nearly so much affected as I was myself."

"Did you examine him?"

"In a cursory way. His pulse was rapid and irregular; not depressed as it would have been had he taken a narcotic. The pupils of the eyes were normal."

"In your opinion, *had* he taken a drug?"

"In my opinion, he had not."

"Thank you; that is all."

("That's torn it," said Evelyn. The prisoner's white face now wore an expression of puzzlement; once he half rose in his chair as though to make an audible protest, and the two warders with him jerked to watchfulness. I saw his lips move soundlessly. The hounds were baying loudly now; and, if he were really innocent, what he must have been feeling was horror.)

H.M. lumbered to his feet and for a full half a minute stood staring at the witness.

"So you examined him 'in a cursory way,' did you?"

H.M.'s voice made even the judge look up.

"Do you examine all your patients 'in a cursory way'?"

"That is neither here nor there."

"It is if they die, ain't it? Do you think a man's life should depend on an examination 'in a cursory way'?"

"No."

"Or that sworn testimony in a court of law should depend on it?"

Dr. Stocking's mouth grew tighter. "It was my duty to examine the body; not to take a blood-test of the prisoner. Dr. Spencer Hume,

I consider, is an authority sufficiently well known for me to accept his considered opinion."

"I see. So you can't give first-hand evidence yourself? It's all based on what Dr. Hume thought—Dr. Hume, by the way, not bein' here now?"

"My lord, I must protest against that implication," cried Sir Walter Storm.

"You will please confine yourself to what the witness says, Sir Henry."

"Begludship's pardon," growled H.M. "I understood that the witness was confinin' himself pretty closely to what Dr. Hume said... Will you *swear* from your own knowledge that he had not taken a drug?"

"No," snapped the witness, "I am not going to swear; I am going to give an opinion; and I swear that the opinion I give shall be an honest one."

The judge's soft, even voice intervened. "I still do not understand. You think it impossible that the prisoner should have taken a drug? That is the matter before us."

"No, my lord, I do not say it is impossible; that would be going too far."

"Why would it be going too far?"

"My lord, the prisoner told me that he took this drug, whatever it was, at about fifteen minutes past six. I did not examine him until nearly eight o'clock. If by any chance he had taken one, the effect would be largely worn off. However, Dr. Hume examined him before seven o'clock—"

"Dr. Hume's opinion has not been presented to us," said Mr. Justice Rankin. "I should like to be quite clear about this, since the matter is vital. If the effect of this mysterious drug would have worn off in any case, I take it that you are hardly in a position to say a great deal about it?"

"My lord, I have said that I can only give an opinion."

"Very well. Proceed, Sir Henry."

H.M., clearly well pleased, went on to other matters.

"Dr. Stocking, there's another side of this business that you've called unlikely to the edge of impossible: I mean any suggestion that the arrow might 'a' been projected. Let's take this question of the position of the body. Do you accept the accused's statement that, at the beginnin', the body was lyin' on its left side facing the side of the desk?"

The doctor smiled grimly. "I believe it is the accused's statements that we are here to examine; not to accept."

"Not under any circumstances, it'd seem. But could you bring yourself to agree with that particular one?"

"I might."

"Is there anything you know of to contradict it?"

"No, I cannot say that there is."

"For the sake of argument, then. Suppose the deceased had been standing on that side of the desk—which would be (look at your plan, there) facin' the sideboard across the room. Suppose he had been bendin' over to look at something on the desk. If while he had been bent forward, the arrow had been discharged at him from the direction of the sideboard: might it have gone into the body just the way it did?"

"It is remotely possible."

"Thanks; nothing else."

H.M. plumped down. The Attorney-General was curt in his re-examination.

"Had matters taken place in any such fashion as my learned friend suggests," observed Sir Walter Storm, "would there have been any signs of a struggle?"

"I should not have expected to find any."

"You would not have expected to find the rumpled collar and tie, the disarranged coat, the grimy hands, the cut on the palm of the right hand?"

"No."

"Can we believe that the cut on the palm of the hand was caused by any attempt to seize in the air at an arrow *fired* at the deceased?"

"Personally, I should call it ridiculous."

"Do you consider it likely that a murderer, equipped with a large cross-bow, was lurking in the sideboard itself?"

"No."

"Finally, doctor, with regard to your qualifications to pronounce on whether or not a drug had been swallowed by the prisoner: you were for twenty years on the staff of St. Praed's Hospital, Praed Street?"

"I was."

The doctor was allowed to stand down, and the Crown then called its most damning witness—Harry Ernest Mottram.

Inspector Mottram had been sitting at the solicitors' table. I had noticed him a number of times without knowing who he was. Inspector Mottram was slow-footed, sure-footed, careful of both manner and speech. He was comparatively young, not more than forty; but his smooth style of replying to questions, never in a hurry to get out an answer too quickly, indicated some experience of court. His manner, as he stood at attention, seemed to say: "I don't particularly like putting a rope around anyone's neck; but let's not have any nonsense; murder is always murder, and the quicker we dispatch a criminal the better it will be for society." He had a square face and a short nose, a face running to jaw, and the expression of his eyes indicated either that they were very sharply penetrating or that he needed glasses. The air of a well-brushed family man, defending society, invaded the court. He took the oath in a strong voice, and fixed his penetrating or near-sighted eyes on counsel.

"I am a Divisional Detective-Inspector of the Metropolitan Police. In consequence of what I was told, I proceeded to 12 Grosvenor Street and arrived there at six-fifty-five p.m. on January 4th."

"What happened?"

"I was conducted to the room called the study, where I found the accused in company with Mr. Fleming, the butler, and Police-Constable

Hardcastle. I questioned the last three, who told me what they have already testified to here. I then asked the accused if he had anything to say. He replied: 'If you will get these harpies out of the room, I will try to tell you what happened.' I asked the others to leave the room. Then I shut the door and sat down opposite the accused."

The statement made by the prisoner, as the inspector quoted it, was much the same as that which had been read by the Attorney-General in his opening speech. As Mottram repeated it in dispassionate tones, it sounded even balder and thinner. When it came to the part about the drugging of the whisky, Sir Walter intervened.

"The prisoner told you that the deceased had given him a glass of whisky-and-soda; that he had drunk over half of it, and then put the glass down on the floor?"

"Yes, by his chair."

"I think, Inspector Mottram, that you are a teetotaller?"

"Yes."

"And," said counsel very gently, "was there any smell of whisky on the prisoner's breath?"

"None whatever."

The thing was so simple, so obvious, that I believe the Crown had been reserving it for a bombshell. It certainly had that effect, for it was a practical and everyday point which came home to the jury.

"Go on, Inspector."

"When he had finished making this statement, I said to him: 'You realise that what you tell me cannot possibly be true?' He replied: 'It is a frame-up, Inspector; I swear to God it is a frame-up; but I cannot see how they can *all* be crooked, or why they should have it in for me, anyway.'"

"What did you understand him to mean by this?"

"I understood that he referred to the other people in the house. He made no difficulty in talking to me; I should describe him as friendly and almost eager. But he appeared to have strong suspicions of every member of the household, or friend of the family, who came near him. I then said to him: 'If you acknowledge that the door was bolted on the inside, and the windows were also locked, how can anyone else have done what you say?'"

"What did he say to this?"

The witness looked mildly bothered. "He began speaking about detective stories, and ways of bolting doors or locking windows from the outside—with bits of string or wire, and things like that."

"Are you a reader of detective fiction, Inspector?"

"Yes, sir."

"Do you know of any such methods as he referred to?"

"Well, sir, I have heard of one or two; and, with a whole lot of luck, they might be practical." Inspector Mottram looked hesitant and a little apologetic. "But none of them could possibly apply in this case."

At counsel's signal, the exhibit of the dummy shutters was again brought forward, and this time the door as well: a solid piece of oak attached to a practical frame.

"I understand that the same evening you removed the shutters and the door, assisted by Detective-Sergeant Raye, and took them to the police-station for purposes of experiment?"

"I did."

"Will you tell us why no such method could apply here?"

It was the old story; but it stood up solid and unbreakable as the Old Bailey itself when Mottram explained.

"After you had questioned him about the door and the windows, Inspector, what did you do?"

"I asked him if he would object to being searched. I observed, when he stood up—he had been sitting down most of the time—a kind of bulge on his right hip under the overcoat."

"What did he say?"

"He said: 'It won't be necessary; I know what you want.' And he opened his overcoat, and reached into his hip pocket, and gave it to me."

"Gave what to you?"

"A .38-calibre automatic pistol, fully loaded," said the witness.

VIII

"THE OLD BEAR WAS NOT BLIND"

A .38-CALIBRE WEBLEY-SCOTT AUTOMATIC WAS HANDED UP FOR inspection and identification. Someone behind us began softly to hum: "O Who Will O'er the Downs with Me?" to words which sounded like: "O Who Said He was Inn-o-cent?" The atmosphere of scepticism was now so heavy that you could feel it in people's very gravity. At the moment I happened to be looking at Reginald Answell, and for the first time an exhibit seemed to interest the prisoner's cousin. He looked up briefly; but his saturnine good looks betrayed nothing except a certain superciliousness. He fell again to playing with the water-carafe on the solicitors' table.

"Is this the pistol he had in his pocket?" pursued Sir Walter Storm. "Yes. Did the prisoner explain how he happened to come for a peaceful discussion of his prospective marriage with a weapon like that in his pocket?"

"He denied that he had brought it. He said that someone must have put it there while he was unconscious."

"Someone must have put it there while he was unconscious. I see. Could he identify the weapon?"

"The accused said to me: 'I know it very well. It belongs to my cousin Reginald. When he is not in the East he always stays at my flat, and I believe that the last time I saw the pistol was a month ago, in the drawer of the sitting-room table. I have not seen it since.'"

After lengthy and convincing testimony had been made as to an examination of the room, the witness was taken to a summing-up.

"What conclusion did you form, from this, as to the way in which the crime had been committed?"

"From the way in which the arrow had been pulled down from the wall, I concluded that it had been dragged from right to left, by a hand holding the arrow in the position where the finger-prints are. This would have put the person who pulled it down on the side of the room a little towards the sideboard. Under these circumstances, I concluded that the deceased had run round the desk, on the left-hand side towards the front of it, in order to get away from his assailant—"

"In other words, to put the desk between himself and his assailant?"

"Yes, like that," agreed Inspector Mottram, making a boxed motion with his hands, and moving them to illustrate. "I concluded that the assailant had then run round the front of the desk. There was then a struggle, with the deceased standing in a position very close to the desk and facing the sideboard. In this struggle the missing piece of feather was broken off, and the deceased also acquired the cut on his hand. The victim was then struck. He fell down beside the desk, getting the dust on his hands when he—he pawed at the carpet just before he died. That is how I believed it to happen."

"Or might he have seized at the arrow, and caught at the shaft to get dust on his hands? What I mean is that there was a part of the arrow you could not test for finger-prints, since it was buried in the deceased's body?"

"Yes."

"The dust on the hands may have come from there?"

"Quite possibly."

"Finally, Inspector. I believe you are a qualified finger-print expert, and were trained for this branch of the service?"

"Yes, that is so."

"Did you take a record of the prisoner's finger-prints: first in Grosvenor Street, using the pad of violet ink provided there, and later at the district police-station?"

"I did."

"Did you compare these with the finger-prints on the shaft of the arrow?"

"I did."

"Please identify these photographs, showing the various sets of prints, and explain the points of agreement to the jury... Thank you. Were the prints on the arrow made by the prisoner?"

"They were."

"Were any finger-prints found in the room other than those of the deceased and the prisoner?"

"No."

"Were any finger-prints found on the decanter of whisky, the syphon, or the four glasses?"

"No."

"Where else were finger-prints of the prisoner found?"

"On the chair in which he was sitting, on the desk—and on the bolt of the door."

After a few more questions relating to the final arrest of Answell, the examination was finished. It had been, in its way, a tightening and summing-up of the whole case. If H.M. had any attack to launch, now was the time to launch it. The clock on the wall up over our heads must be crawling on; for it was growing dark outside, and a few whips of rain struck the glass roof. The white-and-oak of the court-room acquired a harder brilliance from its lights. H.M. got up, spread out his hands on the desk, and asked the following abrupt question:

"Who bolted the door?"

"Excuse me, I did not quite catch that?"

"I said, who bolted the door on the inside?"

Inspector Mottram did not blink. "The prisoner's finger-prints were on the bolt, sir."

"We're not denyin' that he *un*-bolted it. But who bolted it? Were there any other prints on the bolt besides the prisoner's?"

"Yes, the deceased man's."

"So the deceased might 'a' bolted it just as well as the prisoner?"

"Yes, he might: quite easily."

"Now, let's get this story of the crime quite clear. The witness Dyer has testified that at about six-fourteen he heard the deceased say: 'Man, what's wrong with you? Have you gone mad?' and then sounds like a scuffle: hey?... In your opinion, was this the scuffle where Hume got killed?"

Inspector Mottram was not to be caught in any such trap as that. He shook his head, narrowed his eyes, and gave the matter grave attention.

"You want my opinion, sir?"

"Yes."

"From the evidence I have submitted, we concluded that this scuffle was a brief one, terminated when the witness Dyer knocked at the door and asked what was wrong. The door was then bolted on the inside—"

"So that they could continue their fight in peace and comfort, you mean?"

"I cannot say as to that," returned the witness, completely unruffled. "So that no one could go in."

"And they then went on fightin' for fifteen minutes?"

"No, the quarrel may have broken out again fifteen minutes later."

"I see. But if the prisoner bolted the door at six-fifteen, it must have meant that he was ready for business, mustn't it? Would he have bolted the door and then sat down to talk peacefully afterwards?"

"He might."

"You expect the jury to believe that?"

"I expect the jury to believe what my lord tells them is evidence, sir. You are only asking for my opinion. Besides, I have said that the deceased himself might have bolted the door—"

"Oh?" roared H.M. "In fact, you think it likely that he did?"

"Well, yes," admitted the inspector, and squared himself.

"Good. Now, we're asked to believe that the accused went to that house with a loaded gun in his pocket. That'd show premeditation, wouldn't it?"

"People do not usually carry weapons unless they think they may have a use for them."

"But he didn't use that gun?"

"No."

"Whoever killed the victim ran across the room, yanked down an arrow off the wall, and attacked the deceased with it?"

"That is our belief, yes."

"In fact, it's your whole case, ain't it?" demanded H.M., leaning across the desk.

"It is a part of the case; not the whole of it."

"But a vital part?"

"I leave that up to my lord."

H.M. put his hands up to his wig; and lifted one hand and patted the top of his wig with it, as though to cork himself before exploding to the ceiling. The witness's dry, precise voice was never hurried: Inspector Mottram would not say more or less than what he meant.

"Let's take the missin' piece of feather," pursued H.M. in a gentle growl. "You didn't find it anywhere, did you?"

"No."

"Did you search the room thoroughly?"

"Very thoroughly."

"So it couldn't 'a' got away from you if it had been there, eh? No? You agree to that? Where was it, then?"

Inspector Mottram came as near to a smile as the nature of the place would permit. He was watching H.M. warily out of those near-sighted eyes, for foolish testimony in the witness-box will break a police officer; but he seemed to have been prepared for this.

"That had occurred to us, sir," he replied dryly. "Unless, of course, it was removed from the room by someone else—"

"Stop a bit," said H.M. instantly. "Someone else? But in that case it'd have to be by one of the people who have already testified here?"

"Yes, I suppose it would."

"In which case, one of them witnesses was lying, wasn't he? And the case against the accused is partly built on lies?"

The inspector had begun to hit back. "You did not let me finish my answer. I said it only to exclude everything, sir—as we have to do."

"Well, what were you goin' to say?"

"I was going to say that it must have been carried out of the room in the prisoner's clothes. He was wearing his overcoat, a heavy overcoat. The piece of feather could have been entangled in his clothes, unknown to himself."

"Which," said H.M., pointing, "makes it pretty certain it was torn off in a struggle?"

"Yes."

H.M. made a sign towards the solicitors' table. He now seemed to radiate a sort of evil glee. "Inspector, you're a pretty strong man, aren't you? Powerful?"

"As strong as most, I suppose."

"Right. Now, look at what they're holdin' up to you. Do you know what it is? It's a feather—a goose-feather. We got other kinds here too if you want 'em. I'd like you to take that feather in your hands and tear it in half. Try to break it, twist it, pull it, rip it: do anything you like: but break it in half for us."

Inspector Mottram's knuckly hands closed round the feather, and his shoulders opened. He swung from one side to the other, in the midst of a vast silence, and nothing happened.

"Havin' trouble, son?" said H.M. meekly.

The other gave him a look from under jutting brows. "Lean across to the foreman of the jury," pursued H.M., raising his voice, "and have a try at it as though you were strugglin'. Be careful; don't pull each other over the rail... Ah, that's got it!"

The foreman of the jury was a striking-looking man with a grey moustache, but suspiciously vivid brown hair which was parted in the middle. The tug-of-war almost sent him out of the box like a fish on a line. But when the feather eventually began to part it shredded in long wisps and bits which not so much broke the feather as made it resemble a squashed spider.

"In fact," said H.M., in the midst of a startled pause, "it can't be done like that, can it? I use 'em for cleaning pipes, and I know. Now take a look at the broken feather on the arrow that was used for the murder. See it? The break is uneven, but it's absolutely clean and there's not a strand of the feather out of line. You see that?"

"I see it," replied Mottram evenly.

"Will you acknowledge now that the piece of feather couldn't have been broken off like that in a struggle?"

("My God," whispered Evelyn, "he's done it!")

Mottram did not say anything; he was too honest to comment. He stood looking from the shredded pieces of the feather to H.M., and shifted his feet. For the first time the prosecution had received a check. Whatever excitement might have been felt was doused by the cold sanity of Sir Walter Storm.

"My lord, I suggest that my learned friend's test is more spectacular than conclusive. May I see that feather which was used for the test?"

It was passed over to him, while he and H.M. nodded to each other. And now the prosecution was going to fight. So far they had experienced such a complete walk-over that the business looked perfunctory.

H.M. made a rumbling noise in his throat.

"If you got any doubts of it, Inspector, just try the same game on one of the other feathers in the arrow... I repeat: will you acknowledge it could not have been broken off as you said it was?"

"I don't know; I can't say," retorted Mottram honestly.

"But you're a strong man, and *you* couldn't?"

"All the same—"

"Just keep to my questions. The feather WAS broken off: how was it broken off?"

"The guide-feather in that arrow was old and—brittle, like. Dried up. So if—"

"*How was it broken off?*"

"I can't answer you, sir, if you don't give me a chance to. I don't suppose a feather is any irresistible force that can't be broken in two."

"Could you do it?"

"No, not with the feather you gave me."

"Try it with one of those two remainin' old and brittle feathers. Can you manage it? No. All right. Now look at this." He held up the cross-bow. "Suppose you were fittin' an arrow into this bow. You'd put the guide-feather in the middle when you put the arrow into this groove. Wouldn't you?"

Mottram was a trifle rattled. "You might; I can't say."

"I put it to you: you'd shove this arrow back in the groove until it fitted against the projectin' mechanism?"

"You might."

"And consequently, when you wound up the bow, I suggest to you that these teeth on the revolving drum would catch the end of the feather and grip it?"

"I don't know anything about cross-bows."

"But I'm showin' one to you. Here it is. Finally," roared H.M., before counsel could make any objection, "I suggest that the only way a clean break could have been made in that feather—a clean break like the one there—was when the weight of a Toledo-steel catapult flew out and snapped it in two?"

He released the trigger of the cross-bow. There was a vicious snap, and the cords banged across the head of the bow.

"Where is that feather?" enquired H.M.

"Sir Henry," said the judge, "you will please question: not argue."

"If yrludshippleases," growled H.M.

"I further take it that these questions have some relevancy?"

"We think so," said H.M., unmasking his batteries. "At the proper time we're goin' to produce the cross-bow with which we'll suggest that the crime was really committed."

An epidemic of creaking seemed to have afflicted the yellow furniture in the court. Someone coughed. Mr. Justice Rankin remained looking steadily at H.M. for a short space; then he peered back at his notes, and the pen in his plump hand continued to travel. Even the prisoner was looking at H.M., but as though startled and only half interested.

H.M. turned back to Inspector Mottram, who was waiting quietly.

"Take this arrow itself. You examined it as soon as you arrived at Grosvenor Street?"

"I did," answered the Inspector, clearing his throat.

"You've testified, too, that the dust on the arrow wasn't smudged except where you found the finger-prints?"

"That is correct."

"Look at photograph Number 3 in the book, and tell me if you were speakin' the literal truth. What about that pretty thin vertical line that runs down the shaft of the arrow—blurred a little—where there's no dust?"

"I said that there were no other marks in the dust. That was true. There never was any dust in the mark you refer to. That was where the arrow had hung against the wall, and accumulated no dust. Like the back of a picture hanging flat against the wall, you know."

"Like the back of a picture, you say. Did you at any time *see* this arrow when it was hanging against the wall?"

"Naturally not."

"Oh? But you heard the witness Dyer testify that this arrow did not hang flat and dead against the wall; you heard him say it was set out a little on the staples?"

Pause. "I know from my own observation that the other two arrows were flat against the wall."

"Yes. They were two sides to a triangle; they had to be held upright and flat so that they'd stay like that. But what about this one that was the base of the triangle?"

"I do not understand your question."

"Lemme put it like this. Two sides of that triangle were flat on the wall, hey? The third side, the base, *crossed* the bases of the other two arrows. Consequently, it was supported against those arrows and was about a quarter of an inch or more out from the wall. Will you accept Dyer's statement about that?"

"If my lord has admitted it as evidence, I accept it, yes."

"Exactly," rumbled H.M. "But if it was a quarter of an inch out from the wall, it wouldn't be protected from dust, would it?"

"Not entirely."

"Not entirely? You agree it wasn't against the wall? Yes. Then the whole shaft of that arrow would 'a' been covered with dust, wouldn't it?"

"It is a difficult question."

"It is. And the whole shaft of the arrow wasn't covered with dust, was it?"

"No."

"There was a thin vertical line smudged all the way down the shaft?"

"Yes."

"I put it to you," said H.M., holding out the cross-bow, "that the only way a mark like that could 'a' been caused would have been if it had been put into the groove of a cross-bow and fired?"

Still holding out the cross-bow, he drew one finger down the groove in the bow, looked so malevolently round the court that we could see his face, and then sat down.

"Bah," said H.M.

There was a slight sign of released breath in the court. The old bear was not yet blind with blood, and he had made an impression. Inspector Mottram, a quite sincere witness, had been given a bad time. It had not shaken him unduly; it had only solidified the lines of his jaw, and given him a look as though he wished for a give-and-take with claws on more equal terms; but he seemed anxious to receive the Attorney-General's questions in re-examination.

"We have heard several times," began Sir Walter abruptly, "about the 'only way' a certain effect could have been produced. I call your attention to certain evidence in the photographs. It is clear to you that, when the arrow was snatched off the wall, it was jerked violently from left to right? You have already testified as to that?"

"Yes, sir."

"Wrenched so violently that the staples were pulled out?"

"That is so."

"If you were making a motion like that, you would wrench and shake the arrow, and then pull it sideways?"

"Yes, that is what would be done."

"Consequently, you would pull the arrow along the wall—and make a mark like the one indicated?"

"Yes, you would."

Mr. Justice Rankin looked down over his spectacles. "There seems to be some confusion here, Sir Walter. According to my notes, there was first no dust at all. Now we hear that the dust might have been scraped off. Which of these two alternatives are you suggesting?"

"The matter is simple, my lord. Like my learned friend with his cross-bow, I was illustrating. My learned friend insists on speaking of the *only* way a thing could have been done. He can hardly object if I give him way upon way... Now, Inspector. In your own home, I presume, there are pictures on the wall?"

"Pictures, sir? Plenty of pictures."

"They do not hang absolutely flat against the wall, do they?"

"No, they have to be hung up."

"And yet," said the other, glancing towards the women on the jury, "they accumulate practically no dust at the back of the frame?"

"Very little, I should say."

"Thank you. With regard to the *only* way—the only way in the world a feather can be torn in half," counsel went on, with rich and sardonic politeness, "I understand that in preparing this case you acquired some information about archery?"

"I did."

"Yes. I believe that the guide-feather of an arrow—in this case, the one broken off—receives much more wear and tear than the others? What I wish to suggest to you is that it guides the end of the arrow to the string; and is therefore more apt to be chafed and damaged by hand or bowstring?"

"That is so. They have often to be replaced."

"Is it impossible that in a struggle for this arrow between two men, one of them fighting for his life, the central feather should have been broken off?"

"Not at all impossible, I should say; though I will admit—"

"That is all," snapped Sir Walter. He allowed an impressive pause while the witness left the box, and then turned to the judge. "That, my lord, with the accused's statement, concludes the evidence for the Crown."

The worst was over. Despite this re-examination, there had been a very slight lessening of the case against the prisoner: more a feeling of wonder than anything else. But wonder is the beginning of the reasonable doubt. Under cover of the noise, Evelyn whispered excitedly:

"Ken, H.M. is going to bring it off. I tell you I know it! That re-examination was weak. It sounded well, but it was weak; he shouldn't have brought up that business about dust on the backs of pictures. Of course there's dust on the backs of pictures, oodles of it. I was looking at the women on the jury, and I could tell what they were thinking. A little thing like that arrow would have been dust all over unless it had been absolutely flat on the wall. Can't you feel that they're not certain at all now?"

"Ss—t! Quiet!"

The judge was looking at the clock while the clerk's sonorous voice rose:

"Members of the jury, when the prisoner was before the magistrates, he was asked if he had anything to say in answer to the charge; and being told that he need not say anything, but that if he did it would be taken down in writing and used in evidence at his trial, he said: 'I plead not guilty to the charge made against me, and I am advised to reserve my defence. Through this charge I have lost everything in life that was of any value to me; so do what you like; but I am still not guilty. That is all I have to say.'"

"If Sir Henry has no objections," said Mr. Justice Rankin briskly, "we will adjourn the court until tomorrow."

Bumping, shuffling, we all got to our feet as the judge rose.

"All persons who have anything more to do before my Lords the King's Justices of Oyer and Terminer, and general gaol delivery for the jurisdiction of the Central Criminal Court"—the rain was pattering steadily on the glass roof; it was the tired hour when you think of cocktails—*"may depart hence and give their attendance here again tomorrow, at ten-thirty o'clock.*

"God Save the King, and my Lords the King's Justices."

Again the pause broke. The judge turned round, and went stumping along behind the bench at his brisk and pigeon-toed walk. Court-room Number One broke up into individuals, all with lives and thoughts of their own, moving round hats and homes. Someone yawned audibly, and then a voice spoke suddenly with great distinctness:

"*Watch him, Joe!*"

It came with a shock. We all turned round at the commotion in the dock. The two warders had sprung forward with their hands on the shoulders of the prisoner. Nearly at the trap leading down into the cells, Answell had turned round and walked swiftly towards the rail again. We heard his footsteps rap on that dance-floor which has been polished by the feet of so many now dead. But he did not attempt any action. He stood with his hands on the edge of the dock, and spoke with fierce clarity. To hear his voice was like hearing a deaf-and-dumb man speak.

"What's the use of going on with this? That piece of feather broke off the arrow when I stabbed him. I killed the old swine, and I admit it; so let's get this over with and call it a day."

IX

"RED ROBES WITHOUT HURRY"

I F ANYBODY HAD ASKED ME WHAT WOULD PROBABLY HAPPEN IN CASE of a commotion like this, I should have thought of every contingency except what really happened. We all looked at the judge, since the prisoner was speaking to him. By this time Mr. Justice Rankin had nearly reached the door, at the right-hand side behind the bench, by which he entered and left. For perhaps a tenth of a second his brisk step hesitated. For perhaps a tenth of a second he turned his head slightly, with a blank gaze of deafness and non-recognition. Then his red robes—without any hurry—disappeared through the door, and it closed behind his tie-wig.

He "had not heard" the words which the prisoner, with fierce distinctness, was shouting across that void. So we did not hear them either. Like a room of mutes we bent to gather up our hats, our umbrellas, our parcels; we shuffled our papers, and looked at the floor, and pretended to say something to the person beside us...

"My God, won't anybody listen to me? Don't you hear what I'm saying? You—listen—" The jury were going out in sheep-fashion, and not one of them looked round, except one scared woman who was touched on the arm by their guardian. "Please, for God's sake listen to me! I killed him; I'm admitting it; I want you to—"

The soothing mutter of the warder droned. "All right, my lad; all right; down here; easy does it; take him easy, Joe—ee—easy—"

Answell stopped, and seemed to be looking from one warder to the other. Our glances did not go higher than the buttons of his waistcoat, yet you had an impression that he felt more trapped now than he had ever been before. His eyes looked hot and puzzled when they hauled him across to the trap.

"But listen!—wait, I don't want to go—no; wait a bit—I—aren't they going to listen to me? I *admit* it, d'ye hear?"

"Sure, my lad; plenty of time; e-easy there; mind that step—"

We went out in good order, leaving a dead schoolroom full of yellow furniture, and we did not comment. Lollypop, looking white, made a sign to me which I interpreted as: "Downstairs"; I could not see H.M. in the crowd. They began to switch out the lights. A sort of network of shuffling whispers caught us all together.

Someone said in my ear: "—and all over but the hanging."

"I know," muttered another voice. "And yet, for a couple of seconds there, I almost thought—"

"That he mightn't have done it?"

"I don't know: not exactly: and yet—"

Outside Evelyn and I conferred. "They're probably right," she admitted; "and I don't feel so well. I say, I've got to go, Ken. I promised Sylvia to be there at six-thirty. Are you coming?"

"No, I've got a message for H.M. Simply 'yes,' from the Hume girl. I'll wait."

Evelyn drew her fur coat closer. "I don't want to stay now. Oh, *blast* it all, Ken; why did we have to come here? That—that cooks his goose, rather, doesn't it?"

"Depends on whether it's evidence, and apparently it isn't."

"Oh, evidence—!" said Evelyn contemptuously. "Bother evidence! What would you have felt if you had been on that jury? That's what counts. I wish we hadn't come here; I wish we'd never even heard of the case! What is the girl like? No, don't tell me. I don't want to know. That last business— G'bye, darling. See you later."

She hurried away into the rain, and I was left glowering in the crowd.

People were scuttling like chickens at the door of the Old Bailey, though the rain had almost ceased. There was a now-we're-out-of-school look about it. A bitter wind whisked round the corner of the building, and the lines of gas-lamps in Newgate Street were palely solemn. Among the crush of cars waiting for their dignitaries I found H.M.'s closed Vauxhall (not a certain Lanchester of weird memory), with his chauffeur Luigi. I leaned on the car and tried to smoke a cigarette against the wind. Memories were strong tonight. Up there, past St. Sepulchre's Church, ran Giltspur Street: off Giltspur Street was Plague Court, among whose ghosts H.M. and I had walked some years ago: and at that time there had been no thought of murder in James Caplon Answell's mind. The crowd from the Old Bailey thinned slowly. After a general shooting of bolts had begun, a couple of City-of-London policemen—with their humped helmets like firemen's hats in blue cloth—came out and looked the situation over. H.M. was almost the last to leave. He came stumping out with his own unwieldy top-hat stuck on the back of his head, his overcoat with the moth-eaten fur collar flying out behind; and I could tell by the profane movements of his lips that he had been having a talk with Answell.

He pushed me into the car.

"Grub," H.M. said succinctly. He added: "Oh, my eye, the young ass! That's torn it."

"So he's really guilty after all?"

"Guilty? No. Not him. He was only bein' a decent young feller. I got to get him out of this, Ken," said H.M. sombrely. "He's worth saving."

A passing car, as we turned into Newgate Street, merely brushed our mudguard; and H.M. leaned out of the window and cursed with such resonance and imaginativeness that it was an index to his state of mind.

"I suppose," H.M. went on, "he thought he'd only got to come out and confess, and the judge would say: 'O.K., son; that's enough; take him out and string him up,' straightway, d'ye see?"

"But why confess? And, anyway, is it evidence?"

H.M.'s attitude towards this was much like Evelyn's. "Of course it ain't evidence. The point is the effect it's goin' to have, even if old Balmy Rankin tells 'em to disregard it. I got great faith in Balmy, Ken... But did I hear you thinking the worst is over when the Crown gets through with its evidence? Son, our troubles haven't begun. It's the cross-examination of Answell that I'm dreadin'. You ever hear Walt Storm cross-examine? He takes 'em to pieces like a clock and then dares you to put all the little wheels back into place. I'm not legally bound to put Answell into the box; but if I don't I'm wide open to any comments Storm wants to make, and the story of this murder can't be complete unless I do put the feller there. What I'm afraid of is that my own witness may go back on me. If he stands up there and swears what he just said a while ago—well, that WILL be evidence and the old man's licked."

"But I repeat (this damned court-room manner is getting infectious): why did Answell confess?"

H.M. grunted. He was sitting back against the cushion, his unwieldly top-hat tilted over his eyes and his thick arms folded.

"Because somebody's communicated with him. I'm not sure how, but I'm pretty sure who. I mean Our Reginald. Did you notice how he and Reginald kept exchangin' significant glances all afternoon? But you don't know Reginald."

"Yes, I met him this afternoon, at the Humes's place."

A sharp little eye swung round towards me. "So?" said H.M. with heavy inflection. "What d'you think of him?"

"Well—all right. A little on the oh-really and supercilious side, but decent enough."

The eye turned back again. "Uh-huh. And, incidentally, what was the message from the gal?"

"She said to tell you yes, emphatically."

"Good gal," said H.M. He stared at the glass partition from under the brim of his tilted hat. "It may work out well enough. I had some passable luck this afternoon, and also a few nasty jolts. The worst of the jolts was when Spencer Hume didn't turn up as a witness. I was countin' on him: if I had any hair, it'd 'a' been greyer when I heard that. Burn me, I wonder if he's turned tail! I wonder!" He considered. "People think I ain't got any dignity. Fine spectacle it is, hey, of Lollypop and me running about gettin' our witnesses and doin' all the dirty work that ought to be done by solicitors. Nice thing for a barrister, I ask you—"

"Frankly," I said, "the real reason is that you wouldn't work with a solicitor, H.M. You're too anxious to run the whole show yourself."

This, unfortunately, was so true that it provoked a fiendish outburst, especially as his grousing a moment ago indicated that he was worried about something else.

"So that's the thanks I get, is it? That's all the thanks I get? After all the trouble I had runnin' round that railway station like a porter—"

"What railway station?"

"Never mind what railway station," said H.M., checking himself abruptly in mid-flight, and looking austere. But he was so pleased at having caused another point of mystification that he cooled off a little. "Humph. I say, Ken: on the evidence you've heard today, what railway station would *you* have gone to?"

"To take what train? How the subject of railway stations got into this conversation at all," I said, "is not quite clear; but is this a subtle way of hinting that Dr. Hume may have done a bunk?"

"He may have. Burn me, now, I wonder—" For a moment he stared at the glass partition, and then he turned excitedly. "Did you by any chance see Dr. Hume at their place this afternoon?"

"Yes, he was there, full of platitudes and benevolence."

"Did you follow my instructions about spreadin' a little mysterious disquiet?"

"Yes, and I thought I succeeded remarkably well; though what I said that was so effective I can't tell you. Anyway, he certainly told us he was going to testify this afternoon. He said he'd put over a strong intimation that Answell is insane; and, by the way, there was a mental specialist with him, a Dr. Tregannon—"

H.M.'s hat slid so slowly down over his nose and outwards that it was as though he had attempted a balancing-trick with it. He is proud of that hat; but he did not notice when it tumbled to the floor.

"Tregannon?" he repeated blankly. "Dr. Tregannon. Oh, Lord love a duck! I wonder if I'd better go round there?"

"I hope we're not out to rescue any heroines," I said. "Look here, what's up? Are you thinking of the sinister uncle again, or what he might do to Mary Hume for testifying on the side of the defence? I thought of all that too; but it's rubbish. Plain cases, H.M., and sticking closely to the Facts of Life: you don't suppose he'd hurt his own niece?"

H.M. reflected. "No, I don't suppose he would," he replied seriously. "But he's fightin' for his respectability. And psalm-singing Uncle Spencer may turn awful nasty if he discovers she can't find his Turkish slippers... Now, now!"

"Is this allied with the secret and sinister connection between an ink-pad and a railway station and a Judas window and a golf-suit?"

"It is. But never mind. I suppose she's all right, and what I want is grub."

It was some time before he got his wish. As the car drew up before H.M.'s house in Brook Street, a woman was mounting the steps. She wore a fur coat, and her hat was put on crookedly. Then she ran down the steps, rummaging in her handbag. We saw the eager blue eyes of Mary Hume: she was now breathless and on the edge of tears.

"It's all right," she said. "We've saved Jim."

H.M.'s face wore a rather ghoulish expression. "I don't believe it," he said. "Burn me, it ain't *possible* for us to have any luck! The blinkin' awful cussedness of things in general has simply decided that that lad couldn't have a decent stroke of luck if—"

"But he has! It's Uncle Spencer. He's run away, and he's left me a letter, and it practically confesses—"

She was rummaging in her handbag, spilling a lipstick and a handkerchief out on the pavement. When she held out the letter, the wind took it out of her hand, and it was only with a flying catch that I retrieved it.

"Inside," said H.M.

H.M.'s house is one of those ornate and chilly places which seem to exist only to give receptions, and most of the time is occupied only by H.M. and the servants: his wife and two daughters being usually in the south of France. Again, as usual, he had forgotten his latch-key; so he pounded on the door and shouted murderously until the butler came out and asked him if he wanted to get in. In a chilly back-library he seized the letter out of the girl's hand and spread it out on a table under the lamp. It was several sheets of note-paper closely written in a fine and unhurried hand.

Monday, 2 p.m.

Dear Mary:

By the time you receive this I shall be outward-bound; and it will, I think, be difficult for anyone to trace me. I cannot help feeling bitter about this, for I have done nothing—absolutely nothing—of which I need be ashamed: on the contrary, I have tried to do you a good turn. But Tregannon suspects that Merrivale has got at Quigley, and will put him into the witness-box tomorrow; and certain things I overheard at the house this afternoon lead me to the same belief.

I do not wish you to think too hardly of your old uncle. Believe me, if I could have done the least good I should have spoken before. About certain parts of this business I am feeling rather wretched. I can tell you now that it was I who supplied the drug which went into Answell's whisky. It is "brudine," a derivative of scopolamine or twilight-sleep, with which we have been experimenting at the hospital—

"Wow!" roared H.M., bringing his fist down on the table. "This has got it, my wench."

Her eyes were searching his face. "You think that will clear him?"

"It's half of what we want. Now be quiet, dammit!"

—its effects are almost instantaneous, and it ensures unconsciousness for a little under half an hour. Answell woke up a few minutes sooner than had been intended: probably due to the fact that he had to be propped up while the mint extract was poured down his throat to take away the smell of whisky.

"Do you remember what Answell said himself?" demanded H.M. "The first thing the feller noticed when he woke up was that there was an awful taste of mint in his mouth, and he seemed to have slobbered it a good deal. Ever since the Bartlett case there's been arguments as to whether you could pour liquid down the throat of a sleepin' man without choking him."

I still could not make head or tail of it. "But who drugged him? And why? And what in blazes were they trying to do? Either Avory Hume liked Answell or he hated him like poison: but which was it?"

I thought at the time that it was a mistake to load the whole decanter of whisky with the stuff, instead of merely putting it into a glass; because it meant getting rid of the decanter afterwards. Believe me, Mary, the thought that someone afterwards might find the decanter has given me some horribly unpleasant moments.

Finally, I arranged with Tregannon and Quigley to do what was to be done. That is the limit of my dereliction. It is not my fault that my well-meant efforts produced such unfortunate results. But you will see why I could not speak.

At this point, as H.M. turned over the page, a strangled noise escaped him; and then it became a groan. Our hopes went down with a clang like a broken lift.

> *Of course, if Answell had really been innocent, I should have been compelled to speak out and tell the truth. You must believe that. But, as I told you, even the truth would do him no good. He is guilty, my dear—guilty as hell. He killed your father in one of those rages from which his family has been noted for a long time, and I cheerfully let him go to the hangman rather than set him loose on you. Perhaps his protestations of innocence are quite sincere. He may not even know that he killed your father. "Brudine" is still a comparatively unknown quantity. It is quite harmless; but when its effect begins to wear off it often leaves the patient with a partial gap in the memory. I know this will be terrible news for you, but please let me tell you what really happened. Answell thought that your father was drugging him and tricking him in some way. He knew that his drink was drugged as soon as he felt the effects coming on. It remained in his memory, and it was the first thing he remembered when he began to wake up—farther back than his own memory extends now. They had been talking, unfortunately, about killing people with arrows. He got that arrow and stabbed your father before poor Avory knew what was happening: that is how this dear fiancé of yours came to be sitting up in the chair when his memory returned to him. He had just finished his work.*
>
> *Before God, Mary, this is what really happened. I saw it with my own eyes. Good-bye, and bless you forever even if I do not see you again.*
>
> *Your affectionate uncle,*
Spencer.

H.M. put his hands up to his eyes and pressed his forehead. He lumbered up and down beside the table; finally he sat down in a chair. The little worm of doubt was in all of us now.

"But won't it—?" the girl cried.

"Save him?" asked H.M., lifting a dull face. "My dear good wench, if you took that letter into court nothin' in the world could save him. I'm wondering if anything can save him now. Oh, my eye!"

"But couldn't we cut off the last part of the letter and just show them the first part? That's what I thought of."

H.M. regarded her sourly. She was a very pretty piece, and very much more intelligent than this suggestion sounded.

"No, we couldn't," he told her. "Not that I'm above hocus-pocus; but the blazin' bad part of that letter is on the back of the sheet that tells about the drugged whisky. Here's proof—here's evidence—and, burn me, we don't dare use it! Tell me something, my wench. In the face of that letter, do you still believe he's innocent?"

"I most certainly... Oh, I don't know! Yes. No. All I do know is that I love him, and you've got to get him off somehow! You're not going back on me, are you?"

H.M. sat twiddling his thumbs over his paunch and staring at the floor. He sniffed.

"Me? Oh, no. I'm a glutton for punishment, I am. They get the old man in a corner and whack him over the head with a club; and every so often they'll say: 'What, ain't you unconscious yet? Soak him another one'; and yet—burn me, *why* should that chap lie? I mean your good old uncle. He admits it about the whisky. I was lookin' forward, you see, to cross-examinin' him today. I was all ready to tear him to pieces and show up the truth. I could 'a' sworn he knew the truth, and even knew who the real murderer is. But here he is swearin' that Answell..." H.M. brooded. "'I saw it with my own eyes.' That's the part I can't get over. Curse it all, how could he have seen it with his own eyes? He couldn't. He was at the hospital when it happened. He's got an alibi as big as a house; we tested all that. He's lyin'—but if I prove he's lyin' about that, the first part of the letter isn't worth firewood. We can't have it both ways."

"Even at this late date," I said, "will you still keep from giving a hint as to how you mean to defend him? What are you going to say when you get up there tomorrow? What the devil is there to say?"

An expression of evil glee stole over H.M.'s face.

"You don't think the old man can be eloquent, do you?" he enquired. "Just you watch me. I'm going to get up there and look 'em in the face, and I'm goin' to say—"

X

"I CALL THE PRISONER"

"ME LORD; MEMBERS OF THE JURY."

With one hand behind his back, and his feet planted wide apart, H.M. was certainly looking them in the eye. But I could have wished that his manner was not so much that of a lion-tamer entering a cage with whip and pistol, or at least that he would abate his murderous glare at the jury.

Court-room Number One was packed. The rumour of sensational developments had been all over town: since seven o'clock in the morning there had been a queue outside the door to the public gallery up over our heads. Where there had been only a few newspapermen in attendance yesterday, today every paper in London seemed to have put a man in the somewhat inadequate space provided for the press. Before the sitting of the court, Lollypop had spent some time talking with the prisoner over the rail of the dock; he looked shaken but composed, and ended by shrugging his shoulders wearily. This conversation appeared to interest the saturnine Captain Reginald Answell, who was watching them. It was just twenty minutes to eleven when Sir Henry Merrivale rose to open the case for the defence.

H.M. folded his arms.

"Me lord; members of the jury. You're probably wonderin' what sort of defence we're here to offer. Well, I'll tell you," said H.M. magnanimously. "First of all, we'll try to show that not one single one of the statements made by the prosecution could possibly be true."

Sir Walter Storm rose with a dry cough.

"My lord, the assertion is so breath-taking that I should like to be quite clear about it," he said. "I presume my learned friend does not deny that the deceased is dead?"

"Ss-s-t!" hissed Lollypop, as H.M. lifted both fists.

"Well, Sir Henry?"

"No, me lord," said H.M. "We'll concede that as bein' the only thing the Attorney-General has been able to find out about this case unaided. We'll also concede that zebras have stripes and hyenas can howl. Without drawin' any more personal comparisons between hyenas and—"

"The zoology of the matter does not concern us," said Mr. Justice Rankin, without batting an eyelid. "Proceed, Sir Henry."

"I beg your lordship's pardon and withdraw the question," said the Attorney-General gravely; "submitting the accepted fact that hyenas do not howl: they merely laugh."

"Hyenas— Where was I? Ah, I got it. Members of the jury," pursued H.M., leaning his hands on the desk, "the Crown have presented their case to you on two counts. They've said to you: 'If the prisoner didn't commit this crime, who did?' They've also said: 'It's true we can't show you any shadow of a motive for this crime; but *therefore* the motive must have been a very powerful one.' Both of those counts are pretty dangerous for you to go on. They've based their case on a culprit they can't find and a motive they don't know.

"Let's take first this question of motive. You're asked to believe that the prisoner went to Avory Hume's house with a loaded pistol in his pocket. Why? Well, the police-officer in charge of the case says: 'People do not usually carry weapons unless they think they may have a use for them.' In other words, you're subtly asked to believe that the prisoner went there with the straight intention of murdering Avory Hume. But why? As a prelude to married life, it's a little drastic. And what prompted the feller to do that? The only thing you've heard is a telephone conversation—where, mind you, there wasn't one bitter or flamin' word spoken the whole time. 'Considerin' what I have heard, I think it best that we should settle matters concerning my daughter. Can you manage to come to my house at six o'clock' and all the rest of it. Did he say to the prisoner: 'I'll settle your hash, damn you'? He did not. He said it to a dead 'phone; he said it to himself. All the prisoner heard—all anyone says he heard—was a cold and formal voice invitin' him to the house. And *therefore*, you're asked to believe, therefore he grabbed up someone else's gun and rushed round to the house with murder written all over his face.

"Why? The suggestion creeps in that the victim heard something pretty bad about the prisoner. You haven't heard what it was; you've heard only that they can't tell you what it was. They simply say: 'Where there's smoke there must be some fire'; but you haven't even heard about any smoke. They can't supply any reason why Avory Hume suddenly seemed to act like a lunatic.

"But, d'ye see, *I can.*"

There was no doubt that he had caught his audience. He was speaking almost off-handedly, his fists on his hips, and glaring over his spectacles.

"The facts, the actual physical facts in this case, aren't in doubt. It's the causes for these facts that we're goin' to question. We're goin' to show you the real reason for the victim's conduct: we're goin' to show you that it had nothing whatever to do with the prisoner: and we're goin' to suggest that the whole case against this man was a deliberate frame-up from end to end. The Crown can't supply any motive for anybody's actions; we can. The Crown can't tell you what happened to a large piece of feather that mysteriously vanished; we can. The Crown can't tell you how anyone except the prisoner could have committed the crime; we WILL.

"I said a minute ago that the case has been presented to you: 'If the prisoner didn't commit the crime, who did?' But you can't say to yourselves: 'It is very difficult to think that he didn't do it'; if that's what you think, you'll have to acquit him. But I don't mean to bother with merely provin' a reasonable doubt of his guilt; we mean to show that there's no reasonable doubt of his innocence. Why, burn me—"

Lollypop warningly flourished that curious typewritten sheet as H. M. began to thrust out his neck.

"All right, all right! In other words, you'll hear an alternative explanation. Now, it's not my business to indicate who really committed this murder, if the prisoner didn't. That's outside our inquiry. But I'll show you two pieces of a feather, hidden in a place so obvious that nobody in this dazzlin' investigation has thought of looking there; and I'll ask you where you really think the murderer was standin' when Avory Hume was killed. You've heard a whole lot of views and opinions. You've heard all about the prisoner's sinister leers and erratic conduct: first they tell you he's so nervous he can't hold on to his hat, and next he's so coldly cynical that he smokes a cigarette: though why either of them acts should be suspicious is beyond my simple mind. You've heard how first he was supposed to threaten Hume with murder, and then how Hume got up and bolted the door so that he could do it more conveniently. You've heard what he might have done and what he probably did and what he never could have done in this broad green world; and now, by the flaming horns o' Tophet, it's time you heard the truth. I call the prisoner."

While H.M. gobbled at a glass of water, one of the warders in the dock touched Answell's arm. The door in the dock was unlocked, and he was led down through the well of the court. He walked nervously, without looking at the jury as he passed. His neck-tie was a little loose from much fingering; and his hand would go up to it frequently. Again we had an opportunity of studying someone under fire. Answell's light hair was parted on one side; he had good features which showed imagination and sensitiveness rather than a high intelligence; and his only movement, aside from touching his tie or moving his big shoulders slightly, was to glance up at the roof of the witness-box. In this roof there is a concealed mirror—a relic of the days when light was thus focused—and it seemed to fascinate him at times. His eyes looked a little sunken and completely fixed.

Despite H.M.'s truculence—he was drinking water with the effect of gargling it—I knew he was worried. This was the turn of the case. During the time a prisoner is in the box (usually more than an hour and sometimes a day) he carries his fate in his mouth every second. It is a good man who will not falter before the pulverising cross-examination that is waiting for him.

H.M.'s manner was deceptively easy.

"Now, son. Your name?"

"James Caplon Answell," said the other.

Although he was speaking in a very low tone, hardly audible, his voice flew off at a tangent. He cleared his throat a few times, turning his head away to do so, and then gave a half-guilty glance at the judge.

"You've got no occupation, and you live at 23, Duke Street?"

"Yes. That is—I lived there."

"At about the end of December, last, did you become engaged to be married to Miss Mary Hume?"

"Yes."

"Where were you then?"

"At Mr. and Mrs. Stoneman's house at Frawnend, in Sussex."

H.M. led him gently through the part about the letters, but it did not put him at his ease. "On the Friday—that's January 3rd—did you decide to go up to town next day?"

"Yes."

"Why did you decide to do that?"

An indistinguishable mutter.

"You will have to speak up," said the judge sharply. "We cannot hear a word you are saying."

Answell looked round; but the fixed, sunken expression of his eyes never altered. With some effort he found his voice, and seemed to catch up things in the middle of a sentence. "—and I wanted to buy an engagement ring. I had not got one yet."

"You wanted to buy an engagement ring," repeated H.M., keeping his tone to an encouraging growl. "When did you decide to go? I mean, what part of Friday d'jou decide this?"

"Late Friday night."

"Uh-huh. What made you think of this trip?"

"My cousin Reg was going up to town that evening, and he asked me whether he could get an engagement ring for me." A long pause. "It was the first time I had thought of it." Another long pause. "I suppose I should have thought of it sooner."

"Did you tell Miss Hume you were goin'?"

"Yes, naturally," replied Answell, with a sudden and queer ghost of a smile which vanished immediately.

"Did you know that on this Friday evening she had put through a telephone-call to her father in London?"

"No, I did not know it then. I learned it afterwards."

"Was it before or after this call that you decided to come to town next day?"

"Afterwards."

"Yes. What happened then?"

"Happened? Oh, I see what you mean," said the other, as though with relief. "She said she would write a note to her father, and she sat down and wrote one."

"Did you see this note?"

"Yes."

"In this note, did it mention what train you were takin' in the morning?"

"Yes, the nine o'clock from Frawnend station."

"That's about an hour and three-quarters' run, ain't it? Thereabouts?"

"Yes, on a fast train. It is not quite as far as Chichester."

"Did the note mention both the time of departure and the time of gettin' there?"

"Yes, ten-forty-five at Victoria. It's the train Mary herself always takes when she goes up."

"So he knew the train pretty well, eh?"

"He must have."

H.M. was allowing him plenty of time, and handling him with the softest of gloves. Answell, with the same fixed and sunken look, usually started off a sentence clearly, but allowed it to tail off.

"What'd you do after you got to London?"

"I—I went and bought a ring. And some other business."

"And after that?"

"I went to my flat."

"What time did you get there?"

"About twenty-five minutes past one."

"Was that when the deceased rang you up?"

"Yes, about one-thirty."

H.M. leaned forward, humping his shoulders and spreading out his big hands on the desk. At the same time the prisoner's own hands began to tremble badly. He looked up at the edge of the roof over the box; it was as though they were approaching some climax where wires must not be drawn too tightly or they would snap.

"Now, you've heard it testified that the deceased had already rung up your flat many times that mornin', without getting an answer?"

"Yes."

"In fact, he was ringin' up that flat as early as nine o'clock in the morning?"

"Yes."

"You heard Dyer say that?"

"Yes."

"Uh-huh. But he must have known perfectly well he couldn't get you, mustn't he? At nine o'clock you were just leavin' Frawnend, on an hour and three-quarter's journey. There were the times of arrival and departure smack in front of him, on a train his daughter frequently took. He must have known—mustn't he?—that it'd be two hours before he could hope to get you?"

"I should have thought so."

("What on earth is the man doing?" demanded Evelyn in my ear. "Pulling his own witness to pieces?")

"Now let's take this 'phone conversation. What did the deceased say?"

Answell's account was the same as the others'. He had begun to speak with a terrible earnestness.

"Was there anything in what the deceased said that you could take offence at?"

"No, no, nothing at all."

"What'd you think of it, in general?"

"Well, he did not sound exactly friendly, but then some people are like that. I thought he was just being reserved."

"Was there any dark secret in your life that you thought he'd discovered?"

"Not that I know of. I never thought of it."

"When you went along to see him that evenin', did you take your cousin's gun with you?"

"I—did—not. Why should I?"

"You got to the deceased's house at ten minutes past six? Yes. Now, we've heard how you dropped your hat, and seemed in a temper, and refused to take your overcoat off. Son, what was the real reason for all that conduct?"

Mr. Justice Rankin interposed during the prisoner's quick mutter. "If you are to do yourself any good, you must speak up. What did you say? I cannot hear."

The prisoner turned towards him and made a baffled kind of gesture with his hands.

"My lord, I wanted to make as good an impression as I could." Pause. "Especially as he had not sounded—you know, cordial, over the 'phone." Pause. "Then, when I went in, my hat slipped out of my hands. It made me mad. I did not want to look like—"

"Like a what? What did you say?"

"Like a damned fool."

"'Like a damned fool,'" repeated the judge without inflection. "Go on."

H.M. extended a hand. "I suppose young fellers calling on their in-laws for the first time often do feel just as you did? What about the overcoat?"

"I didn't mean it. I didn't want to say it. But after I had said it I could not take it back, or it would have seemed worse."

"Worse?"

"More like an ass," blurted the witness.

"Very well. You were taken back to the deceased? Yes. What was his manner towards you?"

"Reserved and—queer."

"Let's make that clearer, son. Just what d'you mean, 'queer'?"

"I do not know." Pause. "Queer."

"Well, tell the jury what you said to each other."

"He noticed me looking at those arrows on the wall. I asked him if he was interested in archery. He began talking about playing bows and arrows in the north when he was a boy, and how it was fashionable here in London. He said the arrows were trophies of what he called the 'annual wardmote' of the Woodmen of Kent. He said: 'At those meets, whoever first hits the gold becomes Master Forester for the next year.'"

"'The gold?'" repeated H.M. in a rumbling voice. "'The gold?' What did he mean by that?"

"I asked him that, and he said he meant the centre of the target. When he said this, he looked straight at me in an odd kind of way—"

"Explain that. Just take it easy, now..."

Again Answell gestured. "Well, as though he thought that *I* had come fortune-hunting. That is the impression I got."

"As though you'd come fortune-huntin'. But I s'pose, whatever else you could be called, you couldn't be called a fortune-hunter?"

"I hope not."

"What did he say then?"

"He looked at his fingers, and looked hard at me, and said: 'You could kill a man with one of those arrows.'"

"Yes; after that?" prodded H.M. gently.

"I thought I had better change the subject. So I tried to be light about it, and I said: 'Well, sir, I didn't come here to steal the spoons, or to murder anyone unless it becomes absolutely necessary.'"

"OH?" roared H.M. "You used the expression, 'I didn't come here to steal the spoons,' before you said the rest of it. We haven't heard that, y'know. You said that?"

"Yes. I know I said that first, because I was still thinking about 'the gold' and wondering what he had in mind. It was only natural."

"I agree with you. And then?"

"I thought it was no good beating about the bush any longer, so I just said: 'I want to marry Miss Hume, and what about it?'"

H.M. took him slowly through the statement about pouring out the whisky.

"I'm goin' to ask you to be very careful now. I want you to tell us just exactly what he said after he poured out that whisky: every look and gesture, mind, as far as you remember it."

"He said: 'May I wish you prosperity?' and his expression seemed to change, and become—I did not like it. He said: 'Mr. James Caplon Answell,' to the air, as though he were repeating it. Then he looked at me and said: 'That marriage would be advantageous—to both sides, I might say.'"

H.M.'s lifted hand stopped him.

"Just a minute. Be careful. He said: '*That* marriage,' did he? He didn't say: 'This marriage?'"

"No, he did not."

"Go on."

"Then he said: 'As you know, I have already given my consent to it.'"

"Let me repeat that," interposed H.M. quickly. He lifted his blunt fingers and checked off the words. "What he actually said was: '*That* marriage *would* be advantageous; I have already given my consent to it?'"

"Yes."

"I see. And then, son?"

"He said: 'I can find absolutely nothing against it. I had the honour to be acquainted with the late Lady Answell, and I know that your family financial position is sound.'"

"Wait again! Did he say: '*Your* financial position' or 'Your *family* financial position?'"

"It was: 'Your *family* financial position.' Then he said: 'Therefore I propose to tell you—' That was all I heard, distinctly. There was a drug in that whisky, and it got me."

H.M. exhaled a deep breath, and shook his gown; but he kept on steadily in that rumbling monotone.

"Right here let's cut back to the telephone conversation by which you got summoned to Grosvenor Street. The deceased knew you were comin' to London by a train that left Frawnend at nine o'clock?"

"He must have."

"He also knew—didn't he?—that the train wouldn't arrive until ten-forty-five; and that he couldn't possibly get in touch with you before eleven?"

"Mary told him so."

"Exactly. Yet still he kept ringin' up your flat incessantly from as early as nine in the morning—when you hadn't started from Frawnend?"

"Yes."

"When you talked to him over the 'phone at one-thirty on Saturday afternoon, had you ever heard his voice before, or seen him?"

"No."

"I want to hear about the beginnin' of that conversation on the telephone. Just tell us how it began."

"The 'phone rang," replied Answell in a calm voice. "I picked up the receiver" (he illustrated). "I was sitting on the couch, and I reached over after it while I was looking at a newspaper. Mr. Hume spoke. At that time I thought he said: 'I want to speak to Caplon Answell.' So I said: 'Speaking.'"

H.M. leaned forward.

"Oh? You *thought* he said: 'I want to speak to Caplon Answell.' But later, when you looked back on it, did you realise he said something different?"

"Yes, I did. I knew it must be."

"What did he really say, then?"

"Something different."

"Did he really say this? Did he really say: 'I want to speak to CAPTAIN Answell'?"

"Yes."

H.M. dropped his brief on the desk. He folded his arms, and spoke with a ferocious gentleness.

"In short," said H.M., "during that whole conversation, and afterwards at his own house, he thought he was talkin' to your cousin, Captain Reginald Answell: didn't he?"

XI

"IN CAMERA"

FOR PERHAPS TEN SECONDS THERE WAS NOT SO MUCH AS A WHISPER or a creak in the court-room. I imagined I could hear people breathe. The implication penetrated slowly; we had seen it suddenly appear and come closer; but it had to be adjusted to the case, and I wondered whether the judge would allow it. The prisoner, whose tired face now wore a sardonic look, seemed challenging Reginald Answell to meet his eye. Reginald did not. His back was to the witness-box as he sat at the solicitors' table; he had his hand on the water-bottle, and he scarcely appeared to have heard. His saturnine face, with hair the same colour as the prisoner's, showed only a rather bored astonishment.

"Yes, I mean that man there," insisted H.M., drawing attention to him.

Captain Reginald shook his head and smiled contemptuously. Sir Walter Storm rose in full panoply.

"My lord," he snapped, "may I suggest that the prisoner is hardly an authority on what Mr. Hume may or may not have been thinking?"

The judge considered, rubbing his temples lightly with his small hands.

"The point is well taken, Sir Walter. At the same time, if Sir Henry has any evidence to put forward in this matter, I think we may allow him some latitude." He looked at H.M. with sharpness.

"Yes, my lord, we got the evidence."

"Then continue; but remember that the prisoner's suspicions are not evidence."

Although the Attorney-General sat down without attack it was clear that he had declared war. H.M. turned again to Answell.

"About this telephone-call which we're trying to explain: your cousin had come up to London the night before, hadn't he?"

"Yes, from the same place I was staying."

"And, when he was in London, he always stayed at your flat? I think we've heard that testified here?"

"That is true."

"So, if the deceased wanted to get in touch with him, it's natural that he should have rung up your flat as early as nine on Saturday morning?"

"Yes."

"When you went to Grosvenor Street on Saturday evenin', was your first name mentioned at any time?"

"No. I said to the butler: 'My name is Answell'; and, when he announced me, he said: 'The gentleman to see you, sir.'"

"So, when the deceased said: 'My dear Answell, I'll settle your hash, damn you,' you believe he was not speaking about *you* at all?"

"I am sure he was not."

H.M. shuffled with some papers in order to allow this to sink in. Then, beginning with the drinking of the whisky, he went through the story. *We* knew that part of it to be true; but still, was he guilty? The man was not the world's best witness; but there was an air of fierce conviction about everything he said. He conveyed a little of that trapped feeling which must have possessed him if he were innocent. It was a long examination, and Answell would have made a good impression if only—last evening—he had not announced his own guilt from the dock. It hung over every word he said now, even if nobody referred to it. He was a self-confessed murderer before he started. It was as though there were two of him, merging each into the other like figures on a double-exposed photographic plate.

"Finally," growled H.M., "let's take the reasons for various things. When did you first begin to believe that a mistake had been made, and that all that evening the deceased had been mistakin' you for your cousin?"

"I don't know." Pause. "I thought of it that same night, later, but I could not believe it." Pause. "Then I thought about it again. Afterwards."

"Was there a reason why you didn't want to say anything about it, even then?"

"I—" Hesitation.

"Just tell me: did you have a reason?"

(Watch your step, H.M.; for God's sake watch your step!)

"You have heard the question," said the judge. "Answer it."

"My lord, I suppose I did."

Mr. Justice Rankin frowned. "You either had a reason, or you had not?"

"I had a reason."

It was possible that H.M. was beginning to sweat. "Just tell me this: *Do you know why the deceased might have wanted to make an appointment with your cousin and not you?*"

Between counsel and prisoner there seemed to be a scales; and now the scale-pan dipped. The young blockhead squared his shoulders and drew a deep breath. Putting his hands on the rail, he looked with a clear eye round the court.

"No, I don't know," he replied clearly.

Silence.

"You don't know? But there was a reason, wasn't there, why this mistake might have occurred?"

Silence.

"There was a reason, wasn't there, why the deceased may have disliked Captain Answell, and wished to 'settle his hash'?"

Silence.

"Was it because—?"

"No, Sir Henry," interposed the judge into that tightening strain, "we cannot let you lead the witness any further."

H.M. bowed, and leaned his weight on his fists. He clearly saw that it was useless to go on with this. All sorts of speculations must have been buzzing soundlessly in the court, behind those impassive faces banked up round us. The first thing which occurred to me was that it almost certainly concerned Mary Hume. Suppose, for instance, that there had been an affair of striking proportions between Mary Hume and the penniless Captain Answell? And suppose that the practical Avory Hume meant to cut it through to the core before it spoiled a good marriage? It fitted every circumstance; and yet would the prisoner have put his neck in a rope rather than acknowledge it? This was incredible. Let us face it sensibly: it does not happen nowadays. It is carrying chivalry too far. There must be some other reason which concerned Mary Hume—but what it was none of us, I think, then guessed. When we did learn, we understood.

Presently H.M. relinquished his witness, and the formidable Sir Walter Storm rose to cross-examine. For a moment he did not speak. Then in a tone of calm and detached contempt, he threw out one question.

"Have you made up your mind whether or not you are guilty?"

There are certain tones you must not take with any man, even when he is helpless. What nothing else could do, this did. Answell pulled up his head. Across the well of the court he looked the Attorney-General in the eye.

"That is like asking: 'Have you stopped cheating at poker?'"

"It would be irrelevant to question you about your habits with cards, Mr. Answell. Just oblige me by answering my questions," said the other. "Are you guilty or not guilty?"

"I did not do it."

"Very well. I take it that your hearing is normally acute?"

"Yes."

"If I say to you: 'Caplon Answell,' and then, 'Captain Answell'—even in spite of all the unfortunate noise going on in this court—you will be able to distinguish between the two?"

At the solicitors' table Reginald Answell smiled slightly and turned his eyes round. What impression all this had made on him it was impossible to say.

"Please speak up. I take it that you do not have periodic fits of deafness?"

"No. But as it happens, I did not pay much attention at the time. I was looking at a paper. I picked up the 'phone with the other hand, and I did not give it close attention until I heard Mr. Hume's name."

"But you heard *his* name well enough?"

"Yes."

"I have here your statement, exhibit 31. Regarding this theory that the deceased may have said 'Captain Answell' rather than 'Caplon Answell'—did you mention this to the police?"

"No."

"Although you tell us that it occurred to you as early as the night of the murder?"

"I did not think seriously of it at the time."

"What made you think more seriously of it later?"

"Well—I got to thinking it over."

"Did you mention it when you were before the magistrates?"

"No."

"What I am endeavouring to get at is this: When did such an idea first crystallise in your mind?"

"I don't remember."

"What caused it to crystallise in your mind, then? Do you remember that? No? In short, can you give one good and solid reason for this whole extraordinary notion of yours?"

"Yes, I can," shouted the witness, bedevilled out of his torpor. His face was flushed; he looked, for the first time, natural and human.

"Very well; what reason?"

"I knew that Mary had been very friendly with Reg before we met; it was Reg who introduced me to her, at the Stonemans'—"

"Oh?" enquired Sir Walter, with rich suavity. "Are you suggesting that you believed there had been anything improper in their relations?"

"No. Not exactly. That is—"

"Had you any *reason* to suspect anything improper in their relations?"

"No."

Sir Walter tilted back his head, and seemed to be massaging his face with one hand as though to get curious ideas in order.

"Tell me, then, whether I correctly state the various suggestions you have made. Miss Hume was friendly with Captain Answell, there being nothing to which anyone could take exception. Because of this, the eminently reasonable Mr. Hume conceives a violent dislike of Captain Answell and resolves suddenly to 'settle his hash.' He telephones to Captain Answell, but the message is intercepted by you under the mistaken impression that it is for you. You go unarmed to Mr. Hume's house, where he gives you a drink of drugged whisky in the belief that you are Captain Answell. While you are unconscious, someone places Captain Answell's pistol in your pocket and (as I think you have told my learned friend) employs his time in pouring mint-extract down your throat. When you awake, your finger-prints are found on an arrow which you have not touched, and the whisky has flown back into a decanter without finger-prints. Have I correctly stated your position in the matter? Thank you. Can you reasonably expect the jury to believe it?"

There was a silence. Answell put his hands on his hips and glanced round the court. Then he spoke in a natural, off-hand tone. He said:

"So help me, by this time I don't expect anybody to believe anything. If you think everything a person does in life is governed by some reason, just try standing where I am for a while and see how you like listening to yourself."

A sharp rebuke from the bench cut him short; but his nervousness had been conquered and the glazed fixity was gone from his eyes.

"I see," intoned Sir Walter imperturbably. "Do you next suggest that no reason governs any of your own actions?"

"I always thought it did."

"Did reason govern your actions on the night of January 4th?"

"Yes. I kept my mouth shut when they were talking to me as you are now."

It earned another reproof from the bench; but Answell was making a better impression here than under chief-examination. The good impression was quite irrational, for Sir Walter proceeded to tie him into such knots that probably not three people in court believed a word he said. But—after he had let H.M. down badly—there it was. I wondered whether the old man had arranged this to happen exactly as it did.

"You have told us that the reason why you refused to remove your overcoat, and spoke to one witness in a tone that has been described as savage, was because you did not wish to 'look like a damned fool.' Is that correct?"

"Yes."

"Did you think that you would look more like a damned fool with your overcoat off than with it on?"

"Yes. No. I mean—"

"What precisely did you mean?"

"It was the way I felt, that's all."

"I put it to you that the reason why you did not remove that coat was that you did not wish anyone to notice the bulge of the pistol in your hip-pocket?"

"No. I never thought of that."

"You never thought of what? Of the pistol in your pocket?"

"Yes. That is, there was no pistol in my pocket."

"Now, I call your attention again to the statement you made to the police on the night of January 4th. Are you aware that the suggestions you have made today directly contradict this statement you gave to the police?"

Answell drew back, fidgeting again with his tie. "No, I do not follow that."

"Let me read you a few of them," said Sir Walter, with the same unruffled heaviness. "'I went to his house,' you say, 'at six-ten. He greeted me with complete friendliness.' You now imply that his attitude was the reverse of friendly, do you not?"

"Yes, rather."

"Then which of these two attitudes do you wish us to believe?"

"Both of them. This is what I mean: I mean that on that night he took me for someone else, and his attitude was not friendly; but he was actually friendly enough towards myself."

For a moment Sir Walter remained looking at the witness, and then he lowered his head as though to cool it.

"We need not stop to disentangle that; I am afraid you do not appreciate my question. Whoever he thought you were that night, was his attitude during your interview friendly?"

"No."

"Ah, that is what I wished to find out. Then this particular assertion in your statement is false, is it not?"

"I thought it was true at the time."

"But you have completely changed your mind since then? Very well. Again you tell us: 'He said that he would drink my health, and he gave his full consent to my marriage with Miss Hume.' Since you have now decided that he was unfriendly, how do you reconcile this quoting of actual words with an unfriendly attitude?"

"I misunderstood him."

"In other words," said the Attorney-General, spacing his words after a pause, "what you ask the jury to believe now is a direct contradiction to several of the most essential assertions in your statement?"

"Technically, yes."

For a full hour Sir Walter Storm gravely took the witness to pieces like a clock. He went through every bit of testimony with great care, and finally sat down after as pulverising a result as I have ever listened to. It was expected that H.M. would re-examine, in an attempt to rehabilitate his witness. But he did not. All he said was:

"Call Mary Hume."

A warder took Answell back to the dock, where the door was unlocked again, and he was led up into his open pen. A cup of water was brought up from the cells for him; he drank it thirstily, but he peered up with a quick start over the rim when he heard H.M. call the witness.

Where Mary Hume had been during the previous examination you could not tell. She seemed to appear in the middle of the court, as though there should be no hesitation or halt in the shuttle that moved witnesses to and from justice. Answell was already last minute's pattern. And Reginald Answell's expression changed. It was not anything so obvious as a start: only a certain awareness, as though someone had tapped him on the shoulder from behind, and he did not quite want to look round. His long-jawed good looks had a bonier quality; but he assumed a pleasant expression, and his finger tapped slowly on the water-bottle. He glanced up at the prisoner—who smiled.

Mary Hume looked momentarily at the back of Captain Reginald's head as she went up into the witness-box. With the exception of Inspector Mottram, she was (or so it seemed on the surface) the calmest person who had yet testified. She wore sables: a flamboyant display, Evelyn assured me, but she may have been feeling in that mood with defiance. And she wore no hat. Her yellow hair, parted and drawn back sleekly, emphasised the essential softness and odd sensuality of the face, dominated by those wide-spaced blue eyes. Her method of putting her hands on the edge of the box was to grasp it with both arms extended, as though she were on an aqua-plane. In her manner there was no longer any of that hard docility I had seen before.

"You swear by Almighty God that the evidence you shall give—"

"Yes."

("She's frightened to death," whispered Evelyn. I pointed out that she gave not a sign of it, but Evelyn only shook her head and nodded back again towards the witness.)

Whatever the truth might have been, her very presence there indicated thunder on the way. Even her importance seemed emphasised by the fact that she was rather small. A new interest quickened the press-box. H.M., who had difficulty in getting his own voice clear, waited until the stir of interest had died down; only the judge was unimpressed.

"Hurrum! Is your name Mary Elizabeth Hume?"

"Yes."

"You're the only child of the deceased, and you live at 12, Grosvenor Street?"

"Yes," she answered, nodding in a somnambulistic way.

"At a Christmas house-party at Frawnend, in Sussex, did you meet the accused?"

"Yes."

"D'ye love him, Miss Hume?"

"I love him very much," she said, and her eyes flickered briefly. If it were possible to have a more hollow silence than had existed before, it held the court now.

"You know he's here accused of murderin' your father?"

"Of course I know it."

"Now, ma'am—miss, I'll ask you to look at this letter I have here. It's dated, 'January 3rd, nine-thirty p.m.,' the evening before the day of the murder. Will you tell the jury whether you wrote it?"

"Yes, I wrote it."

It was read aloud, and ran:

Dear Father:

Jimmy has suddenly decided to come to London tomorrow morning, so I thought I had better tell you. He will take the train I usually travel by—you know it, nine o'clock here and a quarter to eleven at Victoria. I know he means to see you some time tomorrow.

Love,
Mary.

PS. You will take care of that other matter, won't you?

"Do you know whether your father received this letter?"

"Yes, he did. As soon as I heard he was dead, I came to town, naturally; and I took it out of his pocket the same night—the night he died, you know."

"What was the occasion of your writin' it?"

"On Friday evening—that Friday evening, you know—Jim suddenly decided to go up to town, to get me an engagement ring."

"Did you try to dissuade him, to keep him from goin' to town?"

"Yes, but I could not do too much of it or he would have been suspicious."

"Why did you try to dissuade him?"

The witness moistened her lips. "Because his cousin, Captain Answell, you know, had gone up to London on Friday evening with the intention of seeing my father next day; and I was afraid he and Jim might meet at my father's house."

"Did you have a reason why you didn't want them to meet at your father's?"

"Yes, yes!"

"What was the reason?"

"A little before, in the same week, you know," replied Mary Hume, "Captain Answell had asked me, or rather my father, to pay £5,000 hush-money."

XII

"FROM A FIND TO A CHECK—"

"YOU MEAN THAT MAN THERE?" ASKED H.M., POINTING WITH A BIG flipper and again ruthlessly singling him out.

It was like an inexorable spotlight. Reginald Answell's face had turned a curious colour, a muddy colour, and he sat bolt upright; you could see the rise and fall of his chest. At that moment, looking back on past events, I saw the pattern take form. He had thought he was quite safe: he and this girl were linked together in such fashion that he had thought she would not dare to betray it. She had even promised him, with remarkably well-simulated terror, that she would remain quiet. You could understand now the reason for that hard docility, the meek: "Thanks for everything." A scrap of their conversation came back to me. First his significant: "Fair exchange; it's all agreed, then?" And her colourless: "You know me, Reg," while she contemplated this.

Three voices in the court-room spoke in quick succession.

The first was the Attorney-General's: "Is Captain Answell on trial?"

The second was H.M.'s: "Not yet."

The third was the judge's: "Proceed, Sir Henry."

H.M. turned back to the witness, whose plump and pretty face was composed, and who was looking at the back of Reginald's head.

"So Captain Answell had asked you, or rather your father, to pay five thousand pounds blackmail?"

"Yes. He knew I hadn't got it, of course, but he felt sure he could get it out of father."

"Uh-huh. What reason did he have for blackmailin' you?"

"I had been his mistress."

"Yes, but was there another and stronger reason—much stronger?"

"Oh, yes."

For the second time during that trial, the prisoner sprang to his feet and was about to speak out from the dock. He had not expected this. H.M. made a savage gesture in his direction.

"What was that other reason, Miss Hume?"

"Captain Answell had taken a lot of photographs of me."

"What kind of photographs?"

Her voice was blurred. "Without any clothes on, and in—certain postures."

"I did not catch that," said the judge. "Will you please speak up? What did you say?"

"I said," replied Mary Hume clearly, "without any clothes on, and in certain postures."

The calm inexorability of the judge made everyone in that room squirm.

"What postures?" asked Mr. Justice Rankin.

H.M. intervened. "My lord, just in order to show why the prisoner has been so blamed anxious not to talk about this, and why he's acted in certain ways, I've got one of those photographs here. Across the back of it is written: 'One of the best things she ever did for me,' in what I'd like the witness to identify as Captain Answell's handwriting. Then I'd like to submit it to you to suggest that it can go to the jury as bein' evidence of what we're trying to establish."

The photograph was handed up. While the judge looked at it, there was a hush of such bursting quality that you could hear it. It was to be wondered what the witness was feeling; every eye in the room had glanced at her, just once, and had seen her in other costume—or the lack of it. Sir Walter Storm made no comment or objection.

"You may show this to the jury," said the judge tonelessly.

It travelled along before two lines of impassive faces.

"How many of these photographs are there?"

"A-about a dozen."

"This one here, the one you gave me to put in evidence; is it the only one of 'em you've got?"

"Yes, Reg has the others. He promised to give me the rest if I didn't say anything in court about his trying to get hush-money out of me."

Reginald Answell got slowly to his feet and began to make his way out of the court-room. He tried to walk with equal slowness and casualness. No one, of course, attempted to comment or restrain him. But H.M. deliberately allowed a space while the pressure of the court was focused on him like his own camera. Chairs, people at the solicitors' table, elbows, feet, everything seemed to get in his way, and made him go faster; it was like someone bumping over rows of feet in a theatre, trying to get out without attracting attention along a line of stalls. By the time he reached the door he was running. The policeman on duty there gave him one look, and stood aside. We heard the *whish* of the glass door out into the hall.

"So," observed H.M. in a heavy tone. "Let's take up the story of those pictures. When were they taken?"

Again she moistened her lips. "A-about a year ago."

"Had you broken off your relations with Captain Answell before you met the prisoner?"

"Oh, my God, ages before."

"Did you ask for the photographs?"

"Yes, but he just laughed and said they would do no harm."

"What'd Captain Answell do when he heard you were engaged to the prisoner?"

"He took me aside, and congratulated me. He said it was a really excellent thing, and he approved of it."

"What else?"

"He said that if I didn't pay him five thousand he would show the photographs to Jim. He said he didn't see why he should not get something out of this when everyone else seemed to have so much money."

"This was durin' the week of December 28th—January 4th?"

"That's right."

"Now just go on, if you can, Miss Hume."

"I said he must be c-completely crazy, and he knew I hadn't got five thousand pennies, and never would have them. He said yes, but my father would be willing to pay through the nose. He—he said that my father's one big dream in life was to make a good and wealthy marriage for me, and—"

"And—?"

"—and had got to the point where my father—well, despaired of ever doing it—"

"Steady, ma'am; stop a bit. Had you ever done anything like this before?"

"No, no, no! I'm only telling you what Reg—what Captain Answell said to me. He said my father would not let five thousand pounds stand in the way of my getting a good catch like Jim Answell."

H.M. studied her. "Your father was a pretty inflexible man, wasn't he?"

"He was that."

"When he wanted something, he got it?"

"Yes, always."

"Did your father know anything about these photographs?"

Her wide-spaced blue eyes opened as though she could not understand the stupidity that put such questions, even if they had to be asked for the sake of clearness in a court of law.

"No, no, of course he didn't. Telling him was nearly as bad as—"

"But you did tell him, didn't you?"

"Yes, it had to be done, so I did," replied the witness, summing herself up.

"Explain how that happened, will you?"

"Well, Reg—Captain Answell said he would give me a few days to rake up the money. On—yes, it was on the Wednesday, I wrote to my father and said I had to see him about something horribly urgent and important in connection with my marriage. I knew that would bring him. I couldn't leave the house-party without any explanation, especially as Jim was throwing money right and left to celebrate, and all the local charities were coming to thank us. So I asked my father if he would come down on Thursday morning and meet me in a village near Frawnend..."

"Yes, that's right; go on."

"I met him at an inn called 'The Blue Boar,' I think it was, on the road to Chichester. I expected him to flare up, but he didn't. He just listened to me. He walked up and down the room a couple of times, with his hands behind his back, and then he said that five thousand pounds was absolutely ridiculous. He said he might have been willing to pay something smaller, but he had had a few reverses lately; and in fact he had been looking forward a bit to Jim's money. I said maybe Captain Answell would come down in the price. He said: 'We won't bother with paying him money; just you leave him to me, and I'll settle his hash.'"

"Oho? 'Just you leave him to me, and I'll settle his hash.' What was he like when he said this? How'd he act?"

"He was as white as a sheet, and I think if he had had Reg there he would have killed him."

"H'm, yes. So," observed H.M., jerking his thumb, "the idea of your father settling Captain Answell's hash, and even giving him drugged whisky, don't sound so almighty foolish as it did when my learned friend was discussin' it, eh?" He hurried on before anyone could object to unscrupulous comment. "Did he tell you how he meant to settle Captain Answell's hash?"

"He said he was going back to London, and he wanted a few hours to think. He said to let him know if Reg made any move in the meantime."

"Anything else?"

"Oh, yes; he asked me to try to find out where Reg kept the photographs."

"Did you try?"

"Yes, and I was horribly poor at it. I—that's what brought everything on. Reg just looked at me and laughed, and said: 'So that's the trick, is it? Now just for that, my little lady, I'm going straight to London and see your father.'"

"This was on Friday, wasn't it?"

"Yes."

"What did you do?"

"I telephoned my father early Friday evening—"

"That's the call we've heard about?"

"Yes. To warn him, and ask him what he was going to do."

H.M. made mesmeric passes of some intensity. "I want you to tell us what he said then; every word, as far as you can remember."

"I'll try. He said to me: 'Good; it's all arranged. I will get in touch with him tomorrow morning, and invite him here, and I promise you he will not bother us again.'"

She spoke with extraordinary intensity, so that H.M. allowed a space for the words to sink into the minds of the jury. Then he repeated them.

"Did he tell you what he meant to do about settlin' Captain Answell's hash?"

"No; I asked him, but he would not tell me. The only other thing he said was to ask where he could be certain of finding Reg, and I said at Jim's flat. He said: 'Yes, I thought so; I have already been there.'"

"He said that he had already been there?" H.M. raised his voice. "Did he say anything about pinchin' Captain Answell's automatic pistol out of the flat?"

The effect of this was broken by the judge's interruption.

"The witness has already told you, Sir Henry, that she heard nothing more."

H.M., well satisfied, patted his wig. "And then, on top of all this," he went on, "your *fiancé* all of a sudden decided to go to London as well, and you were afraid somethin' would blow up?"

"Yes, I was half crazy."

"That's why you wrote to your father on Friday night, after the 'phone-call?"

"Yes."

"Does this postscript here, 'You *will* take care of that other matter, won't you?'—does that refer to the effective settling of Captain Answell's hash?"

"Yes, of course."

"One more little point," pursued H.M., with a long and rumbling sniff. "A witness has testified here about the rather odd way your father acted when he got that letter at the breakfast table on Saturday morning. He walked to the window, and he announced in a grim kind o' tone that your *fiancé* was comin' to town that day—and meant to see him. The witness said: 'Oh, then we will not go to Sussex after all; we will invite him to dinner,' or words to that effect. The deceased said that those other two would go to Sussex as arranged. He also said: 'We will not invite him to dinner, or anywhere else.'" H.M. slapped his hand on the table. "What he meant was, then, that they wouldn't invite him to dinner in case the two cousins ran into each other?"

Sir Walter Storm stirred out of his immobility.

"My lord, for the last time I must protest against this constant attempt to question witnesses about things they did not see or words they did not hear, particularly since it is always done in the form of a leading question."

"Do not answer that," said Mr. Justice Rankin.

"In your opinion," said H.M., after the customary form of sardonic apology, "in your opinion, from the things you *have* seen and the things you *have* heard, doesn't what you've just told us show what really did happen on the night of the murder?"

"Yes."

"Would a woman have the nerve to go through with what you've just told us today, unless she believed absolutely that this man is innocent?"

He pretended to listen for an answer, and then sat down with a whack that shook the bench.

There was some whispering behind us, around, beyond, a sound in long grasses which you knew centred in only one thing. Mary Hume must have known it as well; she was drawing patterns with her finger on the edge of the ledge, and looking down. But from time to time she would glance up, briefly, while the Attorney-General was taking some while before beginning his cross-examination. Her pretty face was growing dull red; and, as though unconsciously, she would draw her sables closer round her. How long this mental narcotic would sustain her you could not tell. She had badly damaged many parts of the prosecution's case: you realised that much of Answell's apparent stumbling and foolish testimony must be the solid truth: and it was clear the jury thought so too. But the whispering grew like noise in a forest. Someone inquired plaintively if they were not going to show us the photograph. I noticed that the space reserved for newspapermen was now completely empty, though I could not remember having seen any of them hurry out. It was a matter for headlines and speculations in every British home.

"Hold on to your hat; here we go," whispered Evelyn fiercely, and Sir Walter Storm got up to cross-examine.

Nothing could have exceeded the sympathy and consideration of the Attorney-General's manner. His voice was quietly persuasive.

"Believe me, Miss Hume, we quite appreciate your sincerity in this matter, and your courage in offering this somewhat unusual picture. At the same time, you had no hesitation in posing, I believe, for a dozen of this nature?"

"Eleven."

"Very well; eleven." Again he waited for a time, pushing some books into an even line on the desk. "All these things to which you have testified, Miss Hume—I take it that you were aware of them at the time of the murder?"

"Yes."

"I believe you have stated that, when you learned of your father's death you hurried back from Sussex and arrived at the house on that same night?"

"Yes."

"Quite so," remarked the other, meticulously pushing another book into line. "Yet you did not mention to the police, then or at any other time, the remarkable circumstances to which you have just testified?"

"No."

"Did you mention them to any other person?"

"Only to—" Her slight gesture indicated H.M.

"Are you aware, Miss Hume, that had you given this information to the police, and demonstrated to them that Captain Answell had attempted to blackmail you, it would not have been necessary to bring this photograph into court at all? Or to expose yourself to any such humiliating examination as this must be?"

"Yes, I knew that."

"Oh, you knew that?" inquired Sir Walter, quickening with interest and looking up from the book.

"Yes, I—I read up on it."

"I presume this experience cannot be pleasant for you?"

"No, it is not," replied the girl. Her eyes looked strained.

"Then why did you not mention it, and do the prisoner what good you could without bringing matters to this?"

"I—"

"Was it because you believed the prisoner must be guilty; and therefore that these photographs bore no relation to his actual guilt?"

H.M. got up with painful effort. "Appreciatin' my learned friend's consideration, we'd still like to know what line that question takes. Is it now accepted by the Crown—as we've been suggesting all along—that a mistake was made between Caplon Answell and Captain Answell, and that the deceased got one in attemptin' to settle the hash of the other?"

Sir Walter smiled. "Hardly. We accept the photograph as a fact; we accept the suggestion that Captain Answell took the photograph; but we shall be compelled to deny that these two points have any bearing on the matter in hand—the guilt or innocence of the prisoner."

At my side, Evelyn nudged me sharply.

"But surely they don't dispute that now?" Evelyn asked. "Why, it seems as plain as the sun to me."

I told her she was prejudiced. "Storm's quite sincere: he believes Answell is a common-or-garden variety of murderer, wriggling in front of the facts. He'll show that the girl is simply inventing lies to cover him: that there were goings-on between Reginald and Mary Hume, but no attempt at blackmail by Reginald; and that they're simply making a last-minute effort to construct a defence."

"Well, it sounds silly to me. Do you believe that?"

"No; but look at the two women on the jury."

Black looks from various directions brought us to silence while the Attorney-General proceeded.

"Perhaps I did not make myself quite clear," said Sir Walter. "Let me try again. All the things you tell us here today, you could have told at the very time of the prisoner's arrest?"

"Yes."

"Would they not have been as valuable to him then as my learned friend wishes us to believe they are now?"

"I—I don't know."

"Yet you did not mention them?"

"No."

"You preferred (please excuse the term, Miss Hume, but I fear this is necessary), you preferred to make a show of yourself here rather than to explain all this before?"

"That is a little strong, Sir Walter," interposed the judge sharply. "I must remind you that this is not a court of morals. We have suffered so much in the past from those who appear to have laboured under this impression that I feel constrained to mention it now."

The other bowed. "As you wish, my lord. I myself was under the impression that I remained well within the rights of cross-examination... Miss Hume: you tell us that on Friday evening, January 3rd, Captain Answell left Frawnend for London, in order to see your father on the following day?"

"Yes."

"For the purpose of extracting blackmail money?"

"Yes."

"Why is it, then, that he did not see your father?"

The witness opened her mouth, and stopped. Fragile as she looked, she had been holding up well until now.

"Let me make my question clearer. Several witnesses have testified here—have been pressed to do so, in fact, by my learned friend—that all day Saturday your father received no visitors, no messages, no 'phone calls, except those which have been indicated. Captain Answell did not come near him or attempt to communicate with him. How do you reconcile this with your statement that Captain Answell rushed off to London for the purpose you have declared?"

"I don't know."

The other shot out his hand. "I put it to you, Miss Hume, that on Saturday, the 4th, Captain Answell was not even in London at all."

"But that can't be, I tell you!"

"Will you accept my suggestion, Miss Hume—which comes from the reports of police-officers who have investigated the movements of everyone connected with this affair—that on Friday evening Captain Answell left Frawnend, drove to visit friends in Rochester, and did not arrive in London until nearly midnight on Saturday?"

"No!"

"Will you further accept my suggestion that he announced to several persons in Frawnend his intention of going to Rochester: not London?"

No reply.

"You will agree at least that if he were in Rochester he could not be in London?"

"Perhaps he lied to me."

"Perhaps he did. Let us take another aspect of it. These photographs, you tell us, were taken a year ago?"

"About that, maybe a little more."

"How long afterwards did you sever your relations with Captain Answell?"

"Not long; a month or so; not long."

"And during the entire course of the time afterwards, has he ever attempted to extort money from you?"

"No."

"Or to use these photographs as a threat in any way whatever?"

"No. But didn't you *see* his face when he ran out of here?"

"That is not a matter which can come to our attention, Miss Hume. However, I can conjecture why the subject might be embarrassing to him, for reasons quite apart from blackmail. Can't you?"

"Do not answer that," said the judge, putting down his pen. "Counsel has just informed you that the matter cannot come to your attention."

"You have told us, then, that all this time no suggestion of blackmail was ever made by Captain Answell?"

"Yes."

"Do you know the nature of an oath?"

"Certainly."

"I suggest to you that this entire account of Captain Answell's blackmailing activities, and your father's alleged wish to 'settle his hash,' is an unfortunate fabrication from end to end?"

"No, no, no!"

Sir Walter contemplated her steadily and gently for a moment; then he shook his head, lifted his shoulders, and sat down.

If anyone expected H.M. to re-examine, that person was disappointed. With an almost weary air H.M. got up. "In order to establish this business once and for all," H.M. said very distinctly, "call Dr. Peter Quigley."

I was certain that I had heard the name somewhere before, and recently, but the man who went into the witness-box was a stranger. He was a strong-featured Scotsman with a quiet manner but a voice whose every syllable was distinct. Though he could not have been more than in his early thirties, he gave the impression of being older. H.M. began in his usual off-hand manner.

"What is your full name?"

"Peter Macdonald Quigley."

"Are you a graduate in medicine of Glasgow University, and have you a degree in scientific criminology from the University of Salzburg?"

"Yes."

"H'm. How were you employed durin' the month of December 10th to January 10th, last?"

"I was employed as assistant to Dr. John Tregannon in Dr. Tregannon's private nursing-home at Thames Ditton, Surrey."

"How did you come to be there?"

"I should explain," answered Quigley, spacing his words, "that I am an agent of the International Medical Council, employed in England under the Commissioners in Lunacy, for the purpose of investigating rumours or charges which cannot be substantiated—in the ordinary way—against those practising as mental specialists."

"Is the substance of what you are goin' to tell us contained in your report to the British Medical Council; and is it approved by that body?"

"It is."

"Were you acquainted with the deceased, Avory Hume?"

"I was."

"Can you tell us whether Captain Reginald Answell was attemptin' to extort blackmail money from the deceased?"

"To the best of my knowledge, he was."

"Yes. Now, will you tell us just what you know about this matter?"

"On Friday, January 3rd, last—"

The witness's first words were drowned by the stir in the court, and by Evelyn's whisper. Here was a witness whose credibility they could not shake. With deadly leisureliness, H.M. was taking the Crown's case to pieces. He let them cross-examine as long as they liked; he did not re-examine; and then he went waddling on. Again there came into my head the swinging lines from the song, which H.M. had quoted, and which seemed less like a refrain than like a formula. *"From a find to a check: from a check to a view: from a view to a kill in the morning."*

"On Friday, January 3rd, last—"

XIII

"THE INK-PAD IS THE KEY"

BUT IT WAS TWO O'CLOCK IN THE AFTERNOON, WITH THE SENSAtional testimony which had held the court beyond its morning sitting, before H.M., Evelyn and I sat again at lunch in the upper room of the Milton's Head Tavern, Wood Street. Nearly all of the pattern in this business lay before us: and yet it did not. H.M., a great Chinese image in the firelight, with a cigar stuck at an angle in his mouth, glowered and pushed his plate away.

"Well, my fatheads. You see what happened now, don't you?"

"Most of it, yes. The links in it, no. And how the blazes did you get on to Quigley?"

"By sittin' and thinkin'. Do you know why I took up this case to begin with?"

"Of course," said Evelyn quite sincerely. "Because the girl came to you and burst into tears; and you like to see the young folks have a good time."

"I expected that," said H.M. with dignity. "Burn me, that's the thanks I get from anyone; that's the view you take of a strong silent man who—bah! Now listen to me, because I mean it," and evidently he did believe in it so fiendishly that we listened. "I love to be a Corrector of Cussedness. You've heard me talk a lot in the past about the blinkin' awful cussedness of things in general, and I suppose you thought that was only my way of lettin' off steam. But I meant it. Now, ordinarily, this cussedness is supposed to be funny. You can't help bein' amused even when you kick the waste-paper basket all over the room. I mean that the one morning you've got an important engagement is the one morning you miss the train. The one time you take your best girl out to dinner is the one time you call for the bill and find you've left your wallet at home. But did it ever occur to you to think how that applies to whackingly serious matters too? Just think back over your own life, and see whether most of the important things that happened to you were prompted by anybody's effort to do malice, or anybody's effort to do good, or, burn me, by anybody's effort at all: but simply by the sinful, tearin' cussedness of things in general."

I looked at him with some curiosity. He was smoking furiously—the outburst being produced, I think, by relief. His chief witness had left Sir Walter Storm flat, without a rebuttal in the Attorney-General's nimble brain.

"You don't make a religion of that, do you?" I asked. "For if you think that things in general are all banded together in a conspiracy to administer a celestial kick in the pants, you might as well retire to Dorset and write novels."

"Y'see," said H.M., with ghoulish amusement, "that goes to show that the only sort of cussedness you can imagine is the kind that lands you in the soup. Like the Greek tragedies where the gods get a twist on some poor feller and he's never got a chance. You want to say: 'Hey, fair play!—take a few wallops at him if you must, but don't load the dice so far that the feller can't even go out in a London fog without comin' home with sunstroke.' No, son. Everything works both ways, especially cussedness. Cussedness got Answell into this affair, and the same sort of workin' principle handed me the way to get him out of it. The point is that you'll never explain it rationally—as Walt Storm would like to do. Call the whole process by any fancy name you like: call it destiny or Mansoul or the flexibility of the unwritten Constitution: but it's still cussedness.

"Take this case, for instance," he argued, pointing with his cigar. "As soon as that girl came to me, I saw what must have happened. You probably did too, when you heard the evidence. Jim Answell had got the wrong message and walked straight into the middle of a scheme designed to nobble Our Reginald. But neither Answell nor the Hume gal could realise that at first. They were too close to it; you can't see a piece of grit in your own eye. They only knew the grit was there. But when I sort of dragged the whole story out of her a month ago, and showed what must 'a' happened, it was too late—the case was up for trial. If she had gone to 'em then, they wouldn't have believed her: just as Walt Storm quite honestly and sincerely didn't believe her today."

He sniffed.

"But what the blazes, I ask you, was the girl goin' to think at first? She hears her father is dead. She comes home. She finds her *fiancé* alone with him in a space locked up like a strong-room, with his finger-prints on the arrow and everything pointin' straight to him. How is she goin' to suspect a frame-up against *him*? How is she goin' to connect it with Our Reginald, unless someone points it out to her?"

"And that somebody was you?"

"Sure. That was the position when I first began to sit and think about the case. Of course, it was clear that old Avory Hume himself had arranged that little bit of hocus-pocus with intent to deceive Our Reginald. You heard it all. *He* kept ringin' up the flat as early as nine in the morning—though right in the middle of Answell's original statement to the police is the news that Hume knew he wouldn't arrive until 10.45. *He* gave the cook and the housemaid an unexpected night off. *He* ordered the shutters in the study to be closed, so that nothin' could be seen. *He* called the butler's attention to the fact that there was a full decanter of whisky and a full syphon on the sideboard. *He* bolted the door of the study on the inside, when Answell was alone with him. *He* sang out the words loud enough for the butler to hear, 'What's wrong with you? Have you gone mad?' That was a blunder. For, if you assume Answell really had drunk hocussed whisky, no host in the world would ever naturally say: 'Have you gone mad?' when he saw a feller topplin' into unconsciousness. He'd say: 'Don't you feel well?' or 'Are you ill?' or even: 'Drunk, hey?'

"Granted, then, that Avory Hume was putting up some game. What did he intend to do? He intended to shut Our Reginald's mouth; but he didn't mean to offer money. Do we know anything about Our Reginald that might give an indication? I got it from the gal—as you tell me you overheard it today. Don't we know, for instance, that there was insanity in Reginald's branch of the family?"

For some time there had been in my mind a very vivid memory, of voices rising above the sound of feet shuffling down the stairs of the Old Bailey. Reginald Answell and Dr. Hume were descending together; and between them there was a thick hypocrisy for the common good, with an edge of malice showing through. Reginald Answell had made the thrust, as though casually: "There *is* insanity in our family, you know. Nothing much. Only like a touch of the tar-brush a few generations back—".

"But enough for the purpose," continued H.M. "Oh, quite enough. I wonder what those two chaps were thinking about then? Each of them knowin' the truth; but both of them ruddy well goin' to keep their mouths shut. In any case, let's go on. There's insanity in Reginald's family. And Avory Hume's brother is a doctor. And a very rummy kind of drug must have been required for the purpose. And one of Spencer Hume's closest pals is a Dr. Tregannon, a mental specialist, who's got a private nursing home. And it takes two doctors to certify—"

"And so, as we know, they were going to lock Reginald up as a lunatic," I said.

H.M. wrinkled his forehead.

"Well, there at the start, I was only considerin' the evidence," he pointed out, putting the cigar in his mouth and sucking at it in the fashion of a child sucking a peppermint-stick. "But it looked probable that Avory and Spencer Hume had arranged just that game. Let's see how the hocus-pocus would have worked out. It's true they made a howlin' error and got Jim instead of Reginald. But did that affect the details as we found 'em? Let's see.

"Reginald is to be invited to the house. Why might he, with insanity in his family, be presumed to go off his rocker? That's easy. He was known to be pretty well tied up with Mary Hume; even Jim Answell knew that."

"Did he know about the photographs?" inquired Evelyn, with interest.

"Ho ho," said H.M. "The photographs. No, he didn't know it at the time; he knew it afterwards, in clink—because I told him. It caused me an awful lot of trouble. Jim Answell is no posturin' young hero who'd walk fat-headedly to the rope rather than let it be known his gal had been havin' an affair with another man. But that wasn't it. When it came to the question of the pictures, he couldn't—literally and physically couldn't—*say* all that in court, to be blurted out across the world. He couldn't do it to save his life. Could you?"

"I don't know," I admitted, with visions which must have risen up before Answell. "The more you think about it the more devilish it sounds."

"She could, though," said H.M. with great glee. "That's why I like her: she's a perfectly sincere and natural gal. A nosegay also goes to the judge. When Balmy Rankin made that remark about this not bein' a court of morals—burn me, I almost got up and handed him a box of cigars. Thirty years I've been waitin' for a red judge to acknowledge the facts of life without comment; and I told you I had great faith in Balmy. But stop interruptin' me, dammit! I was telling you about the trick to nobble Our Reginald.

"Where was I? Ah, I got it. Well, it was known Reginald and Mary Hume were tied up together. It was also known he had no money at all, and that Avory Hume had squashed to earth any possibility of marriage. And then his rich cousin James gets engaged to her. And Reginald comes to see the old man—and goes berserk.

"You see the plan Avory had? High words are overheard. Presently witnesses (unprepared witnesses) come chasin' in. They find Reginald with his own gun in his pocket—suggestin' violence. They find his fingerprints stamped on an arrow which has been so obviously (so blinkin' obviously) ripped down from the wall—suggestin' violence of a more than sane kind. They find his hair rumpled, his tie pulled out. They find Avory Hume with all the marks of a struggle on him. And what does Reginald himself say to all this, lookin' wild and a little stupid as though he don't know where he is? He says he's been given a drug, and all this is a frame-up. But here's a medical man to swear there's been no drug taken, and the spotless decanter full of whisky on the sideboard. Short of actually showin' the chap with straws stuck in his hair, I don't see what more could have been arranged.

"Well, I thought to myself, what'll be the watchword when he's found? It'll be: 'Sh-h! Hush! Keep it dark! This thing has got to be kept very quiet, known only to a few witnesses to prove it's genuine.' It mustn't be known that the poor feller has lost his reason. The Commissioners in Lunacy mustn't hear of it. Does the chap keep babblin' something about Mary Hume, and some photographs, and a frame-up? All the more reason why such slanderous ravings mustn't be repeated, mustn't even be breathed by a lunatic. Why not take him to Dr. Tregannon's nursin' home under the charge of Spencer Hume? Even Jim Answell, when it's necessary to break the sad news to him, will hush it up as fierce as anybody. On the eve of his own wedding, he won't want it blared forth that a first-cousin of his had to be taken away under escort.

"Of course, the doctors in charge of the case will also take charge of his personal belongings: clothes, keys and the like. Wherever he's got those photographs stowed away, they'll be found and burnt in pretty quick time." H.M. snapped his fingers, and then sniffed. "And that's all there is to it, my fatheads. It ain't even very expensive. Our Reginald will remain under duress until he promises to be good—and serve him right! It's an awful pity the scheme didn't work. Even if he won't promise, he can't prove anything, and he is still always suspect of a leaky steeple; and Avory Hume's daughter is married. It's happened many times before, y'know. It's the respectable way of hushin' up scandal."

We considered it, more detailed than it had come from the witness-box in the cold voice of Dr. Quigley.

"Avory Hume," I said, "was apparently a tough proposition."

H.M. blinked in the firelight of the old room, surprised.

"Not particularly, son. He was simply respectable. Also, he was a realist. Someone was blackmailing him. Something had to be done about it. And so he did. You heard the father's daughter talkin' in court this afternoon. I don't mind his sort. As I say, in this amusin' little spectacle of dog-eat-dog, I'm rather sorry his scheme didn't come off, and shove our cool Reginald into cooler clink while he reflects that there are ways *and* ways of gettin' money. But I'm an old-fashioned lawyer, Ken, and a whole canine feast ain't goin' to let 'em hang my client. Well, right there at the start, I had to dig up a witness who knew somethin' about the scheme. If necessary, I was prepared to bribe Tregannon himself to spill the beans—"

"Did you say bribe?"

"Sure. But I got Quigley, because the Medical Council had already been after Tregannon. There was someone who actually overheard Avory and Spencer and Tregannon cookin' up the broth; someone planted in Tregannon's nursing home, and waitin' for an opportunity to expose

Tregannon. That was what I meant, a while ago, by speakin' of the cussedness which cuts the other way."

"But what's the line of defence now?"

"Ar!" said H.M., and scowled.

"You've practically established that there was a plot. But will Storm throw up his brief just because of that? Is there any reason why Answell still shouldn't be guilty?"

"No," said H.M. "That's what's got me worried."

He pushed back his chair, lumbered up, and took a few pigeon-toed turns up and down the room.

"So what's the line of defence now?"

"The Judas window," said H.M., peering down over his spectacles…

"Now, now!" he went on persuasively. "Just you look at the evidence, and take it from the beginning as I did. Now that we've established a plot, there'll be a whole heap of helpful suggestions in the way that plot was worked out. I'll give you a hint. One thing in this scheme bothered me a bit. Avory and Spencer are workin' together to nobble Reginald—very well. But, on the night of the trick, Avory manages to get everybody out of the house except the butler. The cook and the maid are out. Amelia Jordan *and* Dr. Hume are goin' off to Sussex. But I said to myself: Here! Spencer can't be going away like that. His brother needs him. Who's goin' to come in and cluck his tongue over the bogus loony: who's goin' to examine the loony: who's goin' to swear he took no drug, if not Dr. Hume? He was the essential part of the scheme; he was the pivot."

"Unless they got Tregannon."

"Yes; but they'd hardly have Tregannon on the premises. It would look much too fishy. And there was the answer to the other question. If Spencer himself were too conveniently hangin' about with his stethoscope, if the whole thing flowed too smoothly, an eyebrow might be raised here and there. It was the Jordan woman, in all accident, who gave the hint away when she was burblin' in court yesterday: I heard her testimony a month ago, and I spotted it then. Remember what she was to do? She was to pick up Spencer in the car—pick him up at the hospital—and they were to drive into the country afterwards. Do you recall that?"

"Yes. What of it?"

"Do you also recall," said H.M., opening his eyes, "what Spencer had asked her to do for him? He'd asked her to pack a suitcase for him, and bring it along to the hospital so that he wouldn't have to bother. And, burn me, I don't recall a neater trick! She intended to go to Sussex; Spencer never did. The one way in this world you can be sure you won't get what you want is to tell someone, off-hand, to pack a suitcase for you. The person does his best, and shoves in what he thinks you'll need. But something is always wrong. In this case, all Spencer needed was a pretext. She was to arrive at the hospital luggin' the suitcase. 'Ah,' said Spencer affably, 'I see you've packed it. Did you put in my silver-backed brushes?' Or it may be his dressing-gown, or his evenin' studs, or anything at all: all he's got to do is wade through the list until he finds something that's been omitted. 'You left that out?' he says. 'Good God, woman, do you think I can travel to the country without my whatever-it-is? My whatever-it-is is absolutely necessary. This is a most unfortunate nuisance'—can't you hear Spencer sayin' that?—'but I am afraid we shall have to go back to the house for it.'"

H.M., patting his stomach and leering down from under lofty eyebrows, was giving such an uncanny impersonation of Spencer Hume that you could almost hear the doctor's voice. Then he broke off. He added:

"So they drive back to the house. And they arrive (accidentally but providentially) just in time to find Avory Hume overcoming a maniac who has tried to kill him. Hey?"

There was a pause.

"It's rather a neat trick, and it would have been convincing," Evelyn admitted. "Was the woman—Amelia Jordan—in on the scheme to nail Reginald?"

"No. Otherwise there'd 'a' been no reason for the hocus-pocus. She was to be one of the unprepared witnesses. The other two were Dyer and Fleming—"

"Fleming?"

Taking the cigar out of his mouth, H.M., with a very sour expression, sat down at the table again. "Look here! You heard what Fleming said in the witness-box. Avory had told him to drop in at the house about a quarter to seven. Hey? All right. With Fleming's habits, he may even suspect that Fleming'll be a few minutes early. Now concentrate on the elegant timing of the whole business, as it was MEANT to happen.

"Avory has told the prospective loony to come to the house at six o'clock sharp; and, considerin' an errand of blackmail, he can ruddy well believe Reginald will be on time. Avory has told Amelia Jordan that she's to start off in the car (which Dyer will bring round from the garage) at soon after 6.15. Gimme a piece of paper, somebody, and a pencil. Avory Hume was awful methodical, and he worked out this piece of crooked work as methodically as he'd have worked out the terms of a mortgage. Like this:

"At 6.0 p.m., Reginald will arrive. He will be seen by Jordan and Dyer. Dyer takes him to the study. Then Dyer will be sent to fetch the car. Dyer will probably linger at the study door for a couple of minutes; he's been warned the visitor is not to be trusted, remember. Dyer will leave the house, say 6.5. He should be back with the car between 6.10 and 6.15. Between 6.15 and 6.20, Amelia Jordan will be drivin' away in it to the hospital.

"It's only a short drive from Grosvenor Street to Praed Street, near Paddington. Amelia Jordan arrives at the hospital, say 6.22. She will hand the suitcase to Spencer, who will discover that his whatever-it-is is missin', and they will drive back. They will arrive back between 6.27 and 6.30.

"By this time the stage is all set. Avory Hume will cut up a row, bring Dyer bangin' at the door—open the door to show the results of a frantic struggle in the study. Reginald, groggy and wild-eyed with the inertia that follows a maniacal outburst, won't be able to say much. The doctor will arrive, clucking his tongue. While the excitement is still high and handsome, Fleming will arrive and be the last witness. So."

H.M. puffed out smoke and waved it away.

"Only it didn't work out like that," I said. "Someone took advantage of that scheme—and murdered the old man."

"That's it. Now I've told you what was meant to happen. Next, to help you along, I'll show you what *did* happen. I'm goin' to give you a time-table for that whole evening, because it's very suggestive. Most of the official times, like the arrival of officers or the times centrin' directly round the fact of the murder, you've already heard in court. Others weren't important as direct evidence, and weren't stressed. But I've got 'em all here, taken down from the police notes; and I've got the comments I wrote opposite 'em after I'd interviewed Answell and Mary Hume. I suggest to you (gor, how I'm beginnin' to hate that expression!) that, if you study 'em with a little cerebral activity, you'll learn a good deal."

From his inside pocket he took out a large, grubby sheet of paper, worn from much pawing-over, and spread it out carefully. It was dated over a month before. The time-schedule, in the left-hand column, had evidently been typed by Lollypop. The comments, in the other column, were scrawled in blue pencil by H.M. Thus:

Table.	Comment.

6.10. Answswell arrives, and is taken to study. — Delay by mist.

6.11. Avory Hume tells Dyer to go and get the car; study door is closed, but not bolted.

6.11–6.15. Dyer remains in passage outside study door. Hears Answell say: "I did not come here to kill anyone unless it becomes absolutely necessary." Later hears Hume speaking in sharp tone, no words distinguishable; but ending loudly: "Man, what is wrong with you? Have you gone mad?" Hears sounds like scuffle. Taps on door and asks if anything is wrong. Hume says: "No, I can deal with this; go away." — No mention of stealing spoons. "Have you gone mad?" Very fishy; look into this. "Scuffle" Answell's fall? Was door bolted at this time? No, or Dyer would have heard sounds made by stiff and unused bolt shot into socket. Very brave of Hume; unco' fishy.

6.15. Dyer goes to get car. — Obedient. Arrives at garage 6.18.

6.29. Amelia Jordan finishes packing own valise and suitcase Dr. Hume has asked her to pack for him. — Shocking. Suppose she left something out? ?

6.30–6.32. Amelia Jordan comes downstairs. Goes into passage towards study door. Hears Answell say: "Get up, damn you!" Tries study door, finds it is bolted; or locked in some way. — Must be bolted. Lock is stuck at "open" position.

6.32. Dyer returns with car.

Table.	Comment.
6.32–6.34. Amelia Jordan tells Dyer to stop them fighting or get Fleming; she goes after Fleming.	
6.34. Finds Fleming coming down steps of own house to go next door.	Rather early; but what of it?
6.35. Fleming accompanies her. They all knock at study door.	
6 36. Answell opens study door.	
6.36–6.39. Examination of body and room. No doubt of door and windows being locked on inside. Answell's cool and dazed behaviour commented on. "Are you made of stone?" Answell says: "Serve him right for drugging (or doctoring) my whisky." Inquiries about whisky. Bottle and syphon found full, glasses untouched; Answell still declaring business a frame-up. Piece of feather found torn off arrow.	Drug still working. Brudine? How did Hume get rid of original syphon? Original decanter too? Answell says nothing put into glass; must have been in decanter. ? N.B.—No hocus-pocus about locks. Door inch-and-a-half thick; big heavy knob and panels; tight-fitting frame; no keyhole. Shutters have bar; no slits; windows also locked. Gobble gobble. Phooey.
6.39. Fleming sends Amelia Jordan to get Dr. Hume. Fleming wants to take Answell's finger-prints. Dyer says there is ink-pad in Dr. Spencer Hume's suit.	Why? Officious busybody?

Table.	Comment.
6.39–6.45. Dyer cannot find ink-pad or suit. Remembers old ink-pad in desk in study. Answell objects to having his finger-prints taken; knocks Fleming across room, finally seems to become dispirited and agrees.	Was that desk searched? (N.B. It was, I find.) Then where is missing piece of feather?
6.45. Dyer goes out into street and calls Police-Constable Hardcastle.	

At this point Evelyn interposed. "I say! Does this mean, in actual times, that it was only nine minutes between the time they went into the room and the time Dyer went out to get the policeman? By the way they talked in court, it sounded much longer, somehow."

H.M. grunted sourly. "Sure. It always sounds longer, because they've got so much to tell. But there's the actual record, as you could 'a' worked it out for yourselves."

"The one thing that's most puzzling here," I insisted, "is why so much rumpus in general is being kicked up on the subject of ink-pads. Ink-pads would seem to have nothing to do with the case. What difference does it make whether Fleming did or didn't take Answell's finger-prints? The police could always do it, and match them with the ones on the arrow. Yet even the prosecution made a point of bringing it up and hammering it home."

Exhaling a cloud of smoke, H.M. leaned back with rich satisfaction and closed one eye to avoid getting smoke in it.

"Sure, they did, Ken. But they weren't concerned with ink-pads. What they wanted to hammer was that, when Fleming tried to get Answell's finger-prints, Answell—far from bein' torpid—flared out murderously and threw Fleming clear across the room. Same kind of attack as he launched on the deceased, d'ye see? But I'm glad they brought it up; if they hadn't, I should have. Because I am most definitely interested in one particular ink-pad. It's pretty well the key to the whole business. You see that, don't you?"

XIV

TIME-TABLE FOR ARCHERS

THAT ARGUMENT, UP IN THE LITTLE LOW-RAFTERED ROOM AT THE "Milton's Head," while we waited for the afternoon session of the court, will always remain a kind of vignette as vivid as anything in the case. The firelight shone on rows of pewter tankards, and on H.M.'s enormous shoes, and on his glasses, and on a face wreathed with fantastic jollity. Evelyn sat with her legs crossed, leaning forward with her chin in her hand; and her hazel eyes had that amused annoyance which H.M. inspires in every woman.

"You know perfectly well we don't," she said. "Now don't sit there chortling and rocking and making faces like Tony Weller thinking what he'd like to do to Stiggins! You know, at times you can be the most utterly exasperating man who ever—ee! *Why* do you take such pleasure in mystifying people? If only Mr. Masters were here, the party would be complete, wouldn't it?"

"I don't take pleasure in it, dammit!" grumbled H.M., and quite seriously believed this. "It's only that people take such unholy joy in doin' me in the eye, that I got to get a bit of my own back." He was soothing. "You stick to business, here. Read the rest of the time-table. I'm merely askin' you: if Jim Answell isn't the murderer, who is?"

"No, thanks," said Evelyn. "I've been had like that before. And much too often. You did it in France, and you did it in Devon. You parade out a list of suspects, and we take our choice; and then it always turns out that you've got someone else altogether. I daresay in this case you'll show the murder was really committed by Sir Walter Storm or the judge. No, thanks."

"Meanin' what?" inquired H.M., looking at her over his spectacles.

"Meaning this. You've called our attention to his time-table, and that's a most awfully suspicious sign. You seem to concentrate attention on people who were actually lurking about the place at the time of the murder. But what about the others?"

"What others?"

"There are at least three others. I mean Reginald Answell, and even Mary Hume herself, and Dr. Hume. For instance, the Attorney-General 'put it to' the Hume girl today that Reginald wasn't in London at all: he was in Rochester: and didn't reach London until nearly midnight. You didn't contradict him—at least, you didn't re-examine the witness. Well, where was he? We know he was at the house at *some* time on the night of the murder, even if it was late: I heard him say so himself, when he was going down the stairs at the Old Bailey. Mary Hume was also there, also late. Finally, there's the doctor, who's missing now. First you rather indicate that Dr. Hume has got an alibi; and last night, Ken tells me, he writes a letter swearing he actually saw the murder committed. How do you propose to straighten out all that?"

"If you'd only read the rest of your time-table—" howled H.M., and then grew reflective. "Some of it's worryin' me," he admitted. "You knew, did you, that there's court order out to arrest Spencer? When we knew he'd run off, Balmy Rankin wouldn't let that pass. If they ketch him, Balmy'll commit him to clink for deliberate contempt of court in a murder case. I thought Walt Storm rather too easily decided to dispense with that witness, when he should 'a' moved an adjournment. Walt must have known he'd done a bunk. But so did Balmy. Burn me, I wonder... never mind. Have you got any ideas, Ken?"

My position was simple. "Not having much sense of social justice, I don't care so much who killed him as how it was done. I'm like Masters: 'Never mind the motive: let's hear about the mechanics.' There are three alternatives: (1) Answell really did stab him after all; (2) Hume killed himself, either by accident or suicide; (3) there's an unknown murderer and an unknown method. H.M., will you answer a couple of straight questions, without technical evasions or double-meanings?"

His face smoothed itself out.

"Sure, son. Fire away."

"According to you, the real murderer made his entrance by means of the Judas window. Is that straight?"

"Yes."

"And the murder was committed with a cross-bow. Is that your argument?"

"That's right."

"Why? I mean, why a cross-bow?"

H.M. considered. "It was the most logical thing, Ken: it was the only weapon that fitted the crime. Also, it was much the easiest weapon to use."

"The easiest weapon? That whacking big clumsy thing you showed us?"

"Easy," said H.M. sharply. "Not in the least big, son. Very broad, yes; remember that; but not long. You saw it yourself: it was the short 'stump' cross-bow. And easy? At a very short distance, you heard Fleming admit himself, not even an amateur could miss."

"I was coming to that. From what distance was the arrow fired?"

H.M. regarded us over his spectacles with a kind of sour whimsicality. "The court-room manner is gettin' infectious. I feel like a medical man said at one trial: 'This is like a college examination under oath.' That, Ken, is the one thing I can't tell you within a couple of inches, since you want me to be so goddam precise. But, just in case I'm accused of evasion, I'll tell you this—not much more than three feet, at the very longest. Satisfied?"

"Not quite. What was Hume's position when the arrow was fired?"

"The murderer was talkin' to him. Hume had been by the desk, bendin' over to look at something. As he bent forward, the murderer casually pulled the trigger of the cross-bow: hence the rummy angle of the arrow, which was shot in rather a straight line. Walt Storm made an awful lot of fun of that, but it's the strict truth."

"Bending over to look at something?"

"That's right."

Evelyn and I looked at each other. H.M., nibbling at the stump of his cigar, pushed the time-table across to me.

"Now that you've got that off your chest, why not pay a bit of attention to matters just as relevant? Spencer Hume, for instance. He's a gap in the proceedings, because he didn't testify in court. Not that he did much of importance when he got back to the house; but what he did is interestin'. Y'know, Spencer must have got one hell of a shock when he learned it really was Jim Answell they'd caught, and not Reginald."

"Did he know either of the cousins by sight?"

"Yes," said H.M., with another odd look. "He knew both of them; and he was the only one in the whole flamin' case who did."

Table.	Comment.
6.46. Spencer Hume arrives in Grosvenor Street.	Uncle Spencer, *vide* police statements, has got an absolutely water-tight alibi. From 5.10 to 6.40 he was walking wards of hospital. At 6.40 he went downstairs and waited in foyer. Finally went out on steps. At 6.43 (fast driving), A. Jordan whizzed up in car and told him to come quickly and take wheel, saying Avory was dead and Mary's *fiancé* was loopy. Uncle Spencer is o-u-t. Gobble gobble.
6.46–6.50. P.C. Hardcastle tries to question Answell; then telephones to police-station.	
6.46–6.50. Spencer Hume takes Amelia Jordan upstairs: doctor necessary.	
6.51–6.55. Spencer Hume goes to study. In presence of Fleming and Dyer, Answell says: "You are a doctor; for God's sake tell them I have been doped." Spencer says: "I can find no sign of it."	Why didn't Spencer own up to truth about drugged drink? Too dangerous?
6.55. Inspector Mottram and Sergeant Raye arrive.	First time study is searched by police.

Table.	Comment.
6.55–7.45. First examination of Answell by Inspector Mottram; other witnesses questioned; study is searched by Inspector Mottram and Sergeant Raye.	No dust in thin vertical line down shaft or arrow. Very rummy; projected? Feather torn in half completely; couldn't be done in struggle; powerful clean break—caught somewhere Mechanism? Projected? What kind of mechanism? Find out what there might be in archer's house. (Later.) J. Shanks, odd-jobs man for three houses, reports cross-bow missing from box in shed in back-garden. Cross-bow missing. Golf-suit missing. 1 + 1 = *Equo ne credite*, o, coppers.
7.45. Divisional Police-surgeon Dr. Stocking arrives.	
7.45–8.10. Examination of body.	Note position of body. Direction of wound? Does not fit. Maybe!
8.15. Spencer Hume telephones to Mary Hume at Frawnend.	Had dinner out, but arrived back in time to get message.
8.10–9.40. Further questioning and search of house. Answell collapses.	
9.42. Answell's cousin Reginald telephoned to.	Reginald had just arrived at flat, motoring from Rochester. Known to have left Rochester about 5.15; says he had early dinner at hotel along way, and took a long time about it; was rather drunk on arriving back. Cannot remember name of hotel or village.

Table.	Comment.
9.55. Reginald Answell arrives in Grosvenor Street.	
10.10. Answell removed to police-station, Reginald going along.	
10.35. Mary Hume, taking first train, arrives back.	
10.50. Body removed to mortuary; at this time two letters formerly in dead man's pocket are discovered missing.	Mary had pinched them; why?
12.15. Answell's final statement taken at police-station.	

Conclusions: From times and facts given above, there is no doubt as to identity of real murderer. Gobble gobble gobble.

"That's fairly sweeping," I commented, and looked hard at him. "Is this supposed to tell us anything? And, by the way, what is the reason for the persistent recurrence of this 'gobble-gobble' business?"

"Oh, I dunno. That's how I felt at the time," said H.M. apologetically. "It showed I was touchin' the fringes of the truth."

Evelyn glanced down the list again. "Well, unless this is a bit of faking on your part, there's someone else you can practically eliminate—I mean Reginald. You say he's proved to have left Rochester at 5.15. Rochester's about thirty-three miles from London, isn't it? Yes. So, while it's theoretically *possible* to drive thirty-three miles in an hour, with all the traffic—and central traffic at that—I don't see how he could have got to Grosvenor Street in time to commit the murder. And you've already eliminated Dr. Hume."

"Eliminated Spencer?" demanded H.M. "Oh, no, my wench. Not a bit of it."

"But you yourself admit he's got a water-tight alibi."

"Oh, alibis!" roared H.M., shaking his fist. He got up and began to waddle about the room, growling. "The Red Widow murderer had a fine alibi, didn't he? The feller who did the dirty in that ten-teacups business also had a pretty good one. But that's not what's really botherin' me. What bothers me is that infernal letter Uncle Spencer wrote to the Hume gal last night—swearin' he actually saw the murder done, and that Answell did it after all. Why did he write that? If he lied, why the blazes *should* he lie? The most insidious bit in it is the suggestion that Answell might be quite sincere about swearin' he's innocent: that he killed Hume and simply doesn't remember it. Oh, my eye! Did you ever hear anyone advance the theory that that was the way Dickens intended to finish *Edwin Drood*?—Jasper bein' the murderer, but not rememberin' it: hence the opium-smoking? It's the same idea Wilkie Collins used in *The Moonstone* for pinchin' the jewel, so I shouldn't be surprised. If my whole great big beautiful theory cracks up on a point like that... but it can't! Burn me, it's not reasonable; or what about the feather? The first person I suspected was Uncle Spencer—"

"You suspected him just because he had an alibi?" I asked.

"It's no good talkin' to you," said H.M. wearily. "You won't see the difficulties. I thought that if he didn't actually commit the murder, he arranged it—"

A new possibility appeared.

"I remember reading about another of these cases," I said; "but it's so long ago that I can't remember whether it was a real happening or a story. A man was found apparently murdered in a room high up in a tower by the edge of the sea. His chest had been blown in with a shot-gun, and the weapon was missing. The only clue was a fishing-rod in the room. Unfortunately, the door of the tower had been under observation, and no one was seen to go in or out. The only window was a small one up a smooth wall above the sea. Who killed him, and what had happened to the weapon?... The secret was fairly simple. It was suicide. He had propped up the shot-gun, facing him, in the window. He stood some feet away and touched the hair-trigger with the fishing-rod. The kick of the gun when it exploded carried it backwards off the window-ledge into the sea: hence it was supposed to be murder and his family collected the insurance. Do you mean that there might have been some device in Avory Hume's study, which he accidentally touched, and it discharged the arrow at him? Or what the devil do you mean?"

"It can't be that," Evelyn protested. "If this isn't more mystification, we're to believe that the murderer was actually talking to Hume at the time."

"That's right," admitted H.M.

"All the same," I said, "it seems that we're straying away from the most important point. No matter who committed the murder, what was the motive? You can't tell me, for instance, that Answell would grab an arrow and stab Hume simply because he believed his future father-in-law had put knock-out-drops in a glass of whisky. Unless, of course, he's as mad as they wanted to make out Reginald was. But there's been remarkably little talk about motive in this case. Who else had a shadow of a motive to kill Hume?"

"Ain't you forgettin' the will?" asked H.M., lifting dull eyes.

"What will?"

"You heard all about it in court. Avory Hume was mad to have a grandson, like most self-made men. Perpetuate the line, and so on. He was goin' to make a will leaving everything in trust—everything, mind—for that hypothetical grandson."

"Did he make the will?"

"No. He didn't have time. So I thought it might be interestin' to go to Somerset House and put down my shilling and get a look at the original will, the one that's been admitted to probate now. Well, the girl is the chief legatee, of course; but everybody else gets a neat slice of the old man's money; he wasn't even cautious over things like that. Even poor old Dyer got a cut, and there was a sizable bequest of £3,500 to build a new ward-house for the Woodmen of Kent, to be delivered to the Secretary and used at his own discretion…"

"So the Woodmen of Kent got together and marched up to London and skewered him with an arrow? Rubbish, H.M.! That's not worthy of you."

"I was only throwin' out suggestions," returned H.M. with surprising meekness. He peered up from under wrinkled brows. "Just to see if anything could possibly stir up your grey matter. You'd never be able to construct a defence, Ken: you can't take a hint out of the evidence, and go straight to where you'd probably find a witness. For instance! Suppose I thought it was pretty vital to get hold of Uncle Spencer? Even if I didn't shove him into the witness-box, suppose I thought it was very necessary to have a little talk with him? How would I go about puttin' my hands on him?"

"God knows. That's one of Masters's favourite jobs of routine. If the police can't find him, I don't see how you can. He got a good head-start, remember. He could be in Palestine by now."

A knock at the door roused H.M. out of his apparent torpor. He dropped the stump of his cigar into the plate, and squared himself.

"Come in," said H.M. "He could be," H.M. added, "but he's not."

The door was opened with some caution. And Dr. Spencer Hume, impeccably dressed, with a bowler hat in one hand and a rolled umbrella hanging from the crook of his arm, came into the room.

XV

"THE SHAPE OF THE JUDAS WINDOW"

IF THE GILDED FIGURE OF JUSTICE ON THE DOME OF THE OLD BAILEY had slid down from the cupola and appeared here, it could have caused no more pronounced effect. But Dr. Hume did not today seem so bland and banal. He looked ill. Though his dark hair was as neatly brushed into place as before, his high colour had gone and his little, sensitive eyes were uneasy. When he saw Evelyn and me sitting in the firelight, he shied badly.

"It's all right, son," H.M. assured him. H.M. was sitting back at the table, one hand shading his eyes. The doctor's glance had gone instinctively towards the window, in the direction of the great building where he was wanted. "These are friends of mine. One of 'em I think you met yesterday. Just sit down and smoke a cigar. There's a very old artillery proverb: 'The closer the target, the safer you are.' Bein' right smack up against the eye of Balmy Rankin, you're all right. You could get in the queue outside the public gallery entrance, and go up in the gallery among the spectators, and you could sit right up over Balmy's head without his knowin' you were anywhere closer than China."

"I—ah—am aware of that," replied Spencer, with traces of a bitter smile. He sat very straight in the chair, and his tubby figure had an odd dignity. He did not accept H.M.'s offer of a cigar, but sat with his hands flat on his knees. "As a matter of strict record, I have been sitting in the public gallery all morning."

"Uh-huh. I was pretty sure I saw you there," observed H.M. casually. The other went a little more white. "It's not a new trick. Charlie Peace did it at the trial of young Habron for the murder of the man Peace really killed. Honestly, you've got more guts than I thought you had."

"But you didn't—speak up?"

"I hate rows in court," sniffed H.M., inspecting his fingers. "It disturbs the nice soothin' atmosphere, and the feelin' of intellectual balance. Still, that's beside the point. I gather you got my message last night?"

Dr. Hume put his hat on the floor, and leaned the umbrella carefully against the side of the chair.

"The point is that you have got me here," he retorted, but without heat. "Now will you answer one question? How did you know where to find me?"

"I didn't," said H.M. "But I had to try the most likely places. You'd done a bunk. But you had time to write a very long, very careful, and very weighty letter to your niece; and people who got to depend on the rush of aeroplanes or boat-trains don't usually have time for that. You knew they'd be after you, and that contempt of court is a criminal offence. There's only one excuse for it—extreme illness. I thought you'd probably run straight to your friend Tregannon, and gone to earth among the bedclothes and the ice-caps in his nursin' home. You can probably produce a certificate now, showin' how ruddy unwell you were yesterday. I've said a good many times that this tracing business is only a glorified version of the old chestnut about the idiot boy findin' the lost horse: 'I just thought where I'd have gone if I had been a horse; and I went there; and he had.' I sent you a message there, and you had."

"Rather a queer kind of message," said Spencer, looking hard at him.

"Yes. That's why it's time we got down to business. I thought there was one person at least you wouldn't want to see hanged."

"You mean myself?"

"Right," agreed H.M., taking his hand away from shading his eyes. He got out his watch, a large cheap one of the turnip variety, and put it on the table. "Listen to me, doctor. I'm not bluffin'. I'll prove it, if you think I am. But in about fifteen minutes I'm due to be in court. I'll wind up the defence of Jim Answell this afternoon. I don't say this as a certainty, mind—but, when I do, I think the betting's about a hundred to six that you'll be arrested for murder."

The other remained quiet for a time, tapping his fingers on his knees. Then, reaching into an inside pocket, he took out a cigarette-case, extracted a cigarette, and closed the case with a rather vicious snap—as he might have closed a different sort of case. When he spoke, his voice was calm.

"That is bluff. I wondered, and now I know."

"It's bluff that I know where the ink-pad and the golf-suit and all the rest of it really disappeared to; and that I've got 'em all in my possession right now?"

With the same impassive expression, H.M. reached into his own side-pocket. He drew out a black ink-pad in its ordinary tin-container, and a long rubber stamp inscribed with someone's name; and he flung them on the table among the plates. For the hundredth time I wondered at the connection, especially at the contrast between the violence of H.M.'s hand and the inscrutability of his face. Dr. Hume did not seem so much taken aback as distressed and puzzled.

"But, my dear sir... yes, of course; but what of it?"

"What of it?"

"Dr. Quigley," answered the other, with quiet bitterness, "disposed of my character in court today. I suppose we shall have to accept his verdict. Granted that you produced every one of those interesting exhibits, what would it prove beyond what has already been proved? The man who has been already drowned views the prospect of a sea-voyage with equanimity." A rather ghastly smile, an edge of the old bouncing and bustling smile, touched his face. "I am not sure whether that is a quotation from Kai Lung. But, since I have already been virtually convicted of one thing, I don't give a damn for your French monkey-tricks."

He lit the cigarette with a sharp jerk of the match across its box. H.M. remained staring at him for a short time, and H.M.'s face altered.

"Y'know—" H.M. began slowly. "Burn me, I'm beginning to believe you really think Answell is guilty."

"I am quite certain he is guilty."

"Last night you wrote to Mary Hume swearin' you saw the murder done. Do you mind tellin' me if that was true?"

The other blew an edge of ash off his cigarette, holding it upright. "I strongly object to giving an opinion even on the weather, as a rule. This much I'll tell you. The thing that has so—so fuddled and—yes, and maddened me throughout this whole affair," he made a fierce gesture, "is that *I* have done absolutely nothing! I tried to help Avory. I tried to help Mary. Granting that it was unethical, I believed it was for everyone's good... and what happened? I am being hounded: yes, sir, I will repeat it: hounded. But even yesterday, when I was forced to go away, I tried to help Mary. I admitted to her that I supplied the brudine, at Avory's request. At the same time I was obliged to point out that James Answell is a murderer; and, if it were with my last breath, I should call him a murderer."

Despite the man's innate love of clichés, his apparent sincerity was such that it overcame even the self-pity in his voice.

"You saw him do it?"

"I had to safeguard myself. If I wrote only the first part of the letter, you would take it into court, and it might help to save Answell—a murderer. So I had to ensure that you did not take it into court."

"Oh," said H.M. in a different tone. "I see. You deliberately shoved that lie in so that we wouldn't dare use it as evidence?"

Dr. Hume waved this aside, and became more calm.

"At considerable risk to myself, Sir Henry, I came here. That was in order to get as much information as I received. Fair play, eh? Surely that is fair? What I wish to know is my legal position in this matter. In the first place, I hold a certificate testifying to my illness yesterday—"

"From a doctor who's goin' to be struck off the register."

"But who is not yet so discredited," replied the other. "If you insist on applying technicalities, I must use them as well. I was actually in attendance this morning, you know. In the second place, the Crown have waived their intention to call me as a witness; and their case is closed."

"Sure. Still, the defence hasn't closed the case. And you can still be called as a witness: it won't matter for which side."

Spencer Hume put down his cigarette carefully on the edge of the table. He folded his hands.

"Sir Henry, you will not call me as a witness. If you do, I will blow your whole case sky-high in just five seconds."

"Oh-ho? So we're doin' a little arguing about compounding a felony, now, are we?" Hume's face tightened, and he looked round quickly at us; but H.M. had only a gleam of benevolent wickedness in his dull eye. "Never mind," H.M. went on. "I'm pretty unorthodox, not to say twisty. Have you got the incredible, stratospheric cheek to threaten you'll go into the box and tell your story about seein' the murder done, if I dare to pull you out of retirement? Wow! Honest, son, I really admire you."

"No," said Hume calmly. "I need only tell a plain truth."

"Comin' from you—"

"No, that will not do," said the other, and raised one finger with a critical air. "It was established this morning, you know, that this is not a court of morals. Because Mary went the way of all flesh, it is no reason why her testimony about a murder should be discredited. Because I intended bloodlessly and painlessly to put a blackmailer where he belonged (a much less heinous offence to British ears, I assure you), that is no reason why my testimony about a murder should be discredited."

"Uh-huh. If you hate blackmailers so much, why try a spot of blackmail on me now?"

Dr. Hume drew a deep breath. "I honestly and sincerely am not. I merely tell you—don't call me as a witness. Your whole case has been based on a missing piece of feather. You have repeatedly and even monotonously thundered at every witness: 'Where is that piece of feather?'"

"Well?"

"*I've* got it," said Dr. Hume simply. "And here it is."

Again he took out his cigarette-case. From under a line of cigarettes he carefully pulled out a piece of blue feather, some inch and a quarter long by an inch broad. He put it on the table with equal care.

"You'll notice," he continued, during the heavy silence while H.M.'s face remained as impassive as ever, "that the edges are a bit more ragged than those on the other piece. But I think they'll fit fairly well. Where was this piece of the feather? God love you, I had it, of course! I picked it up off the floor of the study on the night of the murder. It was no instinct for clues; it was simply an instinct of tidiness. And why didn't I show it to anyone? I can see you getting ready to ask that. My good fellow, do you know the only person who has ever been at all interested in this feather? That's you. The police weren't interested in it. The police never thought greatly about it—like myself. To be quite honest, I forgot all about it. But, if that feather is submitted in evidence, you will readily see the result. Have I convinced you?"

"Yes," said H.M., with a broad and terrifying grin. "At last you have. You've convinced me you really did know about the Judas window after all."

Spencer Hume rose rather quickly to his feet, and his hand knocked to the floor the cigarette on the edge of the table. With an instinct of tidiness he had automatically put his foot on it when there was another knock on the door. This time the door opened more precipitately.

Randolph Fleming, ducking under the low lintel, brought his aggressive red moustache into the room—and stopped in mid-sentence.

"I say, Merrivale, they tell me that you—hullo!"

As though disconcerted at being put off his stride, Fleming stood staring at the doctor. In his own quiet way he was as great a dandy as Spencer Hume: he wore a soft grey hat whose angle just escaped being rakish, and carried a silver-headed stick. His withered jowls swelled out as he regarded Spencer; he hesitated, with an embarrassed air, and ended by making sure that the door was closed behind him.

"Here, hang it!" he said gruffly. "I thought you had—"

"Cut and run for it?" supplied H.M.

Fleming compromised with a blurred statement to Spencer Hume over his shoulder: "Look here, won't you get into a lot of trouble if you turn up now?" Then he faced H.M. in an evident mood to get something off his mind.

"First, like to say this. I'd like to say no offence; I don't hold it against you for pitching into me yesterday in court. That's your business, and all in the day's work. Lawyers and liars, eh? Always has been. Ha, ha, ha! But here's what I want to know. They say—for some reason I don't understand—I may be called as a witness for your side as well. What's up?"

"No," said H.M. "I think there'll be a clear enough identification from Shanks. Even if you do get asked anything, it'll only be a matter of form. I got a cross-bow I want to get identified as belongin' to Avory Hume. Shanks should be able to do that pretty well."

"The odd-jobs man?" muttered Fleming, and brushed up his moustache with the back of his gloved hand. "Look here, would you mind telling me—"

"Not at all," said H.M., as the other hesitated.

"Not to put too fine a point on it," said Fleming, "do you still think poor Hume was killed with a cross-bow?"

"I always did think so."

Fleming considered this carefully. "I don't admit anything to go back on my opinion," he pointed out, after a glowering look. "But I thought I was bound to tell you one thing. I tried some experiments last night, just by way of making sure. And it could be done. It *could* be done, provided the distance was short enough. I don't say it was, but it could be. Another thing—"

"Get it off your chest, son," suggested H.M. He glanced over at the doctor, who was sitting very quietly, and making noises as though he were trying to clear a dry throat without having the sounds become too audible.

"I tried it out three times—shooting arrows from a cross-bow, I mean," insisted Fleming, with an illustrative gesture. "The guide-feather does tend to get stuck in the teeth of the windlass, unless you're damned careful. Once it stuck and pulled the whole feather off the shaft of the arrow when the bow was released. Another time it cut the feather in half—kkk!—like that. Like the one you showed us in court. Mind you," he wagged his finger, "not, as I say, that I'd take back one word I said. But things like that worry me. I'm damned if they don't. I can't help it. I thought to myself: If there's anything fishy in this, I ought to tell 'em about it. Only decent. If you think I like coming here and telling you, you're off your chump; but I'm going to warn the Attorney-General about it too. Then it's off my mind. But still, between ourselves, what did happen to that infernal piece of feather?"

For a short time H.M. looked at him without speaking. On the table, almost hidden by the dishes, lay the piece of blue feather Spencer Hume had put there. Spencer made a quick movement as Fleming spoke, but H.M. forestalled him. Scooping up the feather, H.M. put it on the back of his hand and held it out as though he were going to puff at it.

"It's a very rummy thing about that," remarked H.M., without looking at Spencer. "We were just discussin' the point as you came in. Do you think, for instance, that this could be the missin' piece?"

"Where'd you find it?"

"Well... now. That's one of the points under debate. But, as an expert on the subject, would you just look at this little joker and decide whether it could be the one we want?"

Fleming took it gingerly and rather suspiciously. After a suspicious look between H.M. and Spencer, he carried the feather to the window and examined it in a better light. Several times his sharp little eye moved round during his examination.

"Rubbish!" he said abruptly.

"What's rubbish, son?"

"This is. I mean, any idea that this is the other part of the feather."

Spencer Hume drew a folded handkerchief out of his breast-pocket, and, with an inconspicuous kind of gesture, he began to rub it round his face as though he were polishing that face to a brighter shine than it already had. Something in the expression of his eyes, something that conveyed doubt or misery, was familiar. I had seen just that expression somewhere before, and recently. It was too vivid for me to forget the slide of eyes or hands; but why was it so familiar?

"So?" asked H.M. softly. "You'd say pretty definitely it couldn't be, eh? Why not?"

"This is a turkey-feather. I told you—or rather you got it out of me—that poor old Hume didn't use anything except goose-feathers."

"Is there much difference?"

"Is there much difference! Ho!" said Fleming, giving a fillip to the brim of his hat. "If you go into a restaurant and order turkey, and they serve you goose instead, you're going to know the difference, aren't you? Same with these feathers." A new thought appeared to strike him. "What's going on here, anyhow?"

"That's all right," grunted H.M., and continued without inflection: "We were just havin' a bit of a private conference. We—"

Fleming drew himself up. "I had no intention of staying," he said with dignity. "I came here to get something off my mind. Now I've done it, my conscience is clear again and I don't deny I shall take some pleasure in saying good day. I'll only say that there seems to be something infernally queer going on hereabouts. By the way, doctor. If I do manage to see the Attorney-General, shall I tell him you're back and ready to testify?"

"Tell him anything you like," Spencer answered quietly.

Fleming hesitated, opening his mouth as though he were bedevilled to the edge of an outburst; then he nodded with ponderous gravity, and made for the door. Although he did not know it, it was his own presence which had disturbed the room in a manner we could not analyse. H.M. got up and stood looking down at Spencer Hume.

"Aren't you rather glad you didn't go into court?" he asked quite mildly. "Set your mind at rest. I'm not goin' to call you as a witness. In your present frame of mind, I wouldn't dare. But right here, strictly among ourselves, you faked that evidence, didn't you?"

The other studied this. "I suppose you could call it that, in a way."

"But why the blazes did you fake it?"

"*Because Answell is guilty*," said the other.

And then I knew what the expression of his eyes reminded me of: it reminded me of James Answell himself, and of the same trapped sincerity with which Answell had faced accusations. It made even H.M. blink. H.M. gravely made a gesture which I could not interpret; he kept his eyes fixed on Spencer as he did so.

"The Judas window means nothin' to you?" he insisted, with another incomprehensible gesture at which Spencer peered doubtfully.

"I swear it does not."

"Then listen to me," said H.M. "You've got two courses open to you. You can clear out. Or you can go to court this afternoon. If Walt Storm's waived you as a witness, and if you've really got a medical certificate for yesterday, you can't be arrested unless Balmy Rankin cuts up awful rough—which I don't think he will. If I were you, I'd go to court. You may hear something that will interest you, and will make you want to speak out. But you ought to know where the real piece of feather, the genuine one, is now. There are two parts of that missin' piece. Half of the missin' piece is stuck in the teeth of a cross-bow that I'm goin' to produce in court. The other half was left in the Judas window. If I see the tide startin' to swing against me, I warn you I'll put you into the box no matter how dangerous you are. But I don't think that'll be necessary. That's all I've got to say, because I'm goin' back now."

We followed him out, leaving Spencer sitting by the table with the dying firelight red on his face, pondering. It was at this time yesterday that we had first heard of the Judas window. Before an hour had passed it was to be shown in all its hidden obviousness; it was to loom as large and practical as a sideboard, though of slightly different dimensions: and it was to swallow up Court-room Number One. For the moment we knew only that the room was locked.

On the landing Evelyn seized H.M.'s arm. "There's one thing at least," she said through her teeth, "you can tell. One little question that's so easy it never occurred to me to think of it before—"

"Uh-huh. Well?" enquired H.M.

"What is the shape of the Judas window?"

"Square," said H.M. promptly. "Mind that step."

XVI

"I PUT ON THIS DYE MYSELF"

"SHALL BE THE TRUTH, THE WHOLE TRUTH, AND NOTHING BUT THE truth."

"Ar," said the witness.

The witness did not chew gum; but the continual restless movement of his jaws, the occasional sharp clicking sound he made with his tongue to emphasise a point, gave the impression that he was occupied with an exhaustless wad of it. He had a narrow, suspicious face, which alternately expressed good nature and defiance; a very thin neck; and hair which seemed to be the colour and consistency of liquorice. When he wished to be particularly emphatic, he would jerk his head sideways in speaking, as though he were doing a trick with the invisible chewing-gum; and turn his eye sternly on the questioner. Also, his tendency to address everyone except H.M. as "your Lordship" may have been veiled awe—or it may have been a sign of the budding Communist tendencies indicated by the curl of his lip and the hammer-and-sickle design in his militant tie.

H.M. plunged in.

"Your full name's Horace Carlyle Grabell, and you live at 82, Benjamin Street, Putney?"

"That's right," agreed the witness with cheerful defensiveness, as though he were daring anyone to doubt this.

"Did you use to work in the block of service-flats in Duke Street, D'Orsay Chambers, where the accused lives?"

"That's right."

"What was your job there?"

"I was an Extra Cleaner-Up."

"What's an Extra Cleaner-Up, exactly?"

"It's like this. It's the mess they makes, that the chambermaids don't like. When their ashtrays gets full, they empties 'em into the waste-paper baskets. They sticks their old razor-blades anywhere they can, to get 'em out of sight. They leaves things about—well, you know what I mean. Extra Cleaner-Up, especially when there was parties."

"Were you working there round about the 3rd of January, last?"

"On that date," corrected Horace Carlyle Grabell, with a pounce. "*On* that date, I was."

"Yes. Did you know the deceased, Mr. Hume?"

"I hadn't the honour of his personal acquaintance—"

"Just confine yourself to answering the question," said the judge sharply.

"Very good, your Lordship," said the witness smoothly, and his jaw extended at the same time his upper lip drew away from his teeth. "I was about to say: except once when we got very matey, and he gave me ten pounds to keep my mouth shut about his being a thief."

Several times before a recorder would have had the opportunity of writing the word "sensation." This one, which could hardly be called a full-fledged sensation, since nobody knew what it meant, was all the more pronounced because of the casual way in which Grabell spoke. The judge slowly took off his spectacles, disengaging them from under his tie-wig, folded them up, and contemplated him.

"You quite understand what you are saying?" enquired Mr. Justice Rankin.

"Oh, very good, your Lordship."

"I wished to make sure of that. Proceed, Sir Henry."

"We'll try to make certain of it, my lord," growled H.M. "Now then. How'd you come to know the deceased so well by sight?"

"I used to work at another place—not far away. Every week, Saturday mornings, they used to take the week's takings up to the Capital Counties Bank in a leather bag. I went along; kind of a bodyguard, you see; not that it was ever needed. The deceased, he didn't actually do nothing; I mean, he didn't take the money across the counter or nothing. He would just come out of that little door at the back of the bank, and stand with his hands behind his back, and nod to Mr. Perkins who brought the money, like as if he was giving his blessing to it."

"How many times d'ye think you saw him there?"

"Oh, umpteen."

"A dozen, do you think?"

"More'n that," insisted the witness, shaking his head sceptically and drawing the air through a hollow tooth. "Every Saturday for six months or so."

"Now, where were you on the morning of Friday, January 3rd, last?"

"Cleaning out the dustbin in 3c," answered Grabell promptly. "That's Mr. Answell's flat." He made a sign of quick and saturnine friendliness towards the prisoner, pushing his fist under his own chin as though to keep it up; and instantly checked this with an air of portentous solemnity.

"Where's the dustbin?"

"In the kitchenette."

"This kitchenette opens into the dining-room?"

"Same as usual," agreed Grabell.

"Was the door closed between?"

"Yes. Or very near. Just a crack."

"What'd you see or hear then?"

"Well, I wasn't making much noise. While I was standing in the kitchenette, I heard the door of the dining-room open—that's the other door to the dining-room, leading to the little entry. I thought: ''Ullo!' Because Mr. Answell wasn't expected back. I peeped through and see a man come into the dining-room, walking very soft and quick. You could tell he was up to no good. The blinds was all drawn in the dining-room, too. First he gave a tap on all the walls, like as if he was looking for a safe. Then he started to open the drawers in the sideboard. What he took out I didn't know first going-off, because his back was to me. Then he went over and raised the blind to get a better look. I saw who he was, and I saw what he'd got in his hand."

"Who was it?"

"This deceased, Mr. Hume."

"And what had he got in his hand?" asked H.M. in a louder voice.

"Captain Answell's gun, that you've got down on the table there."

"Hand it up to the witness. Take a closer look, and make sure it's the one the deceased took out of that sideboard on Friday morning."

"That's the one," said the witness, reeling off the serial number of the pistol before it was put into his hand. He pulled out the clip and snapped it back again, turning round the automatic in a way that made the nearest woman juryman shy back. "Why, I had to unload it meself once, when they was getting gay at a party."

"Tell us what happened after you saw Mr. Hume?"

"Couldn't believe my own eyes, that's what. He got out a little note-book and compared something in it, careful as careful; then he stowed away the gun in his pocket. Well, that was too much. I walked out quick and said: 'Hullo.' I'd got no call to be respectful to a chap who was there to steal. It gave him a turn, though he tried not to show it. He turned round with his hands behind his back and his eyebrows pulled down—trying to look like Napoleon, I daresay. He said: 'Do you know who I am?' I said: 'Yes; and I also know you've just pinched Captain Answell's gun.' He said not to be ridiculous; he said it was a joke. I know that tone some of the nobs takes when they've done the dirty and try to carry it off, *I* know it; and that's why I knew he knew it. Why, there was that time Lord Borefastleigh got caught flat with the ace, king, and jack of trumps in his waistcoat pocket—"

"You will omit that," said the judge.

"Very good, your Lordship. I said: 'Joke or not, you're going down to the manager and explain why you've just pinched Captain Answell's gun.' Then he got much quieter. He said: 'All right; but do you know which side your bread is buttered on?' I said: 'I don't know about that, guv'nor; considering as I've never seen any butter in me life.' He said, in a way I'll bet he didn't talk at the bank: 'There's a quid in it for you if you keep your mouth shut about this.' I thought I'd just see what he was up to, and I said: 'I know what that is, guv'nor; that's margarine; and I've had plenty of *that* on me bread.' He said: 'Very well; ten pounds, and that's my limit.' So he went away with the gun."

"Did you take the ten pounds?" enquired the judge.

"Yes, your Lordship, I did," answered Grabell, with defiant querulousness. "What would you have done?"

"It is not a matter on which I dare pass judgment," said Mr. Justice Rankin. "Go on, Sir Henry."

"He went away with the gun." H.M. wagged his head. "And what did you do after that?"

"I knew he was up to no good, so I thought I'd better warn Captain Answell about it."

"Oh? Did you warn Captain Answell about it?"

"Yes. Not that he's good for as much as a bob; but I thought it was my duty to, that's all."

"When did you warn him?"

"I couldn't do it then, him being away in the country. But he turned up unexpected the next day—"

"Uh-huh. So, after all, he was in London on the Saturday of the murder, was he?" said H.M. He allowed a pause, taking the other's movement of the jaws, carried almost to the point of making a face, for a reply. "When did you see him?"

"'Bout ten minutes past six on Saturday evening. He drove into the place behind the block of flats, where they park the cars. There was nobody else about, so I told him Mr. Hume had been there the day before and pinched his gun."

"What did he say?"

"He looked queer for a minute; thoughtful-like; then he said: 'Thanks; that'll be very useful,' and up and handed me half a crown. Then he turned the car round and whizzed out of there."

"Now listen to me, son. The pistol that was found in the accused's pocket—that gun—the gun he's supposed to have taken with him on Saturday night to use on Mr. Hume—was actually stolen out of the flat on Friday by Mr. Hume himself? Is that right?"

"That's as true as God made little apples," retorted the witness, leaning out of the box in response to H.M.'s pointed finger.

H.M. sat down.

Grabell might have been an insolent and garrulous witness, but these facts themselves made an enormous impression. We knew, however, that a tussle was coming. The antagonism which sprang up between this witness and Sir Walter Storm was apparent before the Attorney-General had uttered a word. Due to the Londoner's instinctive awe and reverence before a red robe, which represents a hazy conception of Law-cum-Empire and things deeply rooted, Grabell had shown towards the judge a submissiveness approaching humility. Towards the prosecution he held no such views. They evidently represented to him someone who was merely out to do you down. Grabell must have gone into the box with an eye on them, and ready to bristle. This was not soothed by Sir Walter's—entirely unintentional—lofty stare.

"Ah... Grabell. You tell us you accepted ten pounds from Mr. Hume?"

"Yes."

"Do you think it was an honourable act for you to accept it?"

"Do you think it was an honourable act for 'im to offer it?"

"Mr. Hume's habits are not, I think, in question—"

"Well then, they ought to be. You're trying to hang that poor devil there because of 'em."

The Attorney-General suddenly must have looked so dangerous that the witness drew back a little. "Do you know what contempt of court is, Grabell?"

"Yes."

"In case you do not, my lord may have to make it quite clear to you. To avoid any unpleasant consequences, I must tell you that your business here is to answer my questions—nothing else. Do I make myself understood?"

Grabell, rather pale, looked as though he were straining at a leash; but he jerked his head and made no comment.

"Very well. I am glad you appreciate that." Sir Walter set his papers in order. "I should deduce," he pursued, with a sidelong glance at the jury, "that you are a follower of the doctrines of Karl Marx?"

"Never heard of him."

"Are you a Communist?"

"That's as may be."

"Have you not made up your mind?—Did you, or did you not, accept a bribe from Mr. Hume?"

"Yes. But I went directly and told Captain Answell afterwards."

"I see. Your 'honour rooted in dishonour stands.' Is that what you wish us to believe? Do you wish us to believe that you are all the more trustworthy because you were twice unfaithful to a trust?"

"'Ere, what's all this?" cried the witness, staring round.

"You tell us that round about January 3rd you *were* employed at D'Orsay Chambers, Duke Street. Are you not employed there now?"

"No... I left."

"You left: why?"

Silence.

"Were you dismissed?"

"You could call it that, yes."

"So you were dismissed. Why?"

"Answer the question," said the judge sharply.

"I didn't get on with the manager, and they were overstaffed."

"Did the manager give you a reference when you left?"

"No."

"But if you had left for the reasons you tell us, he must have given you a character, mustn't he?"

Sir Walter Storm had not been prepared for this witness. But, with the knowledge of long experience, he knew exactly where to attack without having any actual information to draw on.

"You tell us that on Friday morning, January 3rd, you were 'cleaning out the dustbin' in the prisoner's flat?"

"Yes."

"How long had Mr. Answell and Captain Answell been away?"

"'Bout a fortnight, maybe."

"About a fortnight. Why, then, was it necessary to clean out the dustbin, if they had been away for so long?"

"They might have come back."

"Yet a moment ago you informed my learned friend that no one was expected back. Did you not?"

"It had to be done sometime."

"It had not been done by anyone during those entire two weeks?"

"No—that is—"

"I put it to you that the dustbin would have been cleaned when the occupants went away?"

"Yes, but I had to make sure. Look here, your Lordship..."

"You further tell us," pursued the Attorney-General, leaning both hands on the desk and settling his shoulders, "that, when you went in to do this, all the blinds were drawn and you made very little noise?"

"Yes."

"Are you accustomed to cleaning out the dustbin in darkness?"

"Look 'ere! I never thought of it—"

"Or being careful to make no noise to disturb anyone in an empty flat? I put it to you that—if you actually were in the flat at the time you say—it was for a purpose other than cleaning out the dustbin?"

"It was not."

"Then you never went into the flat at all?"

"Yes, I did, if you'd let me get in a word edgeways; and what I'm telling you is that old *Hume* was there, and he stole that gun, so help me!"

"Let us see if there is anything else that may help us. There is, I believe, a hall-porter at D'Orsay Chambers?"

"Yes."

"Will you accept my statement that this porter, when questioned by the police, testified he had not seen anyone resembling the deceased in D'Orsay Chambers on Friday or at any other time?"

"Maybe not. He came in by the back stairs—"

"Who came in by the back stairs?"

"Mr. Hume. Anyway, that's how he went out, because I saw him go."

"Did you offer any of this information to the police at the time?"

"No; how could I? I wasn't there. I left my job the next day—"

"You left the next day?"

"I had been under notice for a month, yes, and that was Saturday. Besides, I didn't know it was important."

"Apparently not. There would appear to be a curious notion among several persons as to what may or may not have been important then, but is very important now," said Sir Walter dryly. "When you say you saw Captain Answell in the car-park, was there any other person there who could substantiate the statement?"

"Nobody but Captain Answell himself. Why don't you ask him?"

Mr. Justice Rankin intervened. "The witness's remark, though out of order," he said with some asperity, "would seem pertinent. Is Captain

Answswell in court? Considering that a part of the evidence depends on information that he may be able to give—"

H.M. surged up with a sort of ferocious affability. "My lord, Captain Answell is goin' to appear as a witness for the defence. You needn't trouble to send for him. He's been under subpoena for a long, long time; and we'll see that he is here, though I'm not sure he'll be a very willin' witness for his own side."

("What on earth is all this?" Evelyn asked in a whisper. "You heard the fellow say himself he wasn't to be called as a witness. He must have known he'd been subpoenaed! What is happening?")

It was undoubtedly some trick on H.M.'s part: H.M. being determined to be the old *maestro* if it choked him. Beyond that nothing was known.

"I have no more questions to ask this witness," said Sir Walter Storm abruptly.

"Call Joseph George Shanks," said H.M.

While Grabell was going out of the box, and Joseph George Shanks was going into it, a consultation went on among the counsel for the Crown. The prosecution was in a strange and horned position. They must fight this through. That James Answell had been the victim of a mistake: that Hume had planned a trap for Reginald: even that Hume had stolen the pistol: was now being pushed towards a certainty. But these were details which did not, for everything that was said, in the least demonstrate the innocence of the prisoner. I remembered the words in the summing-up of a great jurist at another *cause célèbre:* "Members of the jury, there is some circumstantial evidence which is as good and conclusive as the evidence of eye-witnesses... If I might give you an illustration: supposing you have a room with one door, and a closed window, and a passage leading from that door. A man comes up the passage, goes through the door into the room, and finds another man standing with a pistol, and on the floor a dead man: the circumstantial evidence there would be almost conclusive, if not conclusive."

We had just such a situation here. The prisoner had still been found in a locked room. The circumstantial evidence of that fact was still conclusive. No doubt had been cast on the central point, which was the only real point at issue. However damaged the case for the prosecution had become, Sir Walter Storm must finish this course.

I was recalled by H.M.'s voice.

"Your name's Joseph George Shanks, and you were odd-jobs man at number 12, Grosvenor Street?"

"Yessir," said the witness. He was a little, broad man, so much like a dwarfed model of John Bull that his Sunday-best clothes sat oddly on him. Two polished knives of white collar stabbed his neck: they seemed to keep his voice light from the effort of keeping his neck high.

"How long did you work there?"

"Ah," said the other, considering. "Six years, more or less, I should think."

"What were your duties, mostly?"

"Mostly keeping Mr. Hume's archery things in order; any repairs to 'em; things like that."

"Take a look at this arrow, which was used to kill the deceased"—the witness carefully wiped his hands on the seat of his Sunday trousers before accepting it—"and tell the jury whether you've seen it before."

"You-bet-I-have, sir. I fastened the feathers on. I remember this one. Dye's a mite dark for the kind I meant."

"You often fastened the deceased's special kind of feathers to the arrows? And dyed the guide-feather? *Mr. Fleming told us that yesterday?*"

"I did that, sir."

"Now, supposin' I showed you a little piece of feather," pursued H.M. with argumentative persuasiveness, "and I asked you to tell me definitely whether it was the piece of feather missing from the middle, there... could you do that?"

"If it was off this feather, I could, sir. Besides, it 'ud fit."

"It would. But—just to take a different sort of question for a minute—you worked in that little workshop or shed in the back garden, didn't you?"

"I'm sure I didn't meant to press you, sir," said the witness generously. "What was that? Ah. Yes, I did."

"Did he keep any cross-bows there?"

The stir of creaking that went through the room affected Shanks with a pleasant sense of importance. He relaxed, and leaned his elbows on the rail of the box. Evidently some stern eye was watching over his conduct from the spectators' gallery over our heads; for he seemed to become sensible of the impropriety of his posture, and straightened up hastily.

"He did, sir. Three of them. Fine nasty-looking things."

"Where'd he keep 'em?"

"In a big box, sir, like a big tool-box with a handle. Under the carpenter's bench." The witness blinked with a painful effort at concentration.

"Tell me: did you go down to that shed on the morning of Sunday, January 5th, the day after the murder?"

"Yes, sir. I know it was Sunday, but even so, considering—"

"Did you notice anything different in the shed?"

"I did, sir. Somebody'd been at that tool-box, or what I call a tool-box. It's directly under the bench, you see, sir; and there's shavings and dust falls on it, like a coating, you see, sir; and so if you look at it you can tell right away, without thinking anything of it, if someone has been *at* it."

"Did you look in the box?"

"Yes, sir, of course. And one of the cross-bows were not there."

"What'd you do when you found this out?"

"Well, sir, of course I spoke to Miss Mary about it; but she said not to bother about such things, considering; and so I didn't."

"Could you identify that cross-bow, if you saw it again?"

"I could, sir."

From his own hidden lair (which he kept jealously guarded) H.M. made a gesture to Lollypop. There was produced a weapon very similar in appearance to the cross-bow H.M. had used yesterday for the purposes of illustration. It was perhaps not quite so long, and had a broader head; steel studs were set in a line down the stock, and there was a little silver plate let into it.

"Is this the cross-bow?" said H.M.

"That's it; yes, sir. Here's even Mr. Hume's name engraved on the little plate."

"Look at the drum of the windlass there, where you'll see the teeth. Just tell me if there's somethin' caught in there—ah, you got it! Take it out. Hold it over so the jury can see. What is it?"

"It's a bit of feather, sir, blue feather."

Sir Walter Storm was on his feet. He was not amused now; only grave, heavy, and polite.

"My lord, are we to assume that this is being suggested as the mysterious piece of feather about which so many questions have been asked?"

"Only a part of it, melord," grunted H.M. "If it's examined, we'll see that there's still a little bit of it missin'. Not much. Only a piece about a quarter by half an inch square. But enough. That, we're suggestin', is the second piece. There are three of them. One's yet to come." After the amenities, he turned back to the witness. "Could you say definitely whether or not the piece you've got in your hand came off that broken guide-feather on the arrow?"

"I think I could, sir," said the witness, and blinked.

"Just look at it, then, and tell us."

While Shanks screwed up his eyes and hunched his shoulders over it, there was a sound of shuffling or sliding in court. People were trying surreptitiously to rise and get a look. The prisoner, his face sharper now and less muddled, was also staring at it; but he seemed as puzzled as anyone else.

"Ah, this is right, sir," declared Shanks. "It come off here."

"You're sure of that, now? I mean, one part of a broken feather might be deceptive, mightn't it? Even if it's a goose-feather, and even if it's got a special kind of dye on it, can you still identify it as comin' from that particular arrow?"

"This one I can; yes, indeed, yes. I put on this dye myself. I put it on with a brush, like paint. That's what I meant by saying it fitted. There's a slip in the paint here that makes a lighter mark in the blue like a question-mark. You can see the upper part of the question-mark, but the little dot and part of the tail I don't see…"

"Would you swear," said H.M. very gently, "would you swear that the part of feather you see stickin' in that cross-bow came from the feather on the arrow in front of you?"

"I would indeed, sir."

"For the moment," said H.M., "that's all."

The Attorney-General got up with a suavity in which there was some impatience. His eye evidently made Shanks nervous.

"The arrow you have there bears the date 1934, I think. Does that mean you prepared the arrow, or dyed it, in 1934?"

"Yes, sir. About the spring, it would be."

"Have you ever seen it since, close enough to examine it? What I mean is this: After winning the annual wardmote in 1934, Mr. Hume hung that arrow on the wall of his study?"

"Yes, sir."

"During all that time since, have you ever been close enough to examine it since?"

"No, sir, not until that gentleman"—he nodded towards H.M.—"asked me to look at it a month ago."

"Oh! But from 1934 until then you had not actually looked at the arrow?"

"That's so, sir."

"During that time you must, I presume, have handled and prepared a good many arrows for Mr. Hume?"

"Yes, sir."

"Hundreds, should you say?"

"Well, sir, I shouldn't quite like to go as far as that."

"Just try to give an approximate number. Would it be fair to say that you had handled or prepared over a hundred arrows?"

"Yes, sir, it might be that. They use an awful lot."

"I see. They use 'an awful lot.' Do you tell us, then, that out of over a hundred arrows, over a space of years, you can infallibly identify one arrow on which you put dye in 1934? I remind you that you are upon oath."

At this tremendous reminder, the witness cast an eye up at the public gallery as though for support. "Well, sir, you see, it's my job—"

"Please answer the question. Out of over a hundred arrows, over a space of years, can you infallibly identify one on which you put dye in 1934?"

"I shouldn't like to say, sir, may I go to he—may I be—that is, to say everything should happen to me—"

"Very well," said the Attorney-General, who had got his effect. "Now—"

"But I'm sure of it just the same, mind!"

"Though you cannot swear to it. I see. Now," continued the other, picking up some flimsy typewritten sheets, "I have here a copy of the prisoner's statement to the police. (Please hand this across to the witness.) Will you take that statement, Mr. Shanks, and read out the first paragraph for us?"

Shanks, startled, took the paper with an automatic gesture. First he blinked at it in the same doubtful way he had shown before. Then he began to fumble in his pockets, without apparent result while the delay he was giving the court evidently preyed worse and worse on his mind, until such a gigantic pause upset him completely.

"I can't seem to find my specs, sir. I'm afraid that without my specs—"

"Do I understand," said the other, who had rightly interpreted that blinking of the eyes, "that without your spectacles you cannot read the statement?"

"It's not exactly to say I *can't*, sir; but—"

"Yet you can identify an arrow on which you put dye in 1934?" asked Sir Walter Storm—and sat down.

This time H.M. did roar up for re-examination, girded for war. But his questions were short.

"How many times did Avory Hume win the annual competitions?"

"Three times, sir."

"The arrow was a special prize on those occasions, wasn't it?"

"Yes, sir."

"So it wasn't just 'one out of over a hundred,' was it? It was a special thing, a keepsake?"

"Yes, sir."

"Did he show you the arrow, and call your attention to it, after he'd won the first-shot competition?"

"Yes, sir."

"Ha," said H.M., lifting his robe in order to hitch up his trousers. "That will do. No, not that way out, son; that's the judge's bench; the warder'll show you." He waited until Shanks had been taken away, and then he got up again.

"Call Reginald Answell," said H.M.

XVII

"AT THE OPENING OF THE WINDOW—"

REGINALD ANSWELL WAS NOT EXACTLY UNDER ESCORT: WHEN THE warder took charge of him, and led him to the box, he seemed a free man. But just behind him I saw a familiar figure whose name eluded me until I remembered Sergeant-Major Carstairs, who guards the entrance to H.M.'s lair at Whitehall. On the sergeant-major's face was the sinister look of a benevolent captor.

Again you could hear the rustle of the wind in trees of scandal; every eye immediately tried to find Mary Hume as well, but she was not in court. Reginald's long and bony face was a little pale, but very determined. I remember thinking then that he looked a tricky customer, and had better be handled as such—whatever H.M. had in mind. But this may have been due to a surge of dislike caused by the slight (manufactured) wave in his dark-yellow hair, or the cool glaze of self-possession on his features: the latter more than the former. He took the oath in a clear, pleasant voice.

H.M. seemed to draw a deep breath. It was to be wondered, in view of the wiles that lay beneath the surface, whether H.M. would find himself cross-examining his own witness.

"Your name is Reginald Wentworth Answell; you have no residence, but when you're in London you live at D'Orsay Chambers, Duke Street?"

"Yes."

"I want you to understand," said H.M., folding his arms, "that you're not obliged to answer any question which will incriminate you—about any activities." He paused. "This question, however, won't incriminate you. When the police talked to you about your general movements on the evenin' of January 4th, did you tell 'em the whole truth?"

"The whole truth, no."

"Are you ready to tell the truth now, under oath?"

"I am," said Reginald with great apparent sincerity. His eyes flickered; there is no other way to describe it.

"Were you in London early in the evenin' on January 4th?"

"I was. I drove from Rochester, and arrived at D'Orsay Chambers a few minutes past six o'clock."

It was possible that H.M. stiffened a little, and an odd air of tensity began to grow again. H.M. tilted his head on one side.

"So-o? I understood it was ten minutes past six o'clock. Wasn't it?"

"I am sorry. It was a little earlier than that. I distinctly remember the clock in the dashboard of my car."

"Had you intended to see the deceased that night?"

"Yes. Socially."

"When you got to D'Orsay Chambers, did you see the witness Horace Grabell?"

"I did."

"Did he tell you about the deceased's visit to your flat on Friday?"

"He did."

"Did he tell you the deceased had taken your pistol, and gone away with it?"

"He did."

"And what did you do then?"

"I could not understand it, but I did not like it. So I thought I had better not see Mr. Hume after all. I went away. I—drove round a bit, and—and before long I left town. I—did not return until later."

H.M. sat down rather quickly. There had been a curious intonation in that "before long"; H.M. had seemed to catch it, for we all did. And Sir Walter Storm was very quick to rise.

"You tell us, Captain Answell," began the Attorney-General, "that you 'drove round a bit,' and 'before long' you left town. How long?"

"Half an hour or a little more, perhaps."

"Half an hour? As long as that?"

"Yes. I wanted to think."

"Where did you drive?"

Silence.

"Where did you drive, Captain Answell? I must repeat my question."

"I drove to Mr. Hume's house in Grosvenor Street," answered the witness.

For a second the implications of this did not penetrate into our minds. Even the Attorney-General, whatever his thoughts might have been, hesitated before he went on. The witness's air of pale candour was that of the "engaging" Reginald Answell I had seen yesterday.

"You drove to Mr. Hume's house, you say?"

"Yes. I hoped you would not ask that." He looked briefly towards the prisoner, who was staring at him. "I told them I could do him no good. I understood I was not to be called as a witness."

"You understand that it is your business to tell the truth? Very well. Why did you go to Mr. Hume's house?"

"I don't know exactly. I thought it was a queer show, a very queer show. I did not intend to go in; I only intended to cruise past, wondering what was—was up."

"At what time did you arrive at the house?" demanded the Attorney-General. Even Sir Walter Storm could not keep his voice quite level, in wondering himself what was up.

"At ten minutes past six."

The judge looked up quickly. "One moment, Sir Walter..." He turned his little eyes on the witness. "If you arrived there at ten minutes past six, that must have been at the same time as the prisoner?"

"Yes, my lord. As a matter of fact, I saw him go in."

There are, I suppose, no degrees of a man's being motionless. Yet I had never seen H.M. convey such a mere impression of absolute stillness as he did then. He was sitting with a pencil in his hand, enormous under his black gown: and he did not even seem to breathe. In the dock, James Answell's chair suddenly scraped. The prisoner made a curious, wild gesture, like a boy beginning to put up his hand in a class-room, and then he checked himself.

"What did you do then?" asked the Attorney-General.

"I did not know what to do. I wondered what was happening, and why Jim was there. He had not spoken about coming here when I saw him last at Frawnend. I wondered if it concerned me, as having been a suitor of Miss Hume's. For what I did," said the witness, drawing himself up, "I do not apologise. Any human being would have done the same. I knew that there was an open passage leading down between Mr. Hume's house and the house next door—"

Sir Walter Storm (be it recorded) seemed forced to clear his throat. He was not now like a man either examining or cross-examining, but one trying to get at the truth.

"Had you ever been to the house before, Captain Answell?"

"Yes, several times, although I had never met Mr. Hume. I had been there with Miss Hume. Mr. Hume did not approve of our acquaintanceship."

"Go on, please."

"I—I—"

"You hear what counsel tells you," said the judge, looking at him steadily. "Continue your story."

"I had heard a great deal of Mr. Hume's 'study' from Miss Hume. I knew that if he entertained Jim anywhere, it would be there. I walked down the passage beside the house—with no motive in mind, I swear, except to get near them. Some way down the passage, on the right-hand side, I found a short flight of steps leading up to a glass-panelled door with a lace curtain over it. The door looks into the little passage outside Mr. Hume's study. As I looked through the curtain, I saw the butler—who was taking Jim there—knock on the study door."

The change in the air was as though a draught had begun to blow and scatter papers on counsel's table.

"What did you do then?"

"I—waited."

"Waited?"

"Outside the door. I did not know quite what to do."

"How long did you wait?"

"From about ten or twelve minutes past six until a little later than half-past six, when they broke in."

"And you," demanded Sir Walter, pointing, "you, like others, have made no mention of this to anyone until this moment?"

"No. Do you think I wanted them to hang my cousin?"

"That is not a proper reply," snapped the judge.

"I beg your Lordship's pardon. I—put it that I was afraid of the interpretation which would be placed on it."

Sir Walter lowered his head a moment. "What did you see while you were outside the glass-panelled door?"

"I saw Dyer come out about fifteen minutes past six. I saw Miss Jordan come down about half-past six, and knock at the door. I saw Dyer return then, and heard her call out to Dyer that they were fighting. And the rest of—"

"One moment. Between six-fifteen, when Dyer left the study, and six-thirty, when Miss Jordan came downstairs, did you see anyone approach the study door?"

"I did not."

"You had a good view of it?"

"Yes, the little passage has no light; but there was a light in the main hall."

"From where you were standing outside that door—hand the witness up a plan—could you see the windows of the room?"

"Yes. They were immediately to my left, as you can see."

"Did anyone approach those windows at any time?"

"No."

"Could anyone have approached those windows without your knowledge?"

"No. I am sorry. I suppose I incur penalties for not telling this—"

I make a pause here, for there was a similar kind of blankness in the room. We have heard much of last-minute witnesses for the defence. This one, though called for the defence, was a last-minute witness for the prosecution who put the rope firmly round the prisoner's neck. James Answell's face was a colour it had not been at any time during the trial; and he was staring at his cousin in a vague and puzzled way.

But there was another kind of pause or change as well—that is, if it did not exist only in my own prejudiced mind. Up to this time, sallow-faced and stiff-lipped Reginald had seemed (in a quiet way) inspired. He compelled belief. He brought to this case what it had heretofore lacked: an eyewitness to support circumstantial evidence. It may have been a certain turn in his last sentence. "I suppose I shall incur penalties for not telling this—" which gave a slightly different glimpse. It did not last long. But it was as though a cog had failed to mesh, or a shutter had been drawn aside, or the same glutinous quality of hypocrisy had appeared in his speech which had appeared once before. The man was lying: I felt convinced of that. More, you could see he had gone into the box with the deliberate intention of lying in just that way. He had made an obvious attempt to draw Sir Walter Storm's attack—

But surely H.M. knew that? H.M. must have been prepared for it? At the moment H.M. was sitting in the same quiet way, his fists at his temples. And the point was its effect, not on H.M. but on the jury.

"I have no more questions," said Sir Walter Storm. He seemed puzzled.

H.M. roused himself to a re-examination which was really a cross-examination of his own witness. And when H.M. did get up, he used words that are not common at the Old Bailey, and have not been since the days of Serjeant Arabin. But there was not only violence in it; there was a sort of towering satisfaction which made him seem about a foot taller.

"I'll give you just two seconds," said H.M., "to admit that you had an attack of delirium tremens, and that everything you said in that examination was a lie."

"You will retract that, Sir Henry," said the judge. "You are entitled to question the witness on any matters that have arisen out of Sir Walter's cross-examination; but you will express yourself in a proper manner."

"If yrludship pleases," said H.M. "It'll be understood why I'm takin' this line when I do question... Captain Answell, do you want to retract any statement you've made?"

"No. Why should I?"

"All right," said H.M. with massive unconcern. "You saw all this through the glass panel of the door, did you?"

"Yes."

"Was the door open?"

"No. I didn't go inside."

"I see. Aside from the night of January 4th, when was the last time you visited that house?"

"Nearly a year ago, it may have been."

"Uh-huh. I thought so. But didn't you hear Dyer testify yesterday that the door with the glass panel,* the old door, had been removed six months ago; and they substituted an ordinary solid wooden door? If you got any doubts on the matter, look up the official surveyor's report—it's

---

* Page 59.

one of the exhibits here—and see what he has to say about it. What do *you* have to say about it?"

The witness's voice seemed to come out of a gulf. "The—the door may have been open—"

"That's all," said H.M. curtly. "At the conclusion of our evidence, my lord, I'm goin' to suggest that somethin' is done about this."

To say that the blow was a staggerer would be to put the matter mildly. A witness had come out of the void to testify to James Answell's certain guilt, and, just eight seconds later, he was caught in flat perjury. But that was not the most important point. It was as though a chemical change had affected the sympathies of the jury. For the first time I saw some of them honestly looking at the prisoner, and that is the beginning of all sympathy. The word "frame-up" was in the air as palpably as though it had been spoken. If H.M. had expected Reginald to play a trick like that, it could have been no more effective. And the sympathy was mounting.

If H.M. had expected...?

"Call your next witness, Sir Henry," said the judge mildly.

"My lord—if the Attorney-General's got no objection—I'd like to ask for one of the Crown's witnesses to be recalled. It's merely for the purpose of identifyin' some articles I'd like to put in in evidence; and it could be done best by a member of the household whose knowledge of the articles has been established."

"I have no objection, my lord," said Sir Walter Storm, who was surreptitiously mopping his forehead with a handkerchief.

"Very well. Is the witness in court?"

"Yes, my lord. I'd like to have Herbert William Dyer recalled."

We had not time to reflect over each new twist of this infernal business when Dyer entered the box. But the prisoner was sitting up, and his eyes were shining. The grave Dyer, as neat as yesterday if in slightly less sombre clothes, bent his grizzled forehead attentively. By this time

Lollypop was busy arranging near the table a series of exhibits mysteriously swathed in brown paper. H.M.'s first move was to display a brown tweed suit with plus-fours—a golf-suit. Evelyn and I looked at each other.

"Ever see this suit before?" questioned H.M. "Hand it up to him."

"Yes, sir," said Dyer, after a pause. "It is a golf-suit belonging to Dr. Spencer Hume."

"Dr. Hume not bein' within call, I presume you can identify it? So. Is that the suit you were lookin' for on the night of the murder?"

"It is."

"Now just feel in the right-hand coat pocket. What do you find there?"

"An ink-pad and two rubber stamps," said Dyer, producing them.

"Is that the ink-pad you were lookin' for on the night of the murder?"

"It is."

"Good. We got some other stuff here," continued H.M. off-handedly: "laundry, and a pair of Turkish slippers, and the like; but that'd be out of your province. We can get it properly identified by Miss Jordan. But tell me if you can identify this?"

This time there was produced a large oblong suitcase of black leather, having the initials stamped in gold on the flap beside the handle.

"Yes, sir," replied Dyer, stepping back a little. "It is undoubtedly Dr. Hume's. I believe it is the one Miss Jordan packed for Dr. Hume on the night of the—circumstance. Both Miss Jordan and I forgot all about it; or at least—she having been very ill afterwards; and, when she asked me what had happened to it, I could not remember. I have not seen it since."

"Yes. But here's just one more thing that *you're* the one to identify. Look at this cut-glass decanter, stopper and all. You'll see it's full of whisky except for about two drinks poured out. Ever see it before?"

For a moment I thought H.M. had got hold of one of the prosecution's own exhibits. The decanter he produced was indistinguishable from the one the Crown had put in in evidence. Evidently Dyer thought so too.

"It looks—" said the witness. "It looks like the decanter which Mr. Hume kept on the sideboard in the study. Like—that other—"

"It does. It was meant to. Between those two, could you swear which was which?"

"I'm afraid not, sir."

"Take one in each hand. Can you swear that my decanter, in your right hand, is not the real one you bought from Hartley's of Regent Street; and that the first exhibit, in your left hand, ain't a copy in inferior glass?"

"I do not know, sir."

"No more questions."

Three witnesses then passed in rapid succession, being not more than five minutes in the box among all of them. Mr. Reardon Hartley, of the firm of Hartley and Son, Regent Street, testified that what H.M. called "my" decanter was the original one supplied by him to Mr. Hume; the prosecution's exhibit was a copy which Avory Hume had bought on Friday afternoon, January 3rd. Mr. Dennis Moreton, analytical chemist, testified to having examined the whisky in "my" decanter, and to having discovered in it one hundred and twenty grains of brudine, a derivative of scopolamine. Dr. Ashton Parker, Professor of Applied Criminology at the University of Manchester, gave the real evidence of the three.

"I examined the cross-bow there, which I was told belonged to Avory Hume. In the groove down the centre of the cross-bow, evidently used for the reception of a missile—here," said Dr. Parker, indicating, "the microscope showed flakes of what I believed to be dry paint. I judged that these flakes had been rubbed off due to the sudden friction when some wooden missile was fired from the bow. Under analysis, the paint was ascertained to be a substance known as 'X-varnish,' used exclusively by Messrs. Hardigan, who sold to the deceased the arrow in question. I present an affidavit to that effect.

"The arrow here was—ah—kindly lent to me by Detective-Inspector Mottram. Here the microscope showed along the shaft of the arrow signs that flakes of paint had been chipped in an irregular line from it.

"In the teeth of the windlass on the cross-bow I found the piece of blue feather which you see there now. This I compared to the broken feather on the end of the arrow. The two pieces made up a complete feather, except for an irregular bit which was missing. I have here photomicrographs of the two pieces, enlarged ten times. The joinings in the fibre of the feather can be seen clearly, and leave no doubt in my own mind that they came from the same feather."

"In your opinion, had the arrow been fired from this cross-bow?"

"In my opinion, it unquestionably had."

This was hard hitting. Under cross-examination, Dr. Parker acknowledged the scientific possibility of an error; it was as far as he would go.

"And *I* acknowledge, my lord," said H.M. in reply to a question from the bench, "that so far we've not shown where this cross-bow or the other articles came from, or what happened to the missin' piece of feather. We'll remedy that now. Call William Cochrane."

("Who on earth is that?" whispered Evelyn. H.M. had said once before that you would no more cause a commotion in Balmy Rankin's court than you would cause one on a chess-board; but the curiosity of the court had now reached as flaming a pitch as it could go. It was stimulated still more by the quietly dressed elderly man who took the oath.)

"Your full name?"

"William Rath Cochrane."

"What's your profession, Mr. Cochrane?"

"I am the manager of the Left-Luggage Department at Paddington Station—the Paddington terminus of the Great West Coast Railway."

"I think we all know the process," rumbled H.M., "but I'll just go over it here. If you want to leave a bag or a parcel or the like for a few hours, you hand it across a counter, and you get back a written slip that allows you to claim the parcel again?"

"That is right."

"Can you tell the date and the time of day when the parcel was handed in?"

"Oh, yes. It is on the ticket."

"Now, suppose," said H.M. argumentatively, "a parcel is handed in, and nobody comes to claim it. What happens to the parcel?"

"It depends on how long it has been left there. If it seems to have been left there indefinitely, it is transferred to a storage-room reserved for that purpose. If it is not claimed at the end of two months, it may be sold and the proceeds devoted to railway charities; but we make every effort to find the proper owner."

"Who is in charge of this department?"

"I am. That is to say, it is under my direction."

"On February 3rd, last, did anybody come to your office and enquire about a suitcase which had been left there at a certain definite time on a certain definite date?"

"Yes. You did," replied the witness with a shadow of a smile.

"Was there anyone else present?"

"Yes, two others whom I now know to be Dr. Parker and Mr. Shanks."

"A week after we had been there, did another person—another person in this case—also call and enquire about it?"

"Yes; a man who gave the name of—"

"Never mind the name," said H.M. hastily. "That's not our business. But about the first people who asked for it. Did you open the suitcase in their presence?"

"Yes, and I was convinced that the suitcase belonged to one of them," said Cochrane, looking hard at H.M. "The contents of the suitcase, not usual contents, were described before the suitcase was opened."

H.M. indicated the big black-leather suitcase inscribed with Spencer Hume's initials. "Will you look at that and tell us whether it's the suitcase?"

"It is."

"I'd also like you to identify some other articles that were in the suitcase at the time. Hand them up as I indicate. That?" It was the golf-suit. "Yes. These?" An assortment of wearing apparel, including a pair of gaudy red-leather slippers. "This?" Up went the decanter H.M. had put in in evidence, the decanter containing drugged whisky from which two drinks were gone. "This?"

"This" was a syphon of soda-water with its contents depleted perhaps two inches. Next came a pair of thin gloves in whose lining the name *Avory Hume* had been written in indelible ink. Next came a small screw-driver. Next, in order, two drinking-glasses and a small bottle of mint extract.

"Finally, was this cross-bow in the suitcase?" demanded H.M.

"It was. It just fitted in comfortably."

"Was this piece of feather caught in the teeth of the windlass?"

"Yes, my attention was called to it. It is the same one."

"Uh-huh. At a certain time of night on Saturday, January 4th, then, a certain person came there and left the suitcase?"

"Yes."

"Could that person be identified, if necessary?"

"Yes, one of my attendants thinks he remembers, because—"

"Thank you; that's all."

For a brief space of time Sir Walter Storm hesitated, risen just half-way to his feet.

"No question," said the Attorney-General.

The whispering of released breath was audible. Mr. Justice Rankin, whose wrist seemed tireless, continued steadily to write. Then he made a careful full-stop, and looked up. H.M. was glaring round the court-room.

"My lord, I've got one last witness. That's for the purpose of demonstratin' an alternative theory as to how a murderer got in and out of a locked room."

("Oh, Lord, here we go!" whispered Evelyn.)

"This witness," continued H.M., rubbing his forehead reflectively, "has been right here in court since the beginnin' of the trial. The only trouble is, it can't talk. Therefore I'm bound to do a bit of explainin'. If there's any objection to this, I can always do it in my closin' speech. But since a couple o' words of explanation will tend to produce another actual bit of evidence—another exhibit for the defence—I'd like the court's indulgence if I say that our evidence can't be completed without it."

"We have no objection to my learned friend's proposal, my lord."

The judge nodded. H.M. remained silent for what seemed a very long time.

"I see Inspector Mottram is at the solicitors' table," said H.M., while Mottram's heavy face turned round abruptly. "I'll just ask him to oblige me by pullin' out one of the Crown's own pieces of evidence. We've had shown here the steel shutters on the windows of the study, and the big oak door as well. Let's have the door out again...

"The inspector—and all policemen here too—will have heard of a little dingus called The Judas Window. It's supposed to be confined exclusively to gaols. The 'Judas window' is in the doors of cells. It's the little square opening, with a panel over it, through which coppers in general can look in and inspect the prisoner without being seen themselves. And it has a good deal of application to the case."

"I do not understand you, Sir Henry," said the judge sharply. "There is no 'Judas window,' as you call it, in the door there before us."

"Oh, yes there is," said H.M....

"Me lord," he went on, "there's a Judas window in nearly every door, if you just come to think of it. I mean that every door has got a knob. This door has. And, as I've pointed out to several people, what a whackin' big knob it is!*...

"Suppose you took the knob off that door; what'd you find? You'd find a steel spindle, square in shape, runnin' through a square hole—like a Judas window. At each end of this, a knob is attached by means of a little screw through a hole in each end of the spindle. If you took everything out, you'd find in the door an opening—in this case, as we'll see, an opening that must be nearly half an inch square. If you don't realise just how big a space half an inch can be, or how much you can see when you look through it, we'll try to indicate it in just a minute. That's why I objected to the word 'sealed.'

"Now, suppose you're goin' to prepare this simple little mechanism in advance. From the outside of the door, you unscrew the knob from the spindle. You notice that there's a very small screw-driver contained in the suitcase that was left at Paddington Station; so I'll just ask the Inspector to do it for us now. Ah! That gives you, in the end of the spindle, a little hole where the screw had been. Through this hole you tie tightly a very heavy length of black thread, with a good length of slack. Then you take your finger and push the spindle through its hole to the other side of the door, the inner side of the door. There's now only one knob—the one inside the door—fastened to the spindle; on the other end is attached your length of thread, and you're playing out the slack. Whenever you want the spindle and knob back up again, you simply pull the thread and up it comes. The weight of the knob inside the door is sufficient to make it hang down dead straight, so you've got no difficulty in gettin' the square spindle back in the square hole; it comes up in a straight line and slides in as soon as the edge of the spindle crosses

---

* Particularly on page 179.

the edge of the Judas window. As soon as it's back in again, you jerk off your thread; you put the *outside* knob of the door back on the spindle again; you screw it up again... It's heart-breakin'ly simple, but the door is now apparently sealed.

"Again suppose you'd prepared the mechanism in advance, with the thread already twined. Somebody is in that room with the door bolted. You start to work your mechanism. The feller inside don't notice anything until he suddenly sees the knob and spindle beginnin' to be lowered a little way into the room. You want him to see it. In fact, you begin to talk to him then through the door. He wonders what the—he wonders what is goin' on. He walks towards the door. He *bends down*, as anyone will when wantin' to look close at a knob. As he bends forward—a target only three feet away from your eye, where you can't miss—"

"My lord," cried Sir Walter Storm, "we are willing to grant all liberties, but we must protest against this argument in—"

"—with your arrow balanced in the opening," said H.M., "you fire through the Judas window."

There was a sort of thunderous pause, while Inspector Mottram stood with the screw-driver in his hand.

"My lord, I've had to say it," said H.M. apologetically, "in order to make clear what I'm goin' to show you. Now, that door has been in the possession of the police ever since the night of the murder. Nobody could 'a' tampered with it; it's just as it was... Inspector, have you unscrewed one knob from that spindle? So. Will you sort of tell my lord and the jury what there seems to be—tied to the hole in the spindle?"

"Please speak up," said Mr. Justice Rankin. "I cannot see from here!"

Inspector Mottram's voice rose, a ghostly kind of effect, in the silence. I am not likely to forget him standing there under the glow of the yellow lights, with the oak panelling, and the yellow furniture, and the tiers of people who were now frankly standing up. Even the white wigs and black gowns of counsel had reared up furtively to obscure our view. At the core of all this, as though in a spotlight under the white dome of the Old Bailey, Inspector Mottram stood looking from the screw-driver to the spindle.

"My lord," he said, "there appears to be a piece of black thread tied to the hole in the spindle, and then wound a few lengths round—"

The judge made a note in his careful handwriting.

"I see. Proceed, Sir Henry."

"And next, Inspector," pursued H.M., "just push the spindle through with your finger—use the point of the screw-driver if it's more convenient—and take the whole thing out. Ah, that's got it! We want to see the Judas window, and... ah, you've found somethin', haven't you? There's somethin' lodged in the opening between the spindle and the Judas window, stuck there? Quick, what is it?"

Inspector Mottram straightened up from inspecting something in the palm of his hand.

"It would appear," he said carefully, "to be a small piece of blue-coloured feather, about a quarter of an inch, triangular in shape, evidently torn off something—"

Every board in the hardwood floor, every bench, every chair seemed to have its own separate creaking. At my side Evelyn suddenly sat down again, expelling her breath.

"And that, my lord," said H.M. quite mildly, "together with the identification of the last piece of feather, will conclude the evidence for the defence. Bah!"

XVIII

"THE VERDICT OF YOU ALL"

4.15 P.M.–4.32 P.M.
*From the Closing Speech for the
Defence, by Sir Henry Merrivale*

"... And so, in what I've just spoken to you about, I've tried to outline what we'll call the outlying phases of this case. You have been told, and I think you believe, that this man was the victim of a deliberate frame-up. You have heard now that, far from taking a pistol to that house, he was goin' to see the one man in the world he wanted most to please. You have heard the details that twisted up everything he said to an extent that will make me, for one, walk warily henceforward. That frame-up has been concealed and elaborated by several people—notably one you heard speak right up before you, and in his own malice try to send this man to the rope. That's a pretty thought to take with you when you consider your verdict.

"But you have nothing to do with pity or sympathy. Your business is justice, plain justice, and that's all I'm asking for. Therefore I'm goin' to submit that the whole point of this case depends on two things: a piece of feather and a cross-bow.

"The Crown ask you to believe that this man—with no motive—suddenly grabbed an arrow down from the wall and stabbed Avory Hume. It's a simple case, and makes a simple issue. Either he did do that, or he didn't. If he did do that, he's guilty. If he unquestionably did not do it, he's unquestionably innocent.

"Take first the feather. When Dyer left the prisoner in that study, alone with Avory Hume, the feather was on the arrow—all of it—intact. That's a simple fact which hasn't been disputed by anyone, and the Attorney-General will acknowledge it to you. When the door was unbolted, and Dyer and Mr. Fleming went into that room, half that feather was gone from the arrow. They searched the room immediately, and the feather was not there: that's also a simple fact. Inspector Mottram searched the room, and the feather was not there, and *that's* a simple fact too. All this time, you remember, the accused had not left the study.

"Where was the feather? The only suggestion the police can make is that it was unconsciously carried away in the prisoner's clothes. Now, I submit to you simply that this couldn't possibly be true. There are two reasons. First of all, you saw it demonstrated here that two people could not possibly tear that feather—in a struggle—in the way it was torn; therefore there wasn't any struggle, and what becomes of the prosecution's case on that score alone? Second, and even more important, we know where the feather actually was.

"You've heard it testified by the manager of the Left-Luggage Department at Paddington that a certain person—*not* the prisoner—left a suitcase at the station early in the evening of January 4th. (In any case, the prisoner was not in a position to go on any errands, having been under the eye of the police from the time the murder was discovered until the followin' morning.) That suitcase contained the cross-bow you've seen; and stuck into the teeth of the windlass was a big part of the missing piece of feather.

"We can't doubt, I think, that this was a part of the feather on the arrow. You've seen micro-photographs in which you can compare every detail, you've heard it identified by the man who attached it to the arrow: in short—as in other things in this case—you've been able to see and decide for yourselves. Well, how did that feather get there? How does this fact square with the prosecution's theory that the prisoner dragged down the arrow and used it as a dagger? That's the picture, I submit, you've got to keep in your minds. If he stabbed the deceased, there are a lot of things I'll submit with my hand on my heart that he didn't do. He didn't tear the feather apart with a power beyond him. He didn't shove one end of it into the teeth of a cross-bow. He assuredly didn't put the whole apparatus into Spencer Hume's suitcase—*which, you recall, was not even packed or brought downstairs until six-thirty.*

"Just a word about that suitcase. I'll suggest to you that in itself it destroys any reasonable doubt of this man's innocence. I'm not suggestin' that Miss Jordan packed a week-end cross-bow among the collar-studs and the slippers. No; I mean that it was standin' downstairs in the hall, and someone used it. But how does this apply to the prisoner? The suitcase was packed and brought downstairs at six-thirty. From that time until the time the three witnesses entered the study, it was always under somebody's eye. Did the prisoner leave the study at any time? He did not. You've heard that too frequently—especially from the prosecution. Did he approach the suitcase, to put in a cross-bow or a decanter or anything else (which, I suggest, were already somewhere else waiting to be put in)? Did he, in short, have anything to do with the suitcase? He did not have an opportunity before the crime was discovered, and he most certainly didn't have an opportunity afterwards.

"Why, burn me—HURRUM—members of the jury, I'll call your attention to another point. Part of the missin' feather is in a suitcase which, we can decide, James Answell's ghost didn't take to Paddington Station. But there's another part of that feather. You know where it was, and is. You saw it there. It was in what, for the sake of convenience, I've called the Judas window. Still keepin' in mind the prosecution's belief that Answell used the arrow as a dagger, how does this square with the presence of the feather in the Judas window?

"It doesn't. There's no doubt the feather is there. There's no doubt it got there at the time of the murder. Inspector Mottram, as you've heard, took away that door on the night of the murder, and has kept it at the police-station ever since. From the time the murder was discovered to the time Inspector Mottram took the door away, there was always somebody in the study; so the feather couldn't have landed there at any time except the time of the murder. Only a minute ago you saw Professor Parker recalled to the witness-box; you heard him identify this feather as undoubtedly the last missin' piece; and he told you why he thought so. It is the feather, then, and it was there. Well, how does my learned friend say it got there? Now, I'm not here to toss dull ridicule at a group of men like Counsel for the Crown, who've conducted their case with scrupulous fairness towards the accused, and given the defence all the latitude we could hope for. But what can I say? Just fix your minds on the stupefyin' suggestion that James Answell wildly arose and killed Avory Hume, and *at the same time* a bit of feather off that arrow managed to get into the hole that supports the knob-spindle in the door. Can you think of any reason for it, however ingenious, that doesn't become mere roarin' comedy?

"You've already heard reasons why the prisoner could not conceivably have come near the cross-bow or the suitcase; in fact, it's never been suggested that he has. The same, in general, applies to the feather in the door and the little mechanism of thread on the spindle. That little mechanism, I think you'll agree, was prepared beforehand. Answell had never been in the house before in his life. That little mechanism was meant to work only from outside, to let the knob down from the other end. Answell was inside the room, with the door bolted. As I say, merely to ridicule is useless; but I'm convinced that the more you think of it the more out of the question it will become, or you're a greater group of fathea—URR—or you're not the intelligent English jury I know you are.

"Still, the feather was there. It got there somehow; and it's not exactly a common place to find one. I'll venture to suggest that you could go home tonight and take the knobs out of all the doors in your own house: and all down the street through your neighbours' houses: and still you wouldn't find a feather in the Judas window. I'll further venture to suggest that there's only one set of circumstances in which you could find both the feather and the thread-mechanism in the Judas window. It's got nothing to do with an arrow snatched down from the wall to stab, except in so far as a drugged man inside could be used as a scapegoat. That set of circumstances is the one I hinted at a while ago: someone who stood outside that bolted door, and fired an arrow into Avory Hume's heart when the murderer was almost close enough to touch him with it.

"With your indulgence, then, I'm goin' to outline to you the way in which we believe the crime was really committed; and I'll try to show you how the facts that have been produced support it and bear against the prosecution's case.

"But, before I do, there's one thing I feel I must face. You can't disregard a beetle on the back of your neck or an unexplained statement in a court of law. Members of the jury, yesterday afternoon you heard the prisoner tell a great big thundering lie: the only lie he has told in this room: the lie that he was guilty. Mebbe he didn't say it under oath; mebbe you were inclined then to believe it all the more because he didn't. But you know now why it was told. Mebbe he didn't care then whether or not he convicted himself; others, you observe, have been tryin' hard enough to do it for him. But you'll judge whether you think the worse or the better of him for saying what he did. And the time has come now when I can stand up and accuse my own client of falsehood. For he said he stabbed Avory Hume with an arrow, whose feather broke off in the struggle. Unless you believe that statement, you cannot and you dare not return a verdict of guilty; and that statement you cannot and you dare not believe; and I will tell you why.

"Members of the jury, the way in which we believe this crime was really committed—"

4.32 P.M.–4.55 P.M.
From the Closing Speech for the Crown, by Sir Walter Storm.

"... thus my learned friend need have no fear. I shall not ask you to wait until my lord addresses you before you learn this: If you are dissatisfied with the story of the prosecution, the prosecution have thereby failed to make out their case and it is your duty to return a verdict of not guilty. I do not think that any of you, having heard my opening speech in this case, could labour under any misapprehension as to that point. I put it before you, then, that the burden of the proof was on the prosecution, as I trust I shall always do when it becomes my duty to lay such a case before a jury.

"But it is likewise my duty to stress against the prisoner such of the material facts as constitute evidence. Facts: as I said in my opening speech. Facts: as I have said all along. Therefore I must ask you, dispassionately: how many of the material facts in this case have been altered or disproved?

"My learned friend has attempted well and eloquently to explain; but I must submit to you that he cannot explain away.

"What remains? It is a fact that the prisoner was found with a loaded pistol in his pocket. He denies that he took this pistol to the house; and what is there to corroborate his denial? There is the testimony of the witness Grabell. You have heard that witness in the box: you have heard his replies to my questions: you have observed his demeanour. He, and he alone, claims to have seen the deceased at D'Orsay Chambers on Friday morning. How did a stranger in those flats escape the attention of every other attendant? How is the deceased presumed to have gained access to the prisoner's flat? How, in fact, did Grabell come conveniently to be cleaning out a dustbin in darkness, when he himself acknowledges that the dustbin would have been cleaned out a fortnight before? Grabell—whose notion of honour and truthfulness you have been able to judge—is the sole witness to this. Is there any other witness who can give even second-hand corroboration to the alleged theft of the pistol by Avory Hume? There is Reginald Answell. But here I confess I am on difficult ground. Members of the jury, I must tell you frankly that, when he told you that story from which you were supposed to infer the prisoner's guilt, I did not believe him. He was (in fact) a witness for the prosecution; and I did not believe him. You will have been able to decide whether or not my learned friend disposed of his testimony in a court where—whether for the prosecution or for the defence—we will not avail ourselves of lies. *But* it is Reginald Answell, this same witness, who testifies to his conversation with Grabell about the pistol. If we believe that a man has borne false witness in the last part of his testimony, shall we therefore believe that he has borne true witness in the first part of it?

"If the prisoner did in fact take that pistol to Mr. Hume's house, there is premeditation. And I suggest to you that he did.

"What other facts remain? There are the prisoner's finger-prints on the arrow. Such things are stubborn. They are marks. They remain. They show beyond doubt that the prisoner's hand was round the arrow—whether or not, as my learned friend has suggested, the finger-prints were placed on the arrow by others while the prisoner was unconscious.

"And what is the evidence as to this alleged unconsciousness, this alleged drugging, on which all deductions from the finger-prints must rest? If you refuse to believe that the prisoner was drugged, then, obviously, I must submit to you that the finger-prints are the most vital evidence in the case. The evidence, then? A decanter similar to the first, filled with drugged whisky, is produced from a suitcase discovered in the Left-Luggage Department at Paddington Station, along with a syphon from which some soda-water is drawn. Doubtless there are many decanters resembling it in London; but I put it before you that what I should like to see is some evidence that the accused had *drunk* any drugged whisky—or any whisky at all. On the contrary, you have heard from the divisional police surgeon that (in his opinion) the prisoner had taken no drug at all. In all fairness I must tell you that the witness who was to have testified to this as well, Dr. Spencer Hume, is missing: and is inexplicably missing: but we cannot say that the two circumstances are connected until we have heard Dr. Hume. That is what I mean by a fact.

"You heard at the time the insinuations that were directed towards Dr. Stocking. Despite this, I do not think that an opinion given by a man of Dr. Stocking's long experience at St. Praed's Hospital should be taken too lightly.

"And other facts? You have heard the witness Dyer's testimony of remarks made by the prisoner to the deceased. 'I did not come here to kill anyone unless it becomes absolutely necessary'; which now appears with the emendation by the prisoner: 'I did not come here to steal the spoons,' and is stressed by my learned friend. You will note that all of Dyer's *other* statements appear to be accepted by my learned friend, even with an accent of welcome, since much of his evidence depends on them. But he will not accept this one. What are we to believe from that? Is Dyer a witness who tells a truth at one o'clock and a falsehood at five minutes past one?

"You understand the fashion, members of the jury, in which I ask you to look at this case. Having made this clear, let me now go over the evidence point by point, line by line, from the beginning...

"... which must bring us, as I have tried to do point by point, to the end of the evidence. Now, as to the suggestions put forward concerning the cross-bow and the triple-feather—this counterblast of which the prosecution had no warning. That the prosecution had no warning was quite legal and ethical, of course; the defence is rightly reserved, though it is customary for the defence to be informed as to the lines on which the prosecution means to proceed. As to the cross-bow and the triple-feather (I say), it is neither my purpose nor my intention to pass comment now. You have heard the evidence for the Crown which it was my duty to lay before you. How the piece of feather—if indeed it is a piece of feather from the arrow before you—how this curious fragment got into the spindle-hole of the door, I do not know. How the other piece of feather—with the same implied reservation—got into the teeth of the cross-bow, I do not profess to know. I say: 'It is there'; and no more. If you believe that these and other matters weigh in the favour of the accused, it is your duty to let your verdict be influenced by them. You cannot convict this man unless you are perfectly clear beyond all reasonable doubt that the case we have outlined points with almost irresistible emphasis to the conclusion that he is guilty. Of course, the last word lies with my lord; and I have little doubt that he will tell you—"

4.55 P.M.–5.20 P.M.

From the Summing-up, by Mr. Justice Rankin.

"... and as you know, members of the jury, we have here a case of circumstantial evidence. Now the real test of the value of circumstantial evidence is this: does it exclude every reasonable possibility? I can even put it higher: does it exclude all other theories or possibilities? If you cannot put the evidence against the accused man beyond a probability and nothing more, then it is impossible for you to say you are satisfied beyond reasonable doubt that the charge is established. There is no muddledom about that; the law there is as plain as a pikestaff. A man cannot be convicted of any crime, least of all murder, merely on probabilities: unless they are so strong as to amount to a reasonable certainty. If you have other possibilities, you cannot come to the decision that the charge is made out. The question is not: who did this crime? The question is: did the prisoner do it? You have heard at some length the evidence in this case, you have heard the speeches of counsel, and it is now my task to make some survey of the evidence. You will remember that you are the judges of the facts; I am not the judge of the facts at all; and you must bear this in mind if I seem to omit or overstress any matter contrary to your view.

"Let us take what may be called the relevant facts from the beginning. Much has been said at the beginning concerning the demeanour of the accused man. As you know, testimony about the look of a man—whether he seemed happy, whether he seemed agitated—is permitted here. You must therefore give it due consideration. But I must tell you that I think it unwise to put too high a value on such statements. You have probably found that it is not always reliable in the affairs of ordinary life. In judging the demeanour of a person, you must suppose that his reactions to a given happening—tragic, peculiar, or even commonplace—will invariably be the same as your own; and I do not need to tell you of the dangers attending that. Taking the facts that have been outlined to you, then…

"… I think, therefore, that this case boils down, not to a question of fact alone but to the interpretation of fact. An arithmetic-book cannot consist of all answers and no sums. A case of this sort cannot consist of all effects and no causes: it is the causes that are under debate. The two original matters you must decide are: first, had Avory Hume formed any plot to drug Captain Answell, arrange the false trappings to suggest a felonious attack on him by Captain Answell, and put Captain Answell under detention as a madman? Second, was the prisoner mistaken for Captain Answell?

"I have just indicated to you my reasons for thinking that there is good evidence in favour of both these things. You have heard Dr. Peter Quigley, an agent of the International Medical Council, as to words he states he heard the deceased speak. The deceased is quoted as saying that he meant to get possession of Captain Answell's pistol: that he meant to invite Captain Answell to his home: that he meant to administer brudine in a drink of whisky and soda: that he meant to get rid of such evidence afterwards: that he meant to create the signs of an apparent struggle: that he meant Captain Answell's finger-prints to be found on an arrow, and the pistol to be found in Captain Answell's pocket. I have quoted to you supplementary evidence which seems to me to make this a reasonable possibility. Do you believe that this happened? If you do not, you will decide accordingly; it is a matter entirely for you. But if you do believe it, you will only be led into a muddle by any talk of 'facts.'

"Did the deceased mean that a pistol should be found in the pocket of the man he was entertaining? If he did, I think we cannot hold against the prisoner the 'fact' that it was actually found there. If he meant to administer drugged whisky, getting rid of the evidence later, and if he succeeded in doing this, I think we cannot hold it against the prisoner that the plan actually succeeded. If he meant finger-prints to be found in the arrow—and if you believe he succeeded in planting them there—then finger-prints are only what we should expect to find. If (to give you an example) A is accused of stealing B's wallet, and the wallet is found in A's pocket, the fact itself would not weigh with you if you were convinced that C put it there.

"In this reading of the evidence, I confess I can see no motive for murder on the part of the prisoner. Indeed, none is suggested except the fact of Mr. Hume's antagonism towards him; and, if you believe this reading, the antagonism did not exist. Without motive or weapon, the prisoner arrives at the house. You have heard evidence which has been construed as the sign of a quarrel in the study, and which you must consider carefully. But if every matter relied on as circumstantial is equally consistent both with the guilt and the innocence of the prisoner, the multiplication of those instances may not take you any further in coming to a conclusion of guilt.

"Taking first the testimony of the individual witnesses...

"... Finally, members of the jury, there is the question whose determining must be the crux of your decision: was the deceased man killed by an arrow held in the hand of the prisoner?

"If the prisoner took the arrow and wilfully stabbed the deceased man with it, he is guilty of murder. On the one hand, you have his fingerprints on the arrow, and the circumstance that door and windows were bolted on the inside. On the other hand, you have the indications with which I have already dealt, and you have an alternative explanation with whose evidence I can deal now. We have heard that, when the prisoner was left alone in the study with Mr. Hume, the guide-feather on the shaft of the arrow was intact. You have heard that, when a search of the room was made immediately after the discovery of the crime, a piece of feather some inch and a quarter long by an inch square was missing. Neither Mr. Fleming nor Dyer found it. It was not found by Inspector Mottram. The suggestion made by the prosecution is that it had lodged in the prisoner's clothing.

"The question now before us is not so much: what happened to the missing piece of feather? The question before us may be put more accurately: do the two pieces of feather produced by the defence—one from a cross-bow, the other from an opening supporting the spindle in the door—constitute what we want? Do they belong to the feather on the arrow used to commit this crime? Are they one feather? If you decide that they are not—or, more properly, that neither of the two pieces belongs to the original—then they do not concern us. The circumstances in which they were found are curious, no doubt; but that is none of our business. On the other hand, if you are satisfied that either or both of them belonged to the original feather, it is difficult not to think that this in itself constitutes a reasonable doubt of the case for the prosecution.

"I confess I do not altogether understand the suggestion of the prosecution here. In my notes I find the suggestion that the first piece of feather, that in the cross-bow, was not a part of the original one; but I have had no further illumination as regards this. Let us take the evidence as it has been presented, and see whether it may not lead irresistibly to the conclusion that—"

5.20 P.M.–5.26 P.M.
From the Record of the Shorthand Writer, by Mr. John Keyes.

The jury, after six minutes' retirement, returned into court.

The Clerk of Arraigns: Members of the jury, are you agreed upon your verdict?

The Foreman of the Jury: We are.

The Clerk of Arraigns: Do you find the prisoner guilty, or not guilty of murder?

The Foreman of the Jury: Not guilty.

The Clerk of Arraigns: You say he is not guilty, and that is the verdict of you all.

The Foreman of the Jury: It is.

Mr. Justice Rankin: James Caplon Answell, the jury, after considering the evidence, have found you not guilty of murder. It is a verdict in which I thoroughly concur. It remains only for me to tell you that you are a free man, and to wish you Godspeed.—The prisoner is discharged.

Notes: Broad grin on Attorney-General's face; he seemed to want this. Old Merrivale standing up and raving and cursing like blazes: can't imagine why: his man's free. Prisoner being handed his hat; can't seem to find his way out. People pressing up to him: including that girl. (???) Gallery wild with delight. "And e'en the ranks of Tuscany could scarce forbear to cheer!"

5.45 P.M.
From the History of the Old Bailey.

In Court-room Number One they were turning out the lights. Two warders, looking very unlike policemen without their helmets, seemed to be alone in a deserted schoolroom. The noise of a vast shuffling was dying away outside the doors; a few echoes came back, as though the echoes moved slowly and hung there. Up on the glass roof the rain was pattering steadily, and you could now hear it with great distinctness. There was a click: one cornice-row of lights vanished, so that the oak panels and the white stone above took duller colours. Two more clicks, and the room was nearly dark. The noise of the rain seemed louder; so did the noise of the warders' footsteps on uncertain hardwood; and their heads moved like high shadows. You could barely see the high, pointed backs of the judges' chairs, and the dull gold of the Sword of State. The vestibule-door creaked in the gloom as one of the warders pushed it open.

"'Ere, stop a bit," said the other suddenly. His voice also had an echo. "Don't close it. There's somebody left behind."

"You seeing ghosts?"

"No, I mean it. Sitting over there—end of that bench—behind the dock. Here! Hoy!"

He might have been seeing ghosts in a house built on the bones of Newgate. Under the greyish-black light, a figure was sitting alone and hunched up at the end of the bench. It did not move, even at the startling echo of the warder's hail. The warder clumped over towards that figure.

"Now then!" he said, with a sort of tolerant impatience. "You'll 'ave to—"

The hunched figure did not look up, but it spoke. "I—don't know if I can. I've just drunk something."

"Drunk something?"

"Some kind of disinfectant. I thought I could face it, but I can't. I—I feel horrible. Can I get to a hospital?"

"Joe!" said the warder sharply. "Come here and lend a hand!"

"You see, I killed him. That was why I drank the stuff."

"Killed who, ma'am?"

"I killed poor Avory. But I'm sorry I killed him; I've always been sorry. I wanted to die, if it didn't hurt so much. My name is Amelia Jordan."

EPILOGUE

WHAT REALLY HAPPENED

"All I'm saying," observed Evelyn, "is that I thought the Attorney-General made the strongest speech of all of you. Even at the last minute I was afraid he might swing it. That man impressed me enormously: I don't care who knows it: and—"

"Ho ho," said H.M. "So that's what you thought, hey? No, my wench. Walt Storm's a much better lawyer than that. I won't say he did it deliberately, but he put it all up so the judge could knock it down. It was as neat a trick of feedin' lines, or arrangin' your chin for the punch, as I've ever seen. He tumbled too late to the fact that the chap wasn't guilty. He might 'a' thrown up his brief; but I wanted the business carried on so it could be proved up to the hilt—with the full story of the crime. So you saw the spectacle of an intelligent man tryin' to make brickbats without straw. It sounded awful impressive; but it didn't mean a curse."

We were sitting, on a boisterous March night, in H.M.'s office up all the flights of stairs of the building overlooking the Embankment. H.M., after having been engaged in brewing whisky-punch (in commemoration, he said, of the Answell case), sat with his feet on the desk and the gooseneck lamp pushed down. There was a good fire, and Lollypop sat by the table in the window corner, evidently making up some accounts. H.M., with the smoke of a cigar getting into his eye and the steam of whisky-punch getting into his nose, was alternately chuckling and strangling.

"Not," declared H.M., "that there was ever any doubt about the verdict—"

"You thought not?" said Evelyn. "Have you any recollection of what you did? When they brought back that verdict, and the court adjourned, someone came to congratulate you, and accidentally knocked a book off your desk. You stood there and you cursed and swore and gibbered for two minutes by the clock—"

"Well, it's always more comfortin' when you get that kind of case off your mind," growled H.M. "I had a few shots still in the locker; but, somewhat to mix the metaphors, you're nervous about a race even if you're dead certain the favourite's comin' in. Y'see, I had to fight it through. I had to get it on so I could make my closin' speech, and I thought a few hints in that speech would have a salutary effect on the real murderer—"

"Amelia Jordan!" I said. We were silent for a short time, while H.M. contemplated the end of his cigar, growled, and ended by taking a gulp of whisky-punch. "So you knew she was guilty all the time?"

"Sure, son. And if necessary I could 'a' proved it. But I had to get the feller in the dock acquitted first. I couldn't *say* she was guilty in court. I wrote on that little time-schedule I gave you that there was only one person who could 'a' committed the murder."

"Well?"

"I'll talk about it," said H.M., shifting in his chair, "because it's such a bleedin' relief not to be governed by any rules in my talk.

"Now, I don't have to retrace the course entirely. You know just about everything up to the time Jim Answell drinks his drugged whisky and tumbles over in Hume's study. You know everything, in fact, except what seem to me pretty solid reasons for believin' a certain person was guilty.

"Back at the beginnin' of the case I had the lunacy-plot part of it worked out straightaway, as I told you. *How* the murder was done, if Answell didn't do it, beat me to blazes. Then Mary Hume made that suggestion—that the thing her feller hated most in prison was the Judas window—and I woke up to the startlin' possibility of a Judas window in every door. I walked up and down, like Satan. I looked at it all round. Then I sat down and made out that time-table; and the whole thing began to unroll.

"As I first saw the business, there were only two persons concerned in the scheme to nobble Reginald Answell: Avory and Spencer. I still think that. It was pretty evident, though, that someone had found out about that scheme, and insisted on comin' into it at the last moment.

"Why? Looky here! If the Judas window was used to do the murder, the murderer must have been workin' with Avory Hume. The murderer must 'a' been at least close enough to know what was going on in the study. It must have been the murderer who carried away an extra decanter—I've made a query about that decanter in my time-table—so that it shouldn't be found by the police. All that implies co-operation with Avory. Someone was in on the plot: someone carried it just so far: and then someone used it neatly to kill the old man.

"Who? Of course, first of all you'd have plumped for Uncle Spencer, since he undoubtedly was a confederate in the plot. But that won't do; at least, as regards Uncle Spencer's committin' the murder with his own hand. He's got a really remarkable alibi, vouched for by half the staff of a hospital.

"Who else, then? It's a remarkable thing, y'know, how the mere certainty of another confederate in the business narrows down the field. Avory Hume was a man with few friends and no intimates, except his own family. He was a great family man. If he went to the extent of confidin' that scheme to someone not necessary to it—even confidin' it under pressure—it must be someone very close to him.

"You understand, at this point I was just sittin' and thinkin'; I'd got no more than an idea to roll about. Someone close to him, says I. Now, while it was theoretically possible for an outsider to have sneaked in and done it (like Fleming, to take an example), still this looked very doubtful. Fleming wasn't an intimate; he wasn't even a close friend, as you can easily tell from the way they speak of each other. Furthermore, an outsider would have had to sneak past a battery of watchful eyes composed of Dyer and Amelia Jordan, one of whom was in the house all the time. Still grantin' that it's *possible*, take the other theory and see where it leads.

"It leads to the belief that the other confederate must 'a' been either Amelia Jordan or Dyer. That's so simple that it takes a long time before it can fully penetrate. But it pretty certainly wasn't Dyer. I'll say nothin' of my own belief that the painfully respectable Dyer was the last person that the painfully respectable Mr. Hume would admit to a peep at any family skeletons from inside the cupboard. As a witness to Captain Reginald's gibberin' lunacy, yes. As a colleague, no. And that it couldn't have been Dyer is clear from the time-table.

"Like this: I'd already come to the conclusion, from reasons you know, that Hume was murdered with that arrow fired from a crossbow. Somebody had to wait until Jim Answell was under the influence of the drug. Somebody had then to go into the study with Hume, assist in pourin' mint-extract down an unconscious man's throat, and get the other decanter and syphon out. Somebody had to make a pretext for takin' the arrow out of the room. Somebody had to get Hume to bolt the door; how Hume was to be persuaded to do this, with the arrow still outside the door, I didn't know. Somebody had to work the mechanism of the Judas window. Somebody had to kill Hume, close up the window, dispose of the cross-bow and the decanter, and generally tidy up. You follow that?

"Well, Dyer let Jim Answell into the house at 6.10 (Established.) It was three minutes at least before Answell took that drugged drink in the study, and longer than that before it hit him over the brain. (Established by Answell himself.) Dyer left the house at 6.15. (Established by me; I put into the right-hand column of my time-table, where I've put only absolutely unquestionable facts, that he got to the garage at 6.18; and, as he himself correctly said at the trial, the garage is a three or four minutes' walk away.) Is it possible to think that in the space of a minute and a half he went through all the hocus-pocus necessitated by Avory Hume's murder? It is not. The time-element makes it impossible.

"Which brought me up against the revealin' fact that Amelia Jordan was the only person who was known to be alone in the house with Hume and an unconscious man. And she was alone there for seventeen minutes, until Dyer returned with the car at 6.32.

"Oho? Think about this woman for a minute. How would she fulfil the specifications for somebody who'd homed into the plot? She'd been livin' with the Humes for fourteen years: fourteen years, my children, which is certainly enough to qualify her as a member of the family. She was, or seemed to be on the surface, fanatically devoted to Avory. When she got excited—as you noticed she did at the trial—she called him by his first name, which was more than anybody except his own brother had the nerve to do. She was in a position to find out a good deal of what was goin' on in that house. If Avory had to confide his design to anybody, the likeliest person seemed to be a practical, swift-workin', hard-workin' woman who'd been there long enough to grow up in the closed circle of the family honour.

"Still only theories, d'ye see: so let's look at what *she* did durin' those mysterious seventeen minutes between 6.15 and 6.32. At 6.30 (she says) she came downstairs after having finished packin' the bags. Here I'll ask you to follow the testimony she gave at the trial, because it was exactly the same testimony she gave the police a long time ago—when I studied it with uncommon close care, like everybody else's testimony. She says she packed a small valise for herself and a large suitcase for Uncle Spencer, and then down she came.

"Now right here is an interestin' bit from Dyer's testimony which fits into that. Dyer returns and finds her standin' in front of the study door—in front of the study door, mark'ee. She flies into a wailin' frenzy, tells him that the fellers inside the study are killing each other, and orders him to run next door after Fleming. At this time, says Dyer, 'she fell over a big suitcase belonging to Dr. Spencer Hume.'

"I rather wondered what that suitcase was doin' back in the passage that leads to the study. The main staircase in that house—you've seen it, Ken—is towards the front. It'd mean that she walked downstairs with the bags; and, intendin' to go to the study to say good-bye to Avory, she walked back into the little passage still carryin' the bags—or at least you notice, the suitcase. What's the game? When people come downstairs with a couple of bags, my experience is that they always plump 'em down at the foot of the stairs where they'll be convenient for the front door. People don't go to the trouble of luggin' 'em to the back of the house and walkin' about with them firmly clutched while they say good-bye.

"Right here I began to get a strange, burnin' sensation at the back of the brain. I began to see things. I wrote a question-mark on my time-schedule opposite Amelia Jordan's activities. Just what did I know, so far, about the murder? For my certain beliefs as opposed to the police's, I knew that (*a*) Hume had been killed with an arrow fired from a cross-bow through the Judas window, and the cross-bow had been missin' from the shed ever since that night; (*b*) Amelia was the only person who had been alone in the house for seventeen minutes; (*c*) Amelia was found near the study door in the inexplicable lovin' company of a large suitcase, which nobody seems to have heard of since that time; and then there fell into my obtuseness the fact that (*d*) Uncle Spencer's fine tweed suit had been missin' out of the house since that night.

"Wow! We even know when that suit was found missin'. Directly after the discovery of the murder, you'll observe, Randolph Fleming conceives the idea of takin' the prisoner's finger-prints. Dyer mentions that there's an ink-pad upstairs in the pocket of Spencer's suit. Dyer flies up to get it—and the suit's gone. Dyer can't understand it, and comes downstairs in a weird state of perplexity. But where was the suit? If everyone hadn't been rattled off balance by the discovery of a murder, where's the first place you'd have thought the suit must be? Hey?"

There was a silence.

"I know," said Evelyn. "You'd know it must have been packed."

"Sure," agreed H.M., spitting out smoke and glowering. "A certain woman had just finished packin' a bag for the owner of that suit. Uncle was goin' into the country for the week-end. Well, what the jumpin' blazes is the first thing you think of shovin' into a suitcase for a man who is goin' to do that? A tweed sports suit, my England.

"Follow this not-too-complicated line of thought. At 6.39, you'll see by your table, Fleming asks Amelia to go to the hospital and get Spencer. At the very same time and in the very same breath, he tosses out the idea of takin' the finger-prints. If only, he says, they had an ink-pad! Dyer mentions the one in the golf-suit, and goes to get it. Mind you, as you'll see in the table, the woman is still there. She hears this. *Why*, therefore, don't she up and say: 'It's no good going up and looking for that suit; I've got it in the suitcase right out in the passage?' (Even if she's taken the ink-pad out of the suit before packin' it, she'd say: 'Don't look in the suit; I've put the ink-pad in such-and-such another place.') In either event, why don't she speak up? She can't have forgotten she packed it so recently; and she's a severely practical soul who's learned to think of everything in Avory Hume's employ. But she says nothin'. Why?

"You notice something else. Not only is the suit missing at this time—but it continues missing. It never turns up at all. Add to this fact the knowledge that a pair of red Turkish slippers (remembered because they're so conspicuous) are also missing; and you begin to see that the whole ruddy suitcase has disappeared.

"That's another why. Do we know of anything else that's vanished as well? We smackin' well do! A cross-bow has also vanished. Let's see: a stump cross-bow, but with a very broad head? It'd be much too big, say, to go into a little valise... but it would fit very neatly into a suitcase, and out of sight."

H.M.'s cigar had gone out, and he drew at it querulously. Privately, I thought this business was among the best bits he had ever done; but I hesitated to say so, for he would only bask woodenly and delight his soul obscurely with more mystification.

"Go on," I said. "You didn't drop any hint to us that Miss Jordan was guilty until your closing speech in court; but you must have your way; so go on."

"Assumin'," said H.M., with as close to a look of pleasure as he could get, "assumin' for the sake of argument that the cross-bow was stowed away in that suitcase, you have a good reason why the woman didn't sing out and tell Dyer the golf-suit wasn't upstairs. She'd hardly tell him to open the suitcase and find the cross-bow. She'd hardly open it herself in the presence of anyone else. Quite to the contrary, what would she do? Dyer was goin' upstairs after the suit. *She'd* think—you can lay a small wager on this—that as soon as he discovered the absence of the suit it'd be all up. The cat would come out of the bag with a reverberatin' yowl. Dyer would think of the obvious thing. He'd say: 'Please, miss, will you open the suitcase and let us have that ink-pad?' Consequently, she would have to get that suitcase out of the house in a blazin' hurry. Fortunately, she had a magnificent excuse to leave the house: she was going for the doctor. Fleming was in the study, Dyer was upstairs: she could snatch up the suitcase and get away to the car without bein' observed.

"So far I thought I was treadin' over pretty safe ground. But—"

"Please wait a bit," interposed Evelyn frowning. "There's one thing I don't understand here, and I've never understood. What did you think was in the suitcase? I mean, aside from Uncle Spencer's clothes?"

"Something like this," said H.M. "One cross-bow. One cut-glass decanter. One syphon partly emptied. One bottle of stuff to destroy the smell of whisky. Probably one screw-driver, and certainly two tumblers."

"I know. That's what I mean. Why did Avory Hume or anyone else need to have a lot of stuff carried out of the house or stowed away? Why did they have to have *two* decanters? Wouldn't it have been easier to have emptied the drugged whisky out of the ordinary decanter, rinsed it, and filled it up with ordinary stuff? Wouldn't it be easier to rinse out the glasses and put them back? And if you simply put a syphon of soda on a shelf in the pantry, what would be suspicious about that?—I don't say anything about the cross-bow, because that wasn't Hume's idea; it was the murderer's; but what about the rest of it?"

H.M. gave a ghostly chuckle.

"Ain't you forgettin'," he enquired, "that originally there was nobody in the scheme except Avory and Spencer?"

"Well?"

"Consider the little pictures we draw," said H.M., gesturing with his dead cigar. "Dyer knows nothin' about the scheme. Neither does Amelia Jordan. The good Reginald Answell will walk in, and be closeted in the study with Avory. Between that time and the time Reginald is discovered as a gibberin' loony, *how can Avory leave the study?* Either Dyer or Jordan will be in the house all the time; Jordan will be there while Dyer goes out after the car, Dyer will be there while Jordan drives off after Spencer. You see it now? Avory couldn't dash out to the kitchen, empty the whisky, rinse the decanter, fill it up again, and walk back—with his guest lyin' unconscious in an open room, and one of his witnesses watchin' him rinse the decanter. You can't do that when there's someone in the house, particularly someone on the alert for trouble: as Dyer was warned to be and as the woman certainly was. Similarly, Avory can't rinse the tumblers, wipe 'em, and put 'em back. He can't go shovin' syphons into pantries.

He's got to lie low in that study. That's why I said, and emphasised: only two people were in the scheme to begin with.

"We'd better deal with that part of the business, and tie it up with my growin' consciousness that Amelia was guilty. As originally planned, Avory had his sideboard all set; duplicates of decanters and glasses in the sideboard underneath, ready to be changed for the others. Lord love a duck, keep one concrete fact in mind! It's this: in Avory's scheme, he had no intention whatever of callin' in the *police!* There wasn't goin' to be any fine-tooth-comb search of the room or even the house. He only meant to fool his own little witnesses, his private witnesses, who wouldn't pry at all. All he had to do in the world was simply to shove decanter, syphon, glasses, and mint-extract into the bottom of the sideboard— and lock the sideboard doors. He could then get rid of the stuff after a dazed Reginald had been led away gibberin'. Don't you remember (see Mottram's notes on the plan) that the key to the sideboard doors was actually found in his pocket?

"But when Amelia stepped into the scheme, *she* had no intention of leavin' it at that. She was goin' to kill him. And that meant the police in. And all those incriminatin' souvenirs couldn't merely be left in the sideboard; they had to be got out of the house, or the blame wouldn't be fastened on the wrong feller who was lyin' unconscious."

"I liked her," said Evelyn suddenly. "Oh, dash it all!—I mean—"

"Listen," said H.M.

He pulled open the drawer of the desk. Taking out one of those terrible blue-bound folders I had seen often enough before (this one had not been there long enough to accumulate dust), he flipped it open.

"You know she died at St. Bartholomew's last night," he said. "You also know she made a statement before she died; the papers have been full enough of it. Here's a copy. Now listen to a paragraph or two.

"'... *I worked for him for fourteen years. I did more than that; I drudged for him. But I did not mind that, because for a long time I thought I loved him. I thought that when his wife died he would marry me, but he did not. I had had other offers of marriage too; but I turned them all down, because I thought he would marry me. And he never said a word about it; he said he would always be faithful to his wife's memory. But there was nothing else to do, so I stayed on at the house.*

"'*I knew that in his will he had left me five thousand pounds. It was the only thing in the world I had to look forward to. Then we learned that Mary was going to get married. All of a sudden he told me this mad idea that he was going to change that will, and to put every penny he had into trust for a son that was not even born. The horrible part was that I suddenly saw he meant it. I could not have stood that, and I did not mean to stand for it.*

"'... *of course I knew all about what he and Spencer and Dr. Tregannon were going to do. I knew about it from the beginning, though Avory did not know I knew; he thought women should not be concerned with things like that, and he would not have told me. There is something else I must tell you, and it is that I like Mary very much. I never would have killed Avory and tried to put the blame on Mr. Caplon Answell; this Reginald Answell was blackmailing Mary and I thought he would get what he deserved if I put the blame on him. How was I to know it was not the right man?'*

"That's true," growled H.M. "It's a good half of the reason why she broke down with brain-fever when she found what she'd done."

"But she didn't own up afterwards," said Evelyn. "She swore there in court that old Avory had been after Jim Answell all the time."

"She was protectin' the family," said H.M. "Does that sound very rummy to you? No, I think you understand. She was protectin' the family as well as protectin' herself."

"*I did not say anything at all to Avory, about my knowing of his scheme, until just about a quarter of an hour before I killed him. When Dyer had gone out of the house to get the car, I came downstairs with the bags. I went straight to the study door, and knocked, and I said: 'I know you've got him in there* drugged with brudine; but there's nobody else in the house, so open this door and let me help you.'

"The odd part of it was that he did not seem terribly surprised. He needed support, too: it was the first crooked thing he had ever done, and when he came to do it he had to lean on me. Well, it was the first crooked thing I had ever done too, but I was much better at it than he was. That was how I was able to make him do what I said.

"I told him he was a very foolish man to think that, when Captain Answell—that is who I thought it was—when Captain Answell woke up, he would not make a terrible fuss and demand to have the house searched. I said Mr. Fleming would be there, and Mr. Fleming was just the man to insist on searching the house for glasses or syphons or things. He knew that was true, and it frightened him. It is about seven years, I think, since I have been in love with Avory; and right then I hated him.

"I said that I had my valise outside, and I was going to the country in a few minutes. I said I would take all the things along, and get rid of them. He agreed to that.

"We put that automatic in the man's pocket—he was lying on the floor—and we tried to pour some stuff down his throat. I was afraid we had choked him. After we had given the arrow a pull and dragged it down, and cut Avory's hand to make it look real... Avory was not a coward, though I should have been afraid to have that done... we had to put finger-prints on it. The hardest part was for me to get the arrow out into the hall now without him suspecting anything. This is how I did it. The decanter and glasses and things were all out there already. I pretended to hear Dyer coming back, and I ran out of the room holding the arrow by the tip, and cried out to him to bolt the door quick. He did it without thinking, because he was an old man and not used to such work.

"Then I had to hurry. I had already put the cross-bow in the dark hall; I meant to take it back to the shed after I had finished. And the thread was already inside the knob on the door..."

H.M. tossed the blue-bound sheets on his desk.

"The worst of it bein'," he said, "that, just as she had finished her work, she *did* hear Dyer comin' back. That was the trouble, I suspected at the time she hadn't allowed for the delay in persuadin' and arguin' with old Avory, and she cut it too fine. Just as she finished sealin' up the door again (with Avory Hume's gloves, which we found in that suitcase), up comes Dyer. She had no intention of shovin' away the cross-bow in the suitcase. The thing to do was take it back to the shed, where nobody'd suspect it. But she hadn't time now. She hadn't even time to disengage the piece of feather from the windlass. Burn me, what was she goin' to do with that bow? In thirty seconds more, Dyer will be there and see everything.

"That was what caused me the trouble at the start, and nearly sent me wrong. She had a little valise and a big suitcase, and both of 'em were back there in the hall. What she intended to do, of course, was put the other preparations in her own valise, disposing of 'em later, and take the cross-bow back to the shed: the best course. But—Dyer appearin' too soon—the bow had to go into Spencer's suitcase; it was too big to fit into the smaller bag.

"It made me suspect (for a long time) that Spencer himself must certainly be concerned in the murder. Hey? She's used his suitcase. When the whole week-end kit suddenly disappears, and later Spencer makes no row about it—"

"He certainly didn't," I said. "On the afternoon of the first day of the trial, he went out of his way to declare he'd sent the golf-suit to the cleaner's."

"Well, I assumed that he must be tangled up in the murder," said H.M. plaintively. "And possibly that he and our friend Amelia planned the whole show together: Spencer carefully preparin' an alibi at the hospital. We've now got the reconstruction of the story up to the time Amelia runs out of the house, to drive to St. Praed's after Spencer; and that whole run of dirty work looked almighty likely.

"But I was sittin' and thinkin', and one thing bothered me badly. She had nipped out of the house with that suitcase, and she couldn't very well bring it back again—on that night, at least—in case anybody got suspicious or still happened to be whistlin' for ink-pads. She had to dispose of it somehow, and to do it in a snappin'-of-your-fingers time; for she had to go direct to the hospital and fetch back Uncle Spencer. If she and Spencer had been concerned together in the murder, you'd have thought she'd have left the suitcase at the hospital: where he would have a room or at least a locker of his own. But that didn't happen. As you see from my note on the time-schedule, the hall porter saw her arrive and drive away with Spencer, and no suitcase was handed out. Then where the blazes did it go? She couldn't chuck it in the gutter or hand it to a blind beggar; and gettin' rid of a suitcase full of dangerous souvenirs (even temporarily) is a devilish difficult trick. There's only one thing that could have been done, in the very limited time the schedule shows you she took. When you're at St. Praed's Hospital in Praed Street, as you know and as has been pointed out to you even if you didn't, you're smack up against Paddington Station. It could have been put into the Left-Luggage Department. This was inevitable, my lads. It had to be.

"Now here was (possibly) a bit of luck. I thought of it 'way back in February. Since the night of the murder, Amelia had been flat on her back with a bad case of brain-fever, and hadn't been allowed out. At that time she still hadn't come out. She couldn't have gone to reclaim the case. As I say, logically the damned suitcase *had* to be there—

"Well, like the idiot boy, I went there; and it was. You know what I did. I took along my old pal Dr. Parker and Shanks the odd-jobs man; I wanted them to be witnesses of the find as well as examiners of it. For I couldn't stop this case from comin' up for trial now. In the first place it was a month under way. In the second and more important place, d'you know what I'd have had to say to the authorities? The old man (never very popular with the Home Secretary or the D.P.P.) would have had to go swaggerin' in and say: 'Well, boys, I got some instructions for you. I want this indictment quashed for the followin' reasons: Amelia Jordan is lyin'. Spencer Hume is lyin'. Reginald Answell is lyin'. Mary Hume has *been* lyin'. In short, nearly every person in the whole ruddy case has been lyin' except my client.' Would they have believed me? Question yourselves closely, my fatheads. I had to put that whole crowd under oath: I had to have a fair field and swords on the green: I had to have, in short, justice. There's my reason; and also the reason for my mysteriousness about it.

"You know where I went to get my witnesses, and why. But one thing still bothered me, and it bothered me up to the second day of the trial. Was Spencer Hume concerned in the dirtier deal of the murder, or wasn't he?

"Here's what I mean. I snaffled the suitcase. But it'd been at Paddington since the night of the murder. Now, if Amelia and Spencer were workin' together, surely she'd have told him to go and reclaim it quickly before some inquisitive feller nosed inside? She hadn't been delirious with fever for over a month. It wasn't until a week after my own visit that a man—*not* Spencer—came and made fumblin' enquiries about it.

"Sometimes I thought one thing, sometimes another: until the evenin' of the first day of the trial I began to get a glimmer. Spencer ran away; but he wrote to Mary, swearin' he actually saw the crime committed by Jim Answell. That letter had a ring of truth that Spencer never got into any of his quotations. Yet I knew it must have been a lie, until (bang!) I saw what it was. Through this case, a vision of simple innocence has been presented by Amelia Jordan. A vision of moustache-twistin' craft has been presented by Spencer. Uncle Spencer's trouble is that he is too innocent. He honestly shouldn't be allowed loose. For fourteen years he's believed every word that's been spoken by that simple and practical woman: perhaps he'd had a right to. *She* told *him* she had actually seen Answell commit the crime; and he believed it. That's all. Don't you realise that that man really believes in all the soundin' platitudes he spouts? Her course had been simple. She told him she joined with Avory in the little plot, and had taken his (Spencer's) suitcase to stow away the decanter, the glasses and the rest of the trappings. She told him she'd had to dispose of that suitcase—into the river, she says here in her statement—and he'd have to get used to the loss. For, if the properties had been found in his bag, he would certainly get into serious trouble. Not a word about the cross-bow, of course. So Spencer shut up. He wouldn't even betray her to the extent of sayin', in his letter to Mary, that his information wasn't first-hand. I think we've misjudged Uncle Spencer. His chivalry was too much."

"But look here!" I protested. "Who was the man who did go to Paddington Station—apparently a week after you did—and asked about the suitcase? You asked the manager about that in the witness-box. I remember, because it threw me off. I was certain a man had committed the murder. Who went to Paddington?"

"Reginald Answell," said H.M. in a satisfied tone.

"*What?*"

"Our Reginald," continued H.M. with ferocious tenderness, "is goin' to serve a couple of years for perjury; you knew that?—Well, he went into the witness-box and swore he had practically seen the murder committed. I wanted him to testify. If he tried any funny business (as I rather hoped he would), I could nail him to the wall quicker than flick a tiddley-wink; and there wasn't enough evidence to indict him for blackmail. Oh, yes. I told him, d'ye see, that the subpoena he'd received was only a matter of form, and he probably wouldn't be called at all. Naturally I didn't want him to run away like Spencer—as he smackin' well would have if I'd let him know I intended to bring up the subject of blackmailin' Mary Hume. So he went smoothly, and tried to repay the compliment by doin' me down. As a result, he'll serve two years for perjury. But the beautiful and glorious and cussed part of it is that, except for the triflin' detail of the person in question, what he said was true: to all intents and purposes, he really did see the murder done."

"What?"

"Sure. He didn't know I knew anything about the interview he had with Grabell—I mean about his knowledge of the pistol Hume pinched—right up until the second day of the trial. He was pretty sick with me already for bringin' up the blackmail question while he sat right at the solicitors' table; so he rounded on me. But the first part of what he said was quite true. He did go down the passage between the houses; *he was* in Grosvenor Street after all. He did go up the steps to the side door. If you'll remember Mottram's notes written on the plan of the rear of the house, you'll remember that door was found unlocked—"

"But, damn it all, you yourself proved that he couldn't have seen anything through a wooden door—"

"And you're still forgettin' something," urged H.M. gently. "You're forgettin' two glasses of whisky."

"Two glasses of whisky?"

"Yes. Avory Hume poured out two drinks, one for himself that he didn't touch (not wantin' to drink brudine), and the other for his guest, who drank only half of it. You've also heard how Amelia Jordan later packed up those glasses in a suitcase. Well, I can tell you one thing she didn't do: she didn't put two drinks of whisky in a suitcase. She had to empty 'em. But there wasn't a sink at hand, and she didn't want to open the windows in case the locked room should be disturbed. So she simply unlocked the side door, opened it, and tossed out the contents of the glasses, thereby—"

"Thereby?"

"Givin' a way in to Reginald, who was prowlin'. You remember what he said when I fired the point about the glass door at him? He turned a little green, and said: 'The door may have been open,' which was quite true. The door *was* open. He didn't even notice what kind of door it was;

he simply remembered the old glass door, and mentioned that because he didn't want to admit he'd stuck his nose into the house. How much he saw I don't know. I doubt very much that he saw the murder committed. But he must have seen enough to give him a handle for blackmail on the person of Amelia Jordan, and he knew very well there was somethin' fishy about that suitcase. The trouble was, the suitcase had disappeared and he didn't know where. Until he did know—until he could find out—he was stuck between Mephistopheles and deep water. It's pretty hard to determine what went on in Reginald's mind, or how far he approached Amelia. She was so bedevilled that I began to be sorry for her; but they weren't goin' to hang my client because of that. I thought it'd be very salutary, however, for her to see the evidence in court. I knew it would be very salutary to put Reginald into the witness-box and make that swine squirm on a hotter griddle than he'd ever dreamed of. Finally, it pleases and soothes me to know that he'll serve a long stretch in clink for tellin' what was, in essentials, the perfect truth."

We stared at H.M. as he gobbled whisky-punch. He had wanted to be the old *maestro*; and, by all the gods, you had to admit he was.

"I am inclined to suspect," said Evelyn, "that you are a disgrace to all the splendid traditions of the fairness of English law. But, since we're all among friends—"

"Yes, I s'pose so," admitted H.M. reflectively. "I technically broke the law when I got my burglar pal, Shrimp Calloway, to break into Inspector Mottram's police-station one fine night and make sure my deductions were right about the piece of feather bein' in the Judas window. It'd never have done to go to court and get my great big beautiful dramatic effect spoiled by the lack of a feather... But still, there it is. The old man likes to see the young folks have a good time; and I rather think Jim Answell and Mary Answell are goin' to be just as happily married as you and your wench there. So why the blazes, burn it all, have you got to pick on me?"

He gobbled whisky-punch again, and lit his dead cigar.

"So our Reginald was laid by the heels," I said, "all by perverting the pure rules of justice; and I begin to suspect that Jim Answell was acquitted by a trick; and the whole thing moves by... by what the devil is it?"

"I can tell you," said H.M. quite seriously. "The blinkin' awful cussedness of things in general."

THE END

ALSO AVAILABLE

"You have to reach for the greatest of the Great Names (Agatha Christie, John Dickson Carr, Ellery Queen) to find Christianna Brand's rivals in the subtleties of the trade."
— Anthony Boucher in the *New York Times*

Night falls in the capital, and a "London particular" pea-souper fog envelops the city. In Maida Vale, Rose and her family doctor Tedwards struggle through the dark after a man has telephoned from Rose's house, claiming to have been attacked. By the time they arrive the victim, Raoul Vernet, is dead. The news he brought from Switzerland for Rose's mother has died with him.

Arriving to the scene, Inspector Cockrill faces a fiendish case with seven suspects who could have murdered their guest—family members and friends with alibis muddled by the suffocating fog and motives wrapped in mystery. Now, the race is on to find the truth before the killer strikes again.

First published in 1952, *London Particular* was Brand's favourite among her own books, and it remains a fast-paced and witty masterpiece of the genre, showing off the author's signature flair for the ruthless twist.

ALSO AVAILABLE

On the eve of Elaine Southey's 21st birthday, the residents and neighbours of the Southeys' historic north London home prepare for the party under a pall of anxiety, while a grim surprise awaits in the basement flat. There lies the insidious charmer Ivan Sweet—whose malign influence held so many in its grasp—dead in suspicious circumstances. While reactions of horror—and relief—spread through the party, the truth that a murderer remains at large seeps in slow and cold.

To bring the ruthless killer to justice, the young Oxford man Superintendent Paul Grainger must untangle the twisted web of Sweet's wrongdoing—and the dark secrets threatening to ruin each suspect's good name. First published in 1960, Sinclair's stylish debut is a classic murder mystery shot through with a chilling vein of the macabre.

ALSO AVAILABLE IN THE BRITISH LIBRARY CRIME CLASSICS SERIES

Big Ben Strikes Eleven	DAVID MAGARSHACK
Death of an Author	E. C. R. LORAC
The Black Spectacles	JOHN DICKSON CARR
Death of a Bookseller	BERNARD J. FARMER
The Wheel Spins	ETHEL LINA WHITE
Someone from the Past	MARGOT BENNETT
Who Killed Father Christmas?	ED. MARTIN EDWARDS
Twice Round the Clock	BILLIE HOUSTON
The White Priory Murders	CARTER DICKSON
The Port of London Murders	JOSEPHINE BELL
Murder in the Basement	ANTHONY BERKELEY
Fear Stalks the Village	ETHEL LINA WHITE
The Cornish Coast Murder	JOHN BUDE
Suddenly at His Residence	CHRISTIANNA BRAND
The Edinburgh Mystery	ED. MARTIN EDWARDS
Checkmate to Murder	E. C. R. LORAC
The Spoilt Kill	MARY KELLY
Smallbone Deceased	MICHAEL GILBERT
The Story of Classic Crime in 100 Books	MARTIN EDWARDS
The Pocket Detective: 100+ Puzzles	KATE JACKSON
The Pocket Detective 2: 100+ More Puzzles	KATE JACKSON

Many of our titles are also available
in eBook, large print and audio editions